ANNIE

'Now, Victoria,' I said sternly, 'I told you that you were going to be spanked and I should imagine that you now realise that this is precisely what is about to happen to you. Your stupidity is matched only by your wickedness. If you had submitted in the first place, we would not have had to ruin your clothes. You would have been far more comfortable across my knees than you are now – and it would all have been over by now. You would be nursing a sore bottom rather than facing the unfamiliar prospect of an even more painful one. I hope that the next half an hour or so will be a salutary lesson to you.'

ANNIE

Evelyn Culber

This book is a work of fiction.
In real life, make sure you practise safe sex.

First published in 1993 by
Nexus
Thames Wharf Studios
Rainville Road
London W6 9HT

Reprinted 1994, 1998 (twice)

Typeset by TW Typesetting, Plymouth, Devon

Printed and bound by
Cox & Wyman Ltd, Reading, Berks

ISBN 0 352 32881 9

PROLOGUE

The old house seemed sad and forlorn, its dusty windows staring blindly out on to the fast-changing world outside, as though its thoughts were turned inwards and its memories of greater importance than its future. With matching sadness, I wandered through the hollow rooms but only heard the vaguest echo of the vitality that had been such a crucial part of my time there so many years ago. I recalled the laughter; the cries of pain; good conversation; maids singing quietly as they went about their duties; sighs of ecstasy — and most memorable of all, that unique, ringing sound of hand on naked bottom-flesh.

With a sigh, I found my way into the garden, forced open the rusting gate that led into the central, walled area. It was tragically overgrown and it was several minutes before I found what I had been seeking. My talisman and early inspiration. She was stained by time, weather and bird-droppings but there was enough of her beauty remaining to bring a smile to my lips. Picking up my skirts, I forced my way through the long grass until I was standing behind her and remembering the emotions of the first time I had gazed at the naked marble curves of her bottom — and how they had helped me take the first steps on a journey of discovery, during which I experienced enormous pleasures, some pain, but above all, love!

It had all begun on the 9th of May, 1889 . . .

1

CHAPTER 1

When the Hackney cab at last turned off the street and into the short drive leading up to the house, I was almost too tired to feel any relief that my long journey from Leicestershire was at an end. I was cold, dusty, my head throbbed and the part of my body which had borne the burden of my weight on the unyielding seat ached numbly.

In addition to my physical weariness, there was an aching void in my heart, mainly the natural sorrow at the untimely death of my beloved parents, but also because my immediate prospect represented a journey into the unknown. Our solicitor had told me that 'Uncle George' and 'Aunt Grace' would be taking care of me and my affairs, which had come as something of a surprise to me, as I had never heard of them!

However, Aunt Grace welcomed me with some warmth and evident sympathy and after a short talk, arranged for a maid to conduct me to the cook. A large, stately woman with a large, gentle face, she sat me down in the kitchen and rapidly produced a jug of refreshing lemonade and a slice of excellent fruit cake, which I eagerly consumed — and I began to recover. What happened next threw me into total confusion. No sooner had I sat back with a contented sigh, when she moved her chair well back from the table and told me to lay myself across her lap! I openly confess that my expression must have been extremely comical as I stared at her in open-mouthed disbelief. Our eyes locked for long moments as my mind whirled, thoughts and questions chasing each other round my head like leaves in an Autumn gale. Eventually I found my tongue:

'Why? What for?'

'Because I'm going to give you a spanking. Now hurry up. You'll want plenty of time to bath and have a rest before dinner.'

She said it as though it was the most natural thing in the world, whereas it struck me as nothing less than extraordinary. Perhaps had I not been so tired, if the sudden death of my parents had not left me feeling so alone and vulnerable, I would have resisted — at least a little. As it was, I rose, stumbled towards the waiting lap and slumped over until my hands were resting on the cool stone floor.

It did not take long. Not that I was in the mood to appreciate any of the various aspects of the experience at the time. I felt no surprise when my skirts and petticoats were swept up until they rested on my back. By the time my chemise was pulled out from under my drawers, I was resigned to this intimate and indelicate item of apparel being exposed to view and if their split gaped open sufficiently to reveal part of the flesh beneath, then I was in blissful ignorance. Not even the impact of her hand made a memorable impression on either my rear or my mind. I was only conscious of fighting back the bubble of bitter humiliation and despair which threatened to burst forth.

Suddenly I was being helped back to my feet, my bottom tingling warmly somewhere in the background of my awareness. Her next actions just added to my confusion — she smiled at me, said: 'You took that well,' then hugged me and kissed me tenderly, swiftly — and on my lips. The maid materialised from nowhere and I followed her unseeingly up stairs and down corridors until we fetched up in a large, well-appointed bedroom, in the middle of which stood the first really welcome sight since the cake and lemonade — a bath, with soft, wispy tendrils of steam floating slowly into the sloping beams from the setting sun.

Luckily my beloved parents' household had left me unaccustomed to the attentions of a personal maid, for when I turned, she had gone, leaving me happily alone to strip off my clothing and sink into the soothing balm of hot water, deliciously scented with some exotic oil.

I must have dozed, because all of a sudden the water was chill and I stood up to wash myself with an energetic haste which lasted until I reached my bottom. Memories and confusion returned in a blushing flood and I stepped out into the modesty of a towel as soon as I could.

My clothes had been taken away! I searched the wardrobe, but it was as bare as I, and my trunks were not to be seen. There was only a tray on a table by the bed, and on it a platter of cold meats, a bowl of blancmange and a bottle of chilled wine, the condensation on its outer surfaces glistening like tiny gems. I ate. I drank.

I then shed the towel and scurried beneath the blankets, as if reluctant to let even the walls see my nudity. I slept.

I remember awaking as the cold, hard light of early dawn glinted through the window and it was as though my mind had no wish to face the day, lest it produce more shocks like the profound one administered by the Cook the evening before. I slipped back into the safety of sleep until the full brightness of the morning sun drew me out of my haven and I lay smiling softly in my rested ease, my limbs loose and my travel-weariness all but gone.

It was the opening of the door which jolted me back to full and wary wakefulness, although recognising Aunt Grace's tall and elegant figure provided some welcome reassurance, especially when she had opened the curtains and the flood of warm light revealed her lovely and equally warm smile. I sat up, saw that my bosom was exposed, grabbed the blankets to pull them up over me, then realised that they were too tightly tucked in to reach and, with a little squeak of embarrassment, slipped back under them. She smiled with even greater warmth and stood there looking at me as I lay looking back at her and the sense of confusion which had been such a part of me since my parents' demise somehow began to ease away.

Was my tiredness the day before responsible for the fact that I had not noticed how strikingly beautiful she was? She was dressed with simple elegance, in a plain white blouse and a slender dark skirt, emphasising the slenderness of her waist and the subtly opulent curves of her hips and bosom, with a black choker round her neck adding an exotic touch to her ensemble.

She walked to the bed, sat down on the edge and looked down at me, her warm brown eyes and smiling lips further soothing away my apprehensions. Then she reached down to cup my cheek, stroking my temple with her thumb at the same time. A new peacefulness wrapped round me like a warm cloak on a winter's day.

'You are truly beautiful, Annie.'

I half believed her. My looks had been commented on before – and she had a quiet air of authority about her, which would have made any denial ring completely false. Her fingertips trickled over my face; her hand stroked my hair; she traced the outline of my lips; tender little tendrils of physical pleasure caressed my skin and I found myself gently pressing my cheek against her palm and then turning my face to kiss it. I lay back against the pillows and closed my eyes as her hand moved like warm silk onto my neck and shoulders. I opened them again when her other hand slipped under the protective shield of the blankets and rested on the upper slopes of my bosom –

but in puzzlement rather than fear or distaste. She was looking down at me with an expression which could only be described as loving.

The morning light bathed her face, her full lips were set in a soft, upward curve and her large brown eyes were full of warmth. She eased the blankets down as far as my waist and I felt a sharp surge of embarrassment at the thought that she was gazing at my naked breasts. Then I felt my nipples stiffen in a way which belied their pink innocence. My breathing quickened as a palm closed gently on the left one, squeezing the flesh, and the tendrils spread and grew more insistent as her other palm cupped my other breast with the same soft, firm warmth. To my amazement, I found that I was raising my back off the bed to push my yearning flesh against her hands. Her voice whispered, echoing round the teeming void that my mind had become:

'So plump and firm . . . Such soft skin . . . Turn over, Annie.'

I obeyed, slowly because her touch had been giving more pleasure than I had ever experienced. She stroked my hair, neck and shoulders and my heartbeat settled down again, the tendrils retracted. It was not the same. It was soothing. It was delightful. But it was not the same. The palm of her hand moved down my spine, kneading the muscles and imparting a languor that was close to sleep — until I became aware of an easing of the weight of the blankets on the small of my back. I had felt no more than a flare of disturbed modesty when she had unveiled my breasts but the imminent laying bare of my bottom sent an unease coursing through me. It did not occur to me to protest, but as I felt the sliding caress of the sheet as it brushed my skin on its downward path, I felt my fleshy mounds clamp together, making their own echoing protest at this unwarranted exposure.

7

She did not stop until the covers were clear of my feet and I was exposed from head to toe. Again, I could feel her eyes studying me. I felt increasingly uncomfortable at this inspection and it came as no surprise when a prickling sensation flared over my face as I blushed in deep embarrassment. And bewilderment. After all, that part of my anatomy presumably providing the focus of her attention was usually described as 'unmentionable' — or rather it had been so by my dear departed mother. One sat on it: as a child one was liable to have it beaten, although I had only suffered such humiliation on perhaps a dozen occasions. And even then I had admitted that the punishment was well-merited. Suddenly the memory of cook's extraordinary behaviour flooded through my bewildered mind. Was Aunt Grace going to spank me? If so, why? I had done nothing to rouse her wrath.

The prickling which had sparkled through my face not long before invaded my lower cheeks and I had to bite the pillow to stifle the moan which was on the verge of escaping and rending the warm silence. Had she not rested her hand on my posterior at that very moment, I know that the suspense would have overcome me. I did jump at the touch and my gasp hissed loudly in my ears, but her touch had a strange quality that calmed my churning thoughts. I felt the easing of the tensions, my clenched buttocks slowly relaxed and then the tendrils of pleasure gradually returned as she glided her palm over the whole surface, barely touching my skin. She then kneaded me firmly with both hands, one on each cheek, shifting the flesh in all directions so that the tendrils tingled ever deeper and further. My panting breath sounded deep and hollow in my ears as strangely pleasurable feelings spread through my lower portions.

I was just beginning to grow accustomed to and enjoy the kneading, when she began to trickle her fingertips all round the skin of my posterior; as soon as I had absorbed this delight, she started to pat the mounds of flesh, and the consequent quivering she induced with this action sent an agitation into some hidden parts whose sensitivity proved a delightful surprise.

My whole body was tingling most pleasingly and I was quietly drifting into a calm, small world of peace and warmth when Aunt Grace gave my bottom a sharp little pat and told me it was time to get up, helping me to my unsteady feet with a firm and steadfast hand. She folded me in her arms; I rested my head on her shoulder while she stroked my hair for a while, letting me recover my breath, settle my heartbeat and try to arrange my thoughts into some kind of reasoned order. The first two disturbances were soon back to normal but everything had been too strange, too new, for me to be able to make any sense of it at that stage. Her hands moved off my shoulders, with one descending to the warm, trembling globe of my bottom and the other stroking up and down my spine. I was not used to caresses. My mother had shown her love for me in her smile and voice and my father with a lightening in his gruffness. My disquiet slept for the moment until she looked me in the face and said:

'You *are* beautiful, Annie. And I believe that you have it within you to move in directions which few will ever know. Do not shutter your mind. Look, observe, learn. Ask me no questions because the knowledge can only come from within you. Now, enough. I shall bath you. Come with me.'

The bath had been removed from my room and so we had to walk down the corridor to the bathroom, where a proper bath emitted a scented, steamy welcome. It was only after I had sunk gratefully into its warm embrace that I realised that I had blithely walked openly from my room in a state of complete nudity. I shuddered at the thought

9

that I may easily have been seen by a passing maid but fortunately had little time to dwell on my narrow escape, for Aunt Grace soon had me standing while she applied a soaped sponge. In spite of what had passed between us, it felt a trifle undignified and I cannot say that I was absolutely at ease, especially when she put the sponge aside and used her hands. She lingered on my bosoms, thighs and buttocks, then made me turn and bend forward. As her slippery hand eased between my bottom cheeks I blushed again at the totally unexpected touch – and yet again when she moved it further forward to wash between my legs. Too soon she commanded me to sit down and rinse off the soap, then to get out while she dried me, before setting back off to my room. Again the possibility of being seen in Eve's costume troubled me until we were safely back in my room, where the first thing I noted was that my trunks had been brought up during my absence and my spirits were raised by the pleasure of having my own possessions. Forgetful of my nudity, I opened the first with little cries of excitement.

Aunt Grace did not seem particularly impressed with my wardrobe. My drawers were pronounced to be 'too baggy', my stays and corsets were 'completely unnecessary – you don't need them, dear,' my dresses generally dismissed as 'shapeless' but in the end we had settled on chemise, my smallest drawers, stockings, one petticoat, a light blouse and my straightest skirt. I will confess that I did enjoy the freedom of being completely uncorseted.

The two of us breakfasted together, after which she suggested that I sit out in the garden for an hour or so before meeting my Uncle George in the library. For what was a town house, albeit one on the outskirts, the garden was pleasingly spacious and cleverly laid out to provide complete seclusion from the neighbouring houses. The centre-

10

piece was an area surrounded by high hedges, with a small summer-house in the middle. Small flower beds provided splashes of colour and the expanse of lawn was of sufficient size to allow croquet or badminton to be played in comfort. To the side of the summer-house there was a fountain, featuring a statue of a naked Greek goddess, poised on the tips of her toes and with extended arms holding a large sea-shell from which the clear water sprayed, bedewing her gleaming white form.

Had it not been for the events of the morning, I probably would have averted my eyes from her exposed figure but, having first made sure that I was not overlooked, I walked carefully round her, curious to see whether her marbled features would provide even the slightest clue to Aunt Grace's apparent fascination with my fleshly ones.

Although I would have been loth to admit it at that time, on occasion I had studied my naked breasts in a looking-glass and so I was able to effect some sort of reasoned judgement on hers. Their shape was indeed delightfully plump and rounded. Marble, however, did not seem a medium which allowed the artist scope to reproduce the nipple with any real accuracy! Similarly, the core of her femininity at the base of her belly was conspicuous by its absence of detail. Recalling Aunt Grace's prolonged attentions to my rear and the unexpected pleasure she had produced in that part of me, and sadly ignorant as to its shape and formation, I passed behind the silent nymph with growing curiosity. I must have been trying to see the statue with the same eyes that Aunt Grace had looked at me earlier and at the same time, searching for any clues which would explain her fascination.

My eyes were first drawn to the long and deep division between the mounds and the way it provided such a strong focal point to the back view. I then studied the buttocks themselves and began to marvel at the range of curves that

11

produced such a subtle effect. The way her hips swelled out from her narrow waist; the sharp in-rolling of each cheek as they met to form that cleft; the way the downward curve began as a gentle slope away from the loins before turning sharply inwards to form delightful folds at the junction with the thighs.

As I walked away to meet Uncle George, the first, tentative beginnings of my understanding were forming and I no longer found Aunt Grace's interest in my body quite as surprising. There had been more than a collection of curves and folds in the shape of the statue's rear view; there was something in the proportions which I found most attractive. Until that moment, the pleasant memories of Aunt Grace's interest in my body had begun to fade, to be replaced by feelings that approached distaste — and were certainly of embarrassment. But having been given an inkling of the essential beauty of the female form, my doubts were lessened by a burgeoning curiosity.

CHAPTER 2

Uncle George was waiting for me in the library and greeted me quietly and rather distantly. He was tall, of slender build, fashionably whiskered and handsome, with a nice smile and the ability to put me immediately at my ease. After we had talked with easy amiability for a while, he said that he would appreciate help in the long-overdue task of cataloguing his various collections and I willingly offered my assistance at any time I was free. As Aunt Grace had made no calls on me, I happily worked with him until the luncheon gong sounded.

There were only the three of us at the large table, waited on by three of the maids, and it was then that I began to ponder on the slightly strange complement which staffed the house. There was no sign of a butler or footman, nor of a valet for Uncle George. There was cook (and a tremor flickered through my buttocks as I remembered our meeting!) and the maids. But the thought left my mind as quickly as it had entered it.

That first day passed without any further incidents of note and I retired early, still in a state of some confusion at the strangeness of my new surroundings — and with more questions and fewer answers. As I drifted into sleep, my body twitched at the memory of Aunt Grace's touch.

I awoke refreshed and completely recovered from the rigours of my journey. The last remnants of my aches and

13

pains had vanished and I lay comfortably at ease with the not unpleasing prospect of another quiet day in the library. I enjoy books and Uncle George's company had proved both undemanding and of interest, for he was a man of wide scholarship. I was beginning to wonder how I could proceed with arranging my bath and had just located a bell-pull above the head of my bed, when the door opened. It was only one of the maids, who drew the curtains, told me that my bath was ready and then disappeared. Grateful for the protection of my nightdress, I walked down the corridor to the bathroom and, welcoming the privacy, stripped and sank into the warm water, which rekindled some of the sensations started by my Aunt's caresses. I settled down and gave out a huge sigh of contentment, although deep within me there was a little question . . . Why was it that I had been caressed so intimately by another woman — and yet had only suffered the smallest pang of guilt?

I ate my breakfast all alone as neither Uncle George nor Aunt Grace had come down. After I had finished, I rose, found my way to the small drawing room, sat for a while before deciding to taste the early morning air in the garden. Was there something about that statue which was calling me? I think there must have been, for I had never been noted for a particular enthusiasm for fresh air and I found that I was standing in front of it without having been conscious of the direction my feet had been taking me. Again I studied those white buttocks, shining and gleaming, the sunlight bejewelling the drops of water as they flew through the air. Again, the memory of Aunt Grace's hands on my flesh came back and I felt a tightening in my throat. It no longer seemed quite so mysterious to me that Aunt Grace had gained so much apparent pleasure from seeing my nakedness. As I gazed at the statue, I resolved that I would offer myself to my Aunt whenever she showed even the slightest desire to see me . . . touch me . . . caress me.

If nothing further in the way of physical contact had occurred during my stay there, perhaps that first morning's activities would have gradually sunk into the hidden depths of my mind and only would have swum to the surface in times of general puzzlement; but after I had re-entered the house, shaking my head as if to clear my mind of the strange fascination of those marbled mounds, Aunt Grace called me up to her bedroom.

I did not notice the other woman in with her — not at first, because Aunt Grace was in her underclothes and considering the relatively late hour, this took me completely by surprise. If I had burst in on her unexpectedly, I would have been covered in confusion at the invasion of her privacy but, as she had summoned me and so clearly expected me to see her in that state, I was able to act with something approaching normality. I stared at her. My features may well have registered the shock I felt at the first sighting but I am sure that my expression did not betray my fast heartbeat as my eyes drank in her intimacies. She was not wearing a chemise, just a small waist corset and drawers, so her full bosom was bare, the pinky-brown nipples seemingly returning my appraisal. More startling was the view of a neat, dark triangle of hair on her lower belly. Her drawers were made of such fine silk that she was not far short of complete nudity — and were so tight that they clung to the full curves of her thighs.

She mesmerised me. If the beauty of her face had come to me relatively slowly, the impact of her figure was immediate, not simply because the combination of pure white skin, richly feminine curves, perfectly round nipples and furry triangle was very striking, but it was the first time I had ever seen another human being in such a state of undress.

I had never seen my mother in anything approaching this level of near-nudity and had I inadvertently done so, I know that I would have been covered in confused embarrassment — and her reaction would undoubtedly have been similar. But not with Aunt Grace. My glance flickered back up from her thighs, lingered momentarily on her love nest, on her bosoms and then I met her eyes, knowing that I was blushing and a little ashamed at my evident lack of sophistication. She was smiling at me. Softly. Gently. Lovingly? And yet I sensed that there was an indefinable challenge in the air. Her enigmatic words echoed in my head — 'Do not shutter your mind. Look, observe, learn. Ask me no questions because the knowledge can only come from within you.' Then she spoke and my thoughts were returned to normality.

'This is my dressmaker, Mrs Savage, and we are going to give you a new and more fitting wardrobe. Please undress completely, Annie.'

I was now on more familiar ground and although none of my previous dressmakers had wished me to strip to complete nakedness, it seemed perfectly natural to do so there. It did not take long and I was soon standing more or less at ease before their expert appraisal, during which I was able to study Mrs Savage in return. If ever a woman was named inappropriately it was her! Small of stature, but pleasingly rounded in breast and hips, she could only be described as meek and mousy. There was even a faintly apologetic air to the manner in which she was staring at my naked form. I moved my focus back to Aunt Grace's infinitely more alluring figure and I sincerely believe that we got equal pleasure from what each of us was seeing! For a woman of nearly forty, she was exceptional. Her breasts were plump and jutted firmly with only a slight — and utterly charming — concession to the laws of gravity. Her neat nipples emerged pointedly from the centre of the two perfect little pink circles. My eyes lingered and then travelled downwards, pausing briefly at the excitingly deep hollow of her belly-button as it peeped cheekily just above the waistband of her drawers; then further down and the breath stopped in my throat as my gaze rested on the centre of her femininity. Her curls were darker than mine but then so were the elegantly coiffed curls on her head. The material of her drawers was enough to prevent detailed observation but the view was still extremely exciting. Just as I was about to make a detailed study of her thighs, I was asked to turn round and my thoughts were turned back to my own body.

I remember clearly feeling at the time that they spent longer in the contemplation of my rear than they had of my front. With only the far wall to look at, my undistracted mind drifted back to the statue in the garden, my unseeing eyes visualising her cold curves as the two pairs of seeing eyes surveyed my fleshly ones. For all her mousiness, I found that I wanted Mrs Savage to approve of my bottom, even though I had little or no idea of what sort of bottom would excite another woman's approval. I knew that Aunt Grace did not find me wanting in this area and this knowledge certainly encouraged me to entertain the thought that there could be a gleam in her eye! I resisted the temptation to turn and see, and gradually my thoughts turned inwards. I began to lose the last vestiges of self-consciousness at my nudity and to enjoy it. The refreshing caress of the air on my skin was the main physical element and I began really to appreciate the sensation, but it was the simple fact of the silent, but indisputable admiration from two much more experienced women which excited me even more.

Eventually the spell was broken as the two ladies worked together on the task of taking measurements. They were meticulous, to say the least. Apart from very careful and painstaking application of the tape, my breasts, tummy, thighs and buttocks were treated to prolonged manual assessment, presumably to check the firmness and resilience of my flesh. I did not dwell on the reason — my mind swayed between enjoyment of the sensations and a certain embarrassment at being treated a little like a prize cow at market.

The final act before I was told to dress was to walk up and down the room. I realised quickly that this was to establish the degree of movement in my hips and buttocks as I walked, as I overheard Mrs Savage commenting on the unusual mobility of my posterior and this made me aware for the first time of the sensual delights of walking naked. The only other time, of course, had been between my room and the bathroom in Aunt Grace's company and on that occasion my mind had been rather overwhelmed by the profusion of new and strange experiences and the fear of being observed had over-ridden all else. This time I could sense the way my buttocks slid together at their in-rolling; the shifting of their fleshy mass with the natural sway and the ensuing gentle wobble as they reversed their direction. It was pleasing, novel and further aroused my growing curiosity about this part of my anatomy.

I was then told to get dressed again and help my Uncle in the library and as I did so, I found renewed enchantment, at the sight of Aunt Grace's naked breasts, and that bewitching triangle of hair. And as I walked along the corridors to the library, I found myself conscious of the movements of my bottom and aware of the difference between walking naked and clothed — and quite looking forward to being naked again! I also found that if I was concentrating on these movements, my actual walk was different. It was slower, a little more sedate and I was really aware of my real femininity for the first time in my life. Until then I had been nothing more than a young girl whom some thought pretty.

Aunt Grace had already changed my attitudes and, because of her influence, I had found her enjoyment very catching. I had felt a lovely all-over tingle while I was parading naked; after one or two early qualms, I had enjoyed feeling Mrs Savage's hands as she measured me with meticulous care; I had felt a simple pleasure while walking up and down while the two ladies studied the movements of my bare bottom.

Then I stopped in mid pace as I realised that if I had been alert to the possibilities, I may well have been able to have seen Aunt Grace's rear view — and in those drawers, her bottom would have been as good as bare. The thought was indeed exciting, if a little forward for a girl only 18 years old. To start with, I felt a trace of guilt at my presumption but this immediately changed to a pang of disappointment at my lack of initiative. I consoled myself with the thought that she had been so composed at my seeing her in just the skimpiest of underclothes that I would probably get another chance before very long.

Smiling secretly to myself, I went into the library.

Two uneventful days passed before Aunt Grace told me that Mrs Savage had finished some of my new clothes and that I should present myself in her room at two o'clock to try them on. The morning spent in the library seemed to last an eternity and was only enlivened by the discovery of several volumes about the lives and works of famous artists. Uncle George was preoccupied at the other end of the room and I was able to leaf quietly through the pages. Whilst fully aware of the artistic merits of the great paintings reproduced, my new-found interest in the female form made me linger with some delight on those featuring the nude. I was particularly taken with Rubens' 'The Judgement of Paris'. The three ladies portrayed exhibited

19

an exciting amplitude of flesh, notably the two showing their rear view and I wondered whether my buttocks were as plump and soft-looking.

During my little post-luncheon rest, I found it extremely hard to settle. Obviously, the main reason was the natural excitement that any young girl feels when there are new clothes in the offing, but I was also aware of a slight tingling in my skin, as though anticipating the probability of having to strip myself right down to my birthday suit.

I pondered on this change in me. Was I unusual in enjoying the complimentary attention that had been plainly expressed by both Aunt Grace and Mrs Savage? Surely not — as long as the praise stops short of flattery, there can be little harm. My mind shied away from lingering further on the physical pleasures that my Aunt's caresses had caused, even though the message from my skin was clearly one of keen hope for her touch. I also hoped that she would be in a similar state of undress as the last time because if her facial beauty had softened any resistance in me from the very beginning, the loveliness of her womanly figure aroused something else within me. Something I had never experienced before and which mystified me. Why, for example, had I felt the sudden surge of regret that I had not caught a glimpse of her bottom?

'Look, observe, learn,' she said. 'Do not shutter your mind.'

I lay back at full stretch on the chaise longue and waited until it was time.

My disappointment at being greeted by a fully-clothed Aunt Grace did not last very long — Mrs Savage's warmly effusive welcome and an impressive collection of new clothes were enough to propel me to the fastest possible disrobing. And when I stood naked before them, the admiring looks on both faces was indeed gratifying, so much so that I felt a surge of warm energy as my blood seemed to race through my veins and I stood before them with a peculiar sense of pride in my display. I went up onto the tips of my toes, raised my arms in an attempt to emulate the pose of the garden goddess; I turned about to show off my naked bottom; I walked to the far end of the room with an exaggerated sway of my hips; I danced and laughed. And they both laughed with me.

In a few moments I was panting from my exertions and we all settled down to the business of my new outfits. First there were drawers, a dozen pairs, mainly white but a couple in wickedly exciting black. Some were all of a piece, with no slit at either front or back; others were of the type I was more used to but infinitely tighter, made of infinitely finer material, so that when I was encouraged to study myself in the pier glass, I could clearly see the triangular shadow of my love nest, although its paler curls made it less of a feature than Aunt Grace's had been earlier.

Then there were two tight bodices, with buttons down the front so that I could arrange a very saucy décolletage. And lightweight skirts which hugged my rear before flaring outwards towards my ankles. We settled on a pair of white, slit drawers, dark stockings which were gartered (in dashing crimson!) about halfway up my thighs, bodice and skirt. I paraded before them in my new finery and immediately felt a transformation in myself. I stood straighter and more confidently; I felt more mature; I walked with a womanly stateliness instead of a rather girlish skip; I felt alluring.

Pleased with my obvious pleasure, Mrs Savage left, promising to have more ready by early in the following week, a promise of greater riches which increased my excitement still further. So it is easy to imagine the deflation I experienced when, the moment the door closed behind her, Aunt Grace turned to me and announced that she was going to spank me!

From grown woman to little girl in the twinkling of an eye. And yet, my trust in her was already such that the shock was sharp but not overwhelming. The instinctive protest died before it passed my lips and I stared at her — pale, I am sure; breathless and with a pounding heart, I know. But I somehow knew that it was part of my education into the strange areas that she had hinted at earlier. The overt reason was probably my excess of vain pride in my new apparel but I did not feel the need to ask. It mattered not. All that did matter was that my powerfully beautiful relative had spoken and that the consequences of refusal would undoubtedly be worse than acceptance. We both held our gaze — mine quietly pleading, for enlightenment rather than mercy; hers steadfast and appraising.

She took my hand and led me over to the place of execution, a chaise longue by the large window, sat down and helped me across her lap. As I sank into the required position, I realised that even at this early stage in the proceedings, there were a number of important differences between this and the last occasion I had been spanked — by Cook. I was not exhausted by two days' travel; I had learnt a little about corporal pleasures, especially those relating to what had hitherto been my private parts; and if my knowledge had increased a little, my curiosity had been considerably aroused. As I settled, I made a conscious effort to open the shutters and learn.

I had gained enough in the way of understanding in the past few days to know that the main object of attention was my bottom, rather than humiliation and pain. Aunt Grace had made no efforts to disguise her admiration for this part of me and my contemplation of the statue in the garden had given me a hint of the reason. With the comfort of this supposition, I was not having to steel myself to withstand a serious assault on my sensitive flesh.

Not surprisingly, my mind was filled with a variety of sensations from my bottom and ignored the hollow sound of my laboured breathing and the pounding echo of my heartbeat. My posterior felt large, prominent and I could tell from the way that the edges of my drawers were digging into my flesh that the curved posture I was adopting had thrust a sizeable part of its middle section through the slit in my underwear. Aunt Grace ran her hand over the seat of my skirt for a few moments then began to tug it steadily up my legs and thighs, over my rump, until she could fold it well out of the way above my waist. My half-naked buttocks started to tingle in anticipation of the spanks which were inevitably about to visit them.

Nothing happened. My breathing grew shallower and quicker as my nerves started jangling quietly before easing again as her hand resumed the soothing stroking, this time producing even more pleasant sensations as her soft palm moved from the taut silk of my drawers onto bare skin, across the division between the cheeks, lingering on the in-rolling curves and then slipping back to silk to complete its journey to my right flank. After four or five similar excursions, I was in thrall to the exceedingly pleasant sensations which were coursing quietly through me.

'I am going to take your drawers down and bare your bottom completely, Annie.'

'Must you, Aunt Grace?'

'Yes.'

My protest had been half-hearted. I had not had time to consider the form my spanking would take, but I think I would have been surprised had she not laid the target area completely bare. Whither my modesty?

Even so, her soft voice, seeming to come from miles above me, renewed the jitters in my nerves and my breathing was distinctly shallower as I felt her fingers

23

carefully loosening the tapes at my waist, before slowly easing my last garment down. Instinctively, my buttocks clamped together, fearing an immediate assault, but when nothing happened, I relaxed them, settling myself on her lap and setting my mind to the exercise of absorbing everything I could possibly learn from this strange experience.

It did not come as a surprise that she did not immediately begin the spanking as by now I was beginning to understand that building up the suspense was a crucial element in the procedure. I sensed that she was studying my bare bottom which seemed to flush hot then go cold under her scrutiny. Little pangs of fear fluttered in my belly and I felt the essential humiliation of my position before her earlier words came back to mind — 'Look, observe, learn'. They helped to stiffen my resolve again. I reminded myself that I was not a silly schoolgirl undergoing merited punishment at the hands of a stern Mistress but virtually a grown woman of eighteen. In a way which I did not fully understand, I was being tested — my field of vision was limited to the small portion of the chaise longue seat close before my eyes but I knew that if I observed and sought to learn from my ordeal, I could perhaps experience something hitherto hidden from me.

The tingling in my bottom intensified. I rested my head on the cradle of my folded arms, closed my eyes and did what I could to anticipate the unknown which lay ahead of me — to force my curiosity to overcome the inevitable pain, to co-operate with Aunt Grace to the best of my ability, although this was a little difficult as I was so ignorant of the whole process of being spanked in such a sensually deliberate manner.

Therefore when the first spank arrived I had had time to prepare myself to some extent, although, because it had been so long since I had been spanked on my bare bottom, I had little idea what I was preparing myself for! Of the several impressions which assaulted my senses more or less simultaneously, the sound of the blow was the most immediate. There was a sharp, ringing quality to it which was quite exciting and in a roundabout way, underlined my nakedness, almost as much as the feeling of her palm strikng my skin. I remember clearly being a little surprised at the extent to which I could feel my bottom quiver at the impact of her hand; then there was the pain. I cannot claim that her first blow was painful, even though it was sharp enough to produce a warm sting, but equally it would not be true to claim that I did not feel it! But I clearly recall my relief that the quality of the pain made it different from what I had expected and at the same time, strangely compelling.

Aunt Grace gave me adequate time to absorb the impact of her first spank before administering the second one to the same area of my right bottom-cheek — on the plumptest part just where the curve begins its downward path towards the thigh. Again she paused for several moments before smacking me for the third time. Then the fourth.

I settled down over her thighs and began to enjoy the firm yet softly yielding support they provided; I grew aware of the feel of her left hand which was resting on the small of my back. It was not holding me down, presumably because I had shown no signs of restless struggle, but was in a peculiar way comforting and reassuring. The spanks were beginning to come more quickly but with less force, dancing across the full expanse of my bottom, moving methodically from the top to base and from one cheek to the other, hard enough to keep my ample mounds perpetually a-quiver, but yet not hard enough to cause a distracting level of pain.

My curious mind moved from sensation to sensation,

trying to savour and appreciate each one as my Aunt's hand beat its incessant rhythm but, in time, the increasing heat in my bottom began to overwhelm everything else. My buttocks seemed to swell and the rest of my body diminish until my whole being apparently consisted of a stark-naked, stinging posterior. And yet, the pain excited me. A small part of my mind could wonder at this for a while, for I have never been noted for my fortitude and my bottom *was* really most sore. I was sighing and gasping but there were no tears in my eyes. I could feel that my hips were moving but I knew that it was not to avoid the spanks but rather to raise the target area to meet them. If I had allowed myself to be put across Aunt Grace's lap without protest, I was now submitting myself to her willingly and was confident that she was finding genuine pleasure in the sight and feel of my bare bottom so close to her. Her pleasure was my pleasure and the waves of heat seemed to be spreading from my buttocks and suffusing my entire being with life.

My vision narrowed so that it was like looking down a long, red tunnel. There was a roaring in my ears that dulled the ringing song of her bare palm on my bare flesh; the pain became pain and I felt as if my bottom would burst; I could hear cries far in the distance — the voice sounded like my own but was too far away. I could feel her arm tightly clamped on my waist and her hand gripping my naked hip, pinning me down on her broad thighs. Then there was peace and I was almost floating, although only for a moment, before my scattered senses began to return. I was sobbing hoarsely, I could feel my whole body tremble and my bottom felt as though some servant had lit a fire on it! It throbbed, burned, ached and stung most abominably. But, in spite of it all, I knew that the shutters had been opened a bit further and that I would learn from my ordeal — even if I was not capable of thinking deeply about the lesson at the time!

If Aunt Grace's right hand had proved exceedingly capable of lighting fires on my buttocks, it was now proving equally adept at extinguishing them. As the burning eased gradually towards the tolerable, I became aware that she was stroking my inflamed flesh with a delightful gentleness. Slowly my sobs died away and all my muscles relaxed and it was as though I was flowing over her lap. Her hand soothed my buttocks, then ran gently up and down the cleft between them, fingering the in-rolling of the heated cheeks and little sparks of tingling pleasure began to flicker through the flames which were still coursing through my whole bottom. In time, my breathing steadied to its usual level and I began to try and come to terms with the kaleidoscope of feelings which were still whirling through me. I again became conscious of the bareness of my buttocks and of the prominent pose they were assuming. Aunt Grace's several examinations and caresses on this part of my body had already accustomed me to their sensitivity and I had soon lost the natural sense of shame at exhibiting my bottom in a state of nature, hence my happy posturing in front of Mrs Savage. But lying face down across her ample thighs, with my skirts tucked up on my back and my drawers in limp surrender at my knees, I felt particularly exposed. But instead of the shame which should have been a vital part of the proceedings — had I actually been the schoolgirl with whom I had compared myself at the beginning, I know that I would have been completely humiliated by having to present my bare bottom right before a Mistress's eyes — there was an exhilaration.

I hoped that I had behaved well under the chastisement. I wanted Aunt Grace to be pleased with me.

I was much reassured when at last she broke the silence:

'Oh Annie, I remember telling you earlier that you had

great promise. You have certainly pleased me so far. There is still much for you to learn but I have few doubts that you will learn quicker than most.'

I lay there, more and more at ease despite the bizarre circumstances, and at last the shutters began to open. I felt more alive than I had ever done in my life; I had offered my beautiful Aunt my bare bottom and she had accepted the offering with obvious delight and, at the same time, had taken part of my soul. I began to love her at that moment. And I sensed that in her own strange way, she loved me a little too. The touch of her hand on my naked flesh hinted it; the tone of her voice suggested it. And her ensuing remarks confirmed it:

'Your bottom is truly magnificent, my dear. Such soft skin, so richly curved . . . lovely deep little folds where your buttocks and thighs meet. And the cleft . . . so tight, deep. And such firm flesh . . . yet properly soft and feminine . . .'

Those few, halting sentences, accompanied by suitable fondling, stroking and pressing, were like music to my ears. I had been complimented on my looks before, especially as a little girl but had never taken a great deal of notice as praise had always seemed to have been accompanied by warnings of vanity! With Aunt Grace it was all so very different. Her comments were so much more than casual observation and so far removed from suspicious flattery that they sent a thrill right through me. My awareness spread from my bottom; I felt that my constricted breasts were tight and swollen, with the nipples sharply pointed and aching with delicious desire. My furry little love nest started to throb as I pressed it against Aunt Grace's thigh, an action which proved pleasing not only because of the pressure on my person but also because of the impression of her thighs gained by my frontal parts. I then lifted my hips before pressing down again and the movements of my bottom added a splendid counterpoint to the pleasures. Aunt Grace obviously found the spectacle attractive for she laughed softly as if in encouragement.

By this stage I was transported into a totally new dimension of physical and emotional feelings. Loving and being loved on both levels, my assaulted flesh no longer burning with the intensity of before but throbbing throughout and with the tingle from the caresses thrilling my skin. I could not imagine that there could be more intense delights — until Aunt Grace's hands moved down to the tops of my stockings and, in perfect concert, smoothed their way from the tight silk and onto the naked skin of my thighs, onwards and upwards until they lingered at the join of thigh with buttock, where the right fingertips stroked the very base of my bottom-cleft, then on to the roundest and plumpest part of each cheek, where they rested. Then they began to knead my mounds, shifting the flesh this way and that, and the movements gently agitated my most secret places until I was gasping and sighing uninhibitedly.

I was so lost in bliss that the significance of her next action did not strike me immediately. I vaguely felt her hands alter their position on my buttocks so that each thumb was resting on each side of their dividing groove. The gradually increasing pressure as she slowly pressed outwards to open up the cleft seemed at first to be no more than an extension of the general kneading which had been giving me such pleasure. As soon as I realised what was being exposed — my little bottom-hole, which to my certain knowledge had not been exposed to anyone's gaze since I was a tiny baby — the surprise was such that I could not even breathe. I froze. Completely. But once again, my newly-awakened sensual curiosity overcame my apprehension, my breath hissed into my strained lungs and my tensed muscles relaxed again. Then I felt the surge of a new and unexpected pleasure. My anus started to produce a distinctive tingle of its own, which added to the maelstrom of other sensations — the warm throbbing in my buttocks, the sweet/sour waves from my love-nest and the tight ache in my breasts. The novelty of this tingle quickly took over, sending the others into the background. She moved the soft halves of my bottom around, gently to begin with and then with slowly increasing vigour, until I was sighing and panting again. Then I felt the feather-like touch of a fingertip running slowly round in decreasing circles, moving closer and closer to the actual opening, the pleasure-waves grew stronger and stronger until they completely dominated me and I was thrusting my bottom upwards against her finger.

I cannot give a detailed account of the next minutes because I surrendered myself, body, soul and mind to Aunt Grace's expert ministrations. I do remember that at some stage she tucked one hand under me and a probing finger wriggled between the swollen lips of my love-nest and found my pleasure spot, while another finger slipped firmly past the tight ring guarding my back passage, so that both my most secret places were under the most delectable assault at one and the same time. After that I was overcome with dizziness and must have been near to fainting, because when I began to regain my senses, her left hand was again holding me down by the hip while her right one was again spanking me.

The smacks were not as hard as they had been but delivered to an already well-warmed bottom and in my post-climax state, they were enough to make me squeak. They were also strangely enjoyable, even though this time there were no other distractions to soften the sting. I tried to keep my bottom still for her but was not successful as it started to bob and weave of its own accord. I started to cry. Not the hot tears of real pain. Perhaps it was a release from the mental pain of my parents' death; or a wordless outpouring of all the questions arising from my strange introduction to my new home. Whatever caused the tears, it was not because I wanted the spanking to stop. When it did, however, my first reaction was one of disappointment, before the burning smart really struck home and my hands flew back to clutch my hot cheeks in a desperate attempt to soothe them. I rubbed away, half crying, half laughing until Aunt Grace helped me back to my feet, sat me down on her lap with my weight supported by my thighs rather than my sore buttocks. She then laid my head on her shoulder and we sat together in loving communion.

Fortunately I was able to slip quietly to my room afterwards. My mind was whirling with all the various and varied impressions of that half hour or so I had spent draped across my Aunt's lap. I eased myself onto my bed, deliberately lying on my back so that the weight of my body would keep the still-flickering fires in my bottom alive for as long as possible. I relived the experience in my mind, selecting an aspect, bringing it to the forefront of my mind to savour it until I was ready to move on to another. There was the surprisingly sensual feeling of lying across her thighs, with my rear end so prominently positioned; there was the pleasure in having my bottom bared with such calm deliberation — and the knowledge that its exposure was keenly anticipated. These were the basic foundations which had supported all the other elements: the sound of Aunt Grace's palm landing on my naked flesh; the quivering of my buttocks on each impact; the slowly increasing sting, which hurt in a way that caused something so much greater than pain.

My bottom felt deliciously warm and heavy and the pleasure waves began to concentrate within my love nest,

31

so that I found my right hand straying into it, pressing the light material of my skirt into its tight slit. And when I found that I could not adequately excite the little button, it took me no time at all to whisk my skirt up, my drawers down and find my own path to that most glorious of sensations.

It was the end of my beginning.

CHAPTER 3

From then on, I truly believe that the shutters over my mind were fully open. I plucked up my courage and asked Aunt Grace if I could have a looking glass in my room. I had thought that there had been some mysterious reason for the absence of one but it turned out that it was no more than a simple oversight. In no time at all, a large and handsome pier glass, a small dressing-table one and a hand one were brought in. I spent some time reflecting on my full-length image and admiring the fit of Mrs Savage's tailoring. I found that craning over my shoulder at my back view was not only difficult but gave me a crick in my neck. It did not take me long, however, to re-arrange the selection of mirrors so that looking into the dressing-table one gave me a clear and easy view of my rear in the pier glass. Having assessed the fit of my new clothes, it seemed a natural progress to remove them. At last I would be able to try and understand properly why Aunt Grace (and Mrs Savage . . . and Cook?) had obtained so much enjoyment from my body.

Standing before the pier glass so that I could observe the full length of my body, I first gave my clothed reflection a long appraisal. I saw a neatly clad young lady, of medium height, with a bosom which was obviously feminine but not overly large. Mrs Savage's talents had emphasised the narrowness of my waist, and the outswelling curves of my hips and the cut of the skirt, allied to

33

its softly clinging material, gave clear hints that my thighs were fully rounded.

It is hard to give any form of considered judgement on one's own face. As I have mentioned, various people in my previous life had commented on my prettiness but my mother had always reminded me that pride was one of the seven deadly sins, so that I had never placed a great deal of reliance on the opinions of those who had passed favourable comments on my looks. However, the image in the mirror before me was certainly striking. My hair was (and still is) the colour of ripe straw or thick honey and hung in free ringlets down to my shoulders, swept back sufficiently to expose a wide, smooth forehead. My eyes were blue and returned my gaze with a steady assurance, which belied the turmoil currently assailing the poor brain behind them! They were wide, well-separated and even in the subdued light, glistened. My nose — well it was really just a nose as far as I could see. It certainly could not be criticised for being too large, nor was it so small that it added little or nothing to my overall appearance. It turned up slightly at the tip but whether this was an enviable feature or not, I did not feel in any way qualified to judge. I did, however, feel that my mouth merited favourable comment. Not noticeably wide, but with full, red lips which curled up slightly at the corners, giving the impression that I found most things in life potentially amusing. In all, a rounded as opposed to a long face, with a healthy pink tint in the cheeks.

I stripped completely and began with a careful study of my front, which of course was reasonably familiar. My breasts were smaller than Aunt Grace's, but nicely plump, with neater and pinker nipples. I noted how my waist curved in dramatically from my lower ribs before flaring out even more dramatically to my hips. I moved closer for a better look at my love-nest, nestling at the junction of my rounded thighs and tummy. The golden curls were not thick enough to conceal the tight slit and I held the lips open and thrust my hips forward until the image of glistening pink flesh was almost touching the reality and then watched with open-mouthed fascination as the fingers of my right hand slipped slowly into the inviting passage and started to excite the little pleasure places. It was bliss, but it was not the right time. My curiosity about my bottom had to be satisfied, so I slowly went back to the rearward-viewing position and focused on the part which seemed to have excited Aunt Grace.

Even though mine was the first living bare bottom I had ever studied, I immediately understood the unique attractions of this part of a girl's anatomy. All the aspects which had intrigued me when I first set eyes on my naked statue were even more splendid when seen 'in the flesh': the tight deep cleft; the variety of curves; the delightful little folds at the junction of each thigh and buttock; the way it swelled out from the waist. Add to these the one element which could never be reproduced in marble — the living, warm, smooth softness of feminine skin and I knew that I could easily share Aunt Grace's enthusiasm.

I tried to watch myself walking away from the pier glass but even using the little hand mirror proved unsatisfactory and, when I walked into the bed and barked my shins quite painfully, a little perilous! I had, however, managed an occasional glimpse of the quivering mobility of my buttocks which gave me some satisfaction.

I may have become absorbed with my own body but the main difference in me after my spanking was that my eyes were much more open to the others in the household, especially the maids, who moved very quickly into the foreground of my awareness. I got to know their names; I studied their faces in a natural attempt to gain some little clues about their personalities; I noted their various uniforms and was immediately struck by the subtle emphasis each version put on their figures. Their white blouses all clung tightly to their bosoms and their skirts, both the short daytime ones (which were astoundingly short!) and the longer ones for the evenings were all tight enough to give a fairly clear impression of the form of their bottoms. At this very early stage in my education, it never occurred to me to want to see them naked but I was aware enough to enjoy what revelations were openly available to me.

I also found that I was able to get on much easier terms with Uncle George, to the extent that after two days or so, I felt no inhibitions at showing him one of the artistic books I was entering into the catalogue and asking his opinion of some of the masterpieces illustrated so beautifully, even though it contained the back view of a nude. Without any embarrassment I found myself asking his opinion of her charms and he responded in an equally open manner, pointing out that the artist had rather exaggerated the curves, 'but the flesh tones are splendidly rich — and the division between her cheeks is almost perfect.'

Perhaps a week after my spanking, I was paying my daily homage to my Goddess's bare buttocks — and was just about to reach through the spray to touch them for the first time when Elspeth, one of the maids, came up to me and told me that Aunt Grace wanted to see me in her room in half an hour. My heartbeat immediately doubled its rate. My breath raced down my tight throat and there was the strangest hollow feeling in my tummy, which the spread to my love-nest. My bottom seemed to double in size and its skin began to tingle. I sat down and gazed up at the swelling lower curves of the shining marble rump above me and once more, but this time knowing what lay ahead of me, anticipated my immediate future. As it was a cool day, I had put on a light petticoat and so there was another layer of clothing for Aunt Grace to remove, and I was wearing a pair of drawers without a slit, so would not experience that delightful sensation of having the centre of my bottom thrusting nakedly into the open as I was curved over her lap. But I was sure that this would not matter. I would know again that extraordinary combination of submission and co-operation as I lay bare-bottomed in the traditional posture.

It proved to be even more exciting, challenging and eventually stimulating than the first one had been, which was fortunate because I realised afterwards that she had not been planning to spank me at all! That she did was my doing entirely and caused by my opening remark as I entered her room:

'I've come for my spanking, Aunt Grace.'

I did not give her a great deal of choice! But as you can imagine, she was not the sort of woman who would miss an opportunity when it had been so clearly offered and, after a couple of blinks, she gave me a dazzling smile and moved over to sit down on the business end of her chaise longue. Smiling shyly back at her, I walked slowly across to her and placed myself across her broad lap, settled down and raised my hips a little to make it easier for her to bare my bottom, which she did even more slowly and deliberately than before. For example, once she had lifted my skirt and petticoat up and folded them neatly on the small of my back, she pulled my drawers right up so that the silken material was forced into the cleft of my bottom and even between the lips of my love-nest. As she stroked my buttocks, I found myself a little concerned that she was going to spank me with them on, and I did not find the thought particularly appealing, as the feeling of having a bottom bared specifically for a spanking had been one of the more memorable aspects of my initiation. I should not have worried, as after a few moments I felt her fingers at the drawstrings at my waist and then the cool air caressing an increasing area of my skin as my final protective garment slipped slowly down to well below the tops of my stockings.

This time my inner fears about my ability to withstand the pain had been laid to rest and although there was a lingering apprehension (which has never left me in spite of the hundreds of spankings I have had since), this served merely to heighten my overall sensitivity, so that the sounds of the spanks rang even more sharply in my ears. I was even more acutely aware of the movements of my fleshy cheeks at every impact. I could pay more attention to the yielding plumpness of her thighs under my naked front — until the stinging warmth in my bottom slowly and gradually became the overwhelming sensation and I began to bob and weave uncontrollably.

I did not cry, although I am sure that she had spanked me as vigorously as she had the first time. There were tears in my eyes, that I cannot deny and when it was over and she turned me and sat me up on her lap, I buried my face in her rounded bosom until the flames in my rear had died down a little. Then, having recovered some of my composure, I raised my head and kissed her soft cheek, as a little gesture of love and appreciation. To my surprise and initial discomfiture, she put a finger under my chin, raised my head and kissed me back — but on the lips! As I said, I was a little taken aback at first, but almost at once, the sweet-tasting softness of her mouth dispelled all doubts and when her hotly moist tongue flickered tantalisingly against my lips it sent a surge of pleasure straight to that secret source of ecstasy buried in the folds of my love-nest. My head was swimming, my bottom was throbbing delightfully, my mouth tingling deliciously and when her hand stole down to my taut and still exposed bottom

with the palm cupping the burning flesh and fingers stroking that core of sensuality between my legs, I was soon
lost in the throes of a shattering 'little death'.

When I had recovered, re-arranged my clothes and given
my beloved Aunt a last thank-you kiss, she frowned for
a moment. Then her expression cleared and the suspicion
that I had not been summoned for a spanking first came
upon me:

'Oh yes, Annie, we have guests tonight and I'm afraid
there won't be room for you at the table. Have a quiet
word with Cook, tell her what you would like to have for
your supper and ask her to have it sent up to your room.
Oh, and you can of course have a bottle of wine.'

'Yes certainly, Aunt Grace,' I replied as easily as I
could. But I knew I was blushing and only hoped that she
didn't think I was upset at my exclusion from the dinner
party. Then I saw the conspiratorial grin on her face, realised that she understood and I blushed again with renewed
vigour.

Cook was very busy with her preparations, so I only
stayed long enough for us to agree on a supper of cold
salmon, a selection of cheeses and a bottle of Moselle,
after which I decided to go up to my room and rest for
a while. I met Elspeth on the stairs and smiled at her. Her
reaction puzzled me to start with, for she reddened slightly
and her eyes slid away from mine before returning, when
her mouth curved upwards in response to my smile. I then
knew that she knew that I had been spanked and I blushed and looked away in my turn: at which point we both
continued silently on our ways. My slight embarrassment
left me as soon as I had closed the door of my room behind
me. If she knew, well there was nothing I could do and
if I felt no shame in being spanked, then there was little
point in getting upset if others found out. As it was not
exactly the most silent of activities in any case, the chances

of it being secret were very remote to start with. I forgot about it immediately when I saw my reflection in the pier glass and had a sudden and overwhelming urge to examine my freshly spanked bottom.

I adjusted the position of my relevant mirrors with almost indecent haste, hauled my skirts up behind with similar urgency and locked my gaze on the seat of my drawers. Unlike the pair of Aunt Grace's that I had seen, mine were not made of the finest silk but were just transparent enough for the shadowy line of my bottom-cleft to be visible, but even more obvious was a red stain over the entire area. Trembling with excitement, I fumbled for the tapes, untied them with fingers suddenly cursed with unusual clumsiness and pushed them down over my buttocks until they started slithering to my ankles. In my innocence, it had never occurred to me that spanking would redden a girl's bottom so dramatically. Nor that the redness would be such a rich, deep shade. I stared, enraptured for several minutes. Then I saw that the discolouration stopped a little way short of the very tops of my cheeks — there was an inch or so of white flesh below the level of the beginning of the cleft. The reason was made clear to me when I bent forward to place my rear closer to the pier glass, and noticed that the cleft got shorter as I did so and that, in this new pose, the whole of my bottom was red. Obviously the same thing would have happened when I was bent across her knees, even though the upper part of my body had been resting more or less flat on the seat of the chaise longue.

My curiosity increased. I stripped myself naked again and moved the mirrors so that I could observe myself in the nearest approximation to that position — lying over my bed — and found the view looking up my white thighs to the scarlet mounds jutting upwards in a wanton display of curved flesh, completely absorbing. And oddly beautiful. I reached back and stroked the still hot skin, trying to concentrate my awareness fully towards the feel of my bottom under my hand, but somehow the feel of my hand on my bottom was distracting, although I was aware of the softness of my skin and flesh. As I lay there, the thought came to me that I would love to watch myself being spanked by Aunt Grace and I wondered if there was any chance of arranging a pair of mirrors to allow me to do just that. Would I have the courage to ask her next time?

After my second serious spanking, I felt even more alive than I had after the first one, with the blood coursing healthily through my veins, all the little frustrations of life dispersed, the quiet love of Aunt Grace, the friendship of Cook and the maids and the satisfying work with Uncle George in the library, all combining to produce a perpetual song in my heart. There were also the newly discovered sensual delights available from my own body. If I often stared at my naked reflection for minutes on end, I reject any accusations of vanity. I was not looking at, or for, perfection in myself but for knowledge and understanding of the many fascinations that the female body contains — although it would be dishonest to deny that I knew that mine represented quite a high standard of beauty and equally so not to admit that my search was a pleasant task!

As things turned out, I did not have to ask Aunt Grace to spank me in front of a mirror. Only a day or so later, we were in her drawing room waiting for afternoon tea and talking happily away about nothing of any great importance. At precisely four o'clock there was a knock on the door and Maria, one of the older maids and a quiet girl with a gentle, round face, came in with the tray. I can remember quite clearly that I idly watched her rear view as she walked past me to set the tray down on the table by Aunt Grace, and noticed that she was broad and rounded in the beam. As I have said, at that stage, my

41

thoughts were very inward-looking and it had not occurred to me even to wonder at the shape and quality of the maids' flesh — in spite of my momentary regret that I had not seen my Aunt's near-naked behind when Mrs Savage was measuring me. I also spotted a subtle exchange of little smiles between the two of them but thought no more of it until a long time later, because Aunt Grace's next words came like a bolt of lightning which drove any other thoughts from my mind:

'Maria! Why on earth haven't you cut the crusts off the sandwiches? How many times do I have to tell you? Now go and cut them properly — then I'll give you the sound spanking you thoroughly deserve.'

I sat very still. All the usual signs of sensual excitement arrived at one and the same time: restricted breathing; a rapid rise in my heartbeat; a prickling feeling in my face as I blushed and an immediate tingling throb between my thighs. Then an awful thought occurred to me. Aunt Grace could well decide to reduce Maria's humiliation and ask me to leave. I would certainly stay close to the door in the hope of hearing the sound of her hand on the girl's bottom but that would be but a poor substitute for actually watching her being so suitably and entertainingly punished. My mind raced through the various alternatives before deciding that boldness was more likely to succeed than staying as quiet as possible in the hope that my presence would not intrude. I cleared my throat nervously:

'Er, would it be in order, Aunt Grace, if I . . . I mean, I'm sure that it would be, er, interesting and instructional if I could actually . . . well, watch you spank her . . . if that's all right. Aunt Grace, er, you know, it would, I am sure, be helpful to me in showing me how to present and conduct myself better the next time you spank me . . .'

As a firm, positive statement it may have left a little to be desired but it did not matter. Aunt Grace favoured me with another of her special smiles, then laughed:

'Oh dearest Annie, of course you can watch. She's quite used to others watching her having her bottom well warmed, and your presence will add a little extra spice to her chastisement. Not that you have a great deal to learn about conducting yourself, in any case . . . you took both spankings remarkably well — and the second one noticeably better than the first. I have been meaning to ask you, by the way — how do you feel about being put across my knee . . now that you have been there twice?'

'It is not easy to describe, Aunt. I suppose basically I wanted to please you . . . you had said that you liked my bottom . . . then your little strokes were very pleasant and feeling it gradually being bared was strangely exciting. I knew that you weren't punishing me . . . more testing me. I still don't fully understand . . . but it enabled me to withstand the pain which wasn't like normal pain. My bottom seems to feel things differently to other parts of my body . . . although I cannot help feeling that if I were being punished by a schoolmistress for example, I would have felt it simply as humiliating and agonising — but not with you. And afterwards, when the stinging had died away . . .. and you caressed me . . . you know . . . um down there . . . the pleasure was almost more than I could bear. And after that, for quite a long time, I felt very different. Especially after the second one. Far more alive, somehow . . . I felt loved, however odd that may sound.'

At that point, I blushed again and looked down at the floor, unable to believe that I had opened my heart so easily. I had a sudden dread that she would laugh at me, and that would have been very hard to bear. There was no sound from her. I sneaked a quick glance — and she was looking at me in a most heart-warming way, with a soft gentle smile.

'I told you that you had it in you to discover many things

43

which normal people could not even imagine, let alone understand. You're right, my dear it *is* difficult to explain. But not everything about it is in the mind. You see . . .'

At that very point, Maria came back in with the plate of correctly made sandwiches and was told to pour our tea and then stand in the corner until we were ready. The conversation did not flow as it had been doing up until then. It was not helped by the fact that my eyes were constantly straying to the seat of her skirt, studying the way it subtly hinted at the shape of her posterior and trying to imagine the true form and colour of the twin mounds. I sincerely hoped that Aunt Grace would lay her bottom bare for the punishment and did my level best to eat and drink with some sort of composure. This was, however, tested almost to the limit when she was told to pour us both a second cup — and to refill my plate. After which, she had to go back in the corner but this time with hands resting on the top of her head, which pulled her skirt a little more tightly over her rear and made the view even more tantalising.

About an hour later — well, it seemed at least as long but I suppose it couldn't have been — Aunt Grace put her empty cup on the tray, stood up, fetched an armless chair from a corner, placed it sideways-on right in front of my chair and sat down. I sat back and, trying to look as calm and nonchalant as possible, waited for the next stage in my education to commence. Thanks to the delay in the proceedings — however frustrating it seemed at the time — I was in a much more composed frame of mind than I would have been if Maria had had to present her bottom immediately. Aunt Grace did not say much but I noted the calm and almost sympathetic tone of her voice: 'Come here, Maria.'

She stood in front of my aunt, facing her, so that I was looking at their profiles and could watch both their facial expressions — and cast the occasional glimpse at the curve of the maid's seat. 'Now you really know by now how to cut my sandwiches. It was pure carelessness and I hope that this punishment will smarten you up a bit — in more ways than one. As I said earlier, I am going to spank you. Quite hard. On your bare bottom. Now come here and place yourself across my lap.'

As the full details of the sentence were announced, I gave a little sigh of relief. Maria blushed and her mouth assumed an even more pronounced downward curve.

She gave me a shy and sweet little smile, moved round to Aunt Grace's right — with her back to me — and slowly but gracefully laid herself across those splendid thighs, her skirt momentarily tightening nicely across the broadened bottom as she did so, until she was in position, her hands and feet on the floor, the target area in the centre of Aunt Grace's lap, her legs slightly apart. Her black-clad rump loomed up in a sweeping curve from her thighs and I instinctively leaned forward to get a closer view. My Aunt, with a little smile on her face, stroked the taut seat for a moment, squeezed the flesh underneath and then began to prepare it, lifting the skirt, then the petticoat and folding them neatly on the middle of Maria's back. We both studied the result. Her drawers were as loose and baggy as my old ones and by chance, they had folded themselves to cover her buttocks completely in spite of the up-thrust position of her hips and the movements of her outer clothing. Aunt Grace's right hand then slipped quietly into the slit and I was treated to the rather tantalising sight of it moving around under the material as she reminded herself of the qualities of the skin and flesh underneath.

Fortunately, she did not take long on what seemed to be a pleasurable exercise and was soon setting about the task of loosening the ribbons at the waist and slowly pulling the drawers down until they lay limply at Maria's ankles.

I gazed with delight at the first naked bottom I had ever properly seen and let out a deep, long sigh. Due to her posture, it jutted less dramatically than my statue's but still displayed a delightful range of curves, all covered in skin of an alabaster whiteness and the smoothness of silk. The cleft dividing the cheeks provided an even more vivid centre of attention than the marble one, with its pinkish shade and impression of feminine softness.

I suppose that one is born with tastes that will emerge later in life if the right stimulus is found — and so my rapid conversion to the appreciation of the human buttocks probably started deep within me and the events of the past few weeks had simply brought them to the surface. Similarly, some people will take to eating fish or listening to opera, whatever their education in such matters, whereas others will be completely indifferent to their attractions. Whatever the cause, I was very moved at the sight of Maria's bare bottom as it waited so patiently for its spanking and needed nobody to point out its attractions.

Nor did watching it as it was spanked do anything but increase my pleasure. The ringing impact of Aunt Grace's hand was known to me of course but the other effects were not similar. The most immediately obvious was the way her fat cheeks wobbled so noticeably at every smack. I had felt the movement of my own flesh but the extent of the agitation surprised me. Then there was the spreading red stain as the spanking progressed. Although I had obviously expected this, having inspected my bottom in the mirror not long before, the imprint left by Aunt Grace's palm and the way each one began to merge with the marks of previous visitations was something I found utterly charming. Then my vision expanded from her posterior to her whole being and I noted her calm and ready acceptance of the punishment, the way she presented herself, mostly as still as she could manage, except when her left flank was being attended to and she tilted her body to her right to allow proper access to this area. The sound of the spanks was enough to tell me that I had got off relatively lightly and the stoic way she kept her bottom presented — and as still as she could — impressed me, and I vowed to myself to do all I could to match her courage when it was my turn again.

Her whole bottom was a deep scarlet colour before Aunt Grace stopped. Maria lay passively across her lap while the effects were closely studied by her audience, gasping and panting as the stinging heat throbbed through her flesh but otherwise remarkably composed. Which is rather more than could be said about my feelings! I had found the whole thing exceedingly exciting and that increasingly familiar sweet and sour ache was spreading from my love-nest, to the extent that I can only vaguely recall seeing her clamber back to her feet, re-arrange her clothing and leave.

As soon as I could, I returned to my room, stripped naked and turned my back on the pier glass. At last I had some basis on which to make some sort of comparison between my bottom and another, and I did feel that mine was distinctly more rounded than Maria's although whether this was a good or bad thing, I did not feel qualified to judge. Without caring if a passer-by should overhear, I arranged the various mirrors so that I could bend over the side of my bed and watch my own hand bring that lovely flush to my cheeks — after which I lay back and brought about another journey to physical heaven.

When I eventually went to bed, my last waking thought was the hope that I would again be allowed to watch a maid being spanked.

It did not occur to me to wish that I would ever be able to spank one of them myself.

CHAPTER 4

I probably had a week to assimilate the lessons of the various experiences that had been visited upon me. At first, my relationship with Maria had been a little awkward. The excitement I had felt before and during her chastisement had faded to a sympathy with her natural sense of shame at having to proffer such a private area of her flesh with me as an avid witness but, very shortly, her complete acceptance of the incident communicated itself to me and a bond grew between us. I began to spend more and more time in the kitchen and the slight awkwardness which had made conversation with all the maids initially a little stilted gradually disappeared. Cook proved to be a lovely, jolly woman, who always seemed to have a titbit for a hungry girl — as well as a happy jest and a warm welcome.

It was unlike any kitchen I had ever visited. The maids were all very pretty young women, with ages varying between the 19 years of Elspeth and Agatha's 32, were all nicely spoken, seemed to have had a fair level of education and exhibited a mental brightness which made the general atmosphere completely different to all the other below-stairs establishments I had known. In this one, I was treated with warm politeness as opposed to the slightly nervous respect I had been used to, even as a young girl. In short, they were not the type of maid I was accustomed to!

Uncle George and I worked happily away in the library

and our discussions on the merits of the figures of the naked ladies depicted in the illustrations of his collection of art books grew more frequent, more detailed and involved — and more entertaining.

Aunt Grace seemed busy and I saw relatively little of her but, when we did have a chance of some conversation, there was an easy, warm intimacy between us which did a great deal to heal the scar left by the loss of my dear mother, although I was beginning to realise that perhaps my relationship with that calm and rather distant lady had not been as close as I had thought. I certainly found that it was far easier to ask Aunt Grace's advice and opinion about all manner of subjects — and that her replies were often of an open and candid nature which my mother would have found shocking. The only subject which did not elicit her usual frankness was our kinship. When I tried to question her, she changed to another conversational topic and all I could gather was that she had known both my parents for a long time. I suspected that she was not an aunt in the true sense at all. At first this supposition renewed my feelings of loneliness and vulnerability but the atmosphere of this strange house had captured me to such an extent that I no longer felt the lack of a family. I had a comfortable home, I was on the threshold of making real friends and, first and foremost, I had discovered that the human body was capable of intense physical pleasures, that the female form could be uniquely beautiful and that, to me at least, both these factors were most evident when concentrated on the bottom.

At this point, my buttocks began to tingle at the memories of the treatment already meted out to them. I raised them and hauled my nightgown up to my waist, before turning onto my side so that my hand could pass over the naked flesh, stroking, squeezing, patting and pinching the yielding mounds until the blood flowed hotly and the waves of pleasure slowly intensified. I turned right over and kicked the blankets down to the end, so that the night air could play over the skin and send cooling tendrils into the warmth of the dividing cleft. I slowly reached back with both hands, one on each cheek, and drew them apart, revelling in the gradual exposure of my bottom-hole. I extended the middle finger of my right hand and and trickled the tip over the gently wrinkled area surrounding it, and then treated the opening itself to the nearest approximation to Aunt Grace's feathery caress that I could manage. Doing it with my own hand was nowhere near as tantalising as hers had been but, even so, it was a thrilling sensation which soon sent those flickering tendrils into my fast-moistening love nest. Almost of their own accord, my knees moved upwards until my bottom was thrust into the air, opening the deep cleft, making it easier for my finger to slip a little way past the tight ring which so ably protected this very private little passage. My other hand moved underneath to the throbbing button and, with my gasps of ecstasy whistling in my ears, I rode the waves of my climax.

The following morning I awoke early and with all my senses alert. I ate a hearty breakfast, enjoyed a stroll in the garden and a lingering assessment of the glistening marble buttocks which had provided me with so much inspiration. I then decided that a quiet morning in the library was too dull a prospect and so made my way to the kitchen, in the hope that the bustling, cheery atmosphere usually to be found there would provide some amusement.

Cook had already left to organise the weekly shopping, the other maids were busy about the house, leaving only Elspeth, who was sitting quietly enjoying a cup of tea. As I entered, her dear little face split into an especially cheery grin and she drew another chair up to the range and poured me a cup. We chatted easily enough for several minutes and then she moved over to the sink to wash up our cups, giving me the opportunity to calmly study her neat rear. She was dressed in the normal daytime costume with the short skirt only just covering her knees. Her legs were in perfect keeping with her slender figure but her calves were shapely enough to fill her dark stockings and the way that the skirt arranged itself about her thighs suggested that there was a satisfactory degree of fleshly curve beneath it. Naturally my gaze moved rapidly upwards till it rested happily on her seat. I recalled the similar view I had had of Maria when I had witnessed her spanking and could therefore surmise with some confidence that Elspeth was not as well endowed, although the gentle shake which agitated this part of her as she scrubbed the mugs was not only enchanting, but also indicated that she could well be deceptively plump.

Suddenly I felt an irresistable urge to see and touch her. My period of abstinence from fleshly stimulation and the way I had brought that period to an end the night before, had combined to make me long for physical contact. I did not want to upset a burgeoning friendship and I was still unsure of my exact place in this strange household, so was not confident that I could use social superiority to bend her to my will. She was also older than I, even if only a year or so. On the other hand, she showed every sign of liking me and was clearly aware that Aunt Grace had spanked me — and I could not believe that Maria had not told them all that I had witnessed her punishment. So, taking my courage in both hands, I rose, walked over to her, rested my right hand on her hip and said: 'I love the way your bottom shook while you were washing the cups.'

She had turned her head towards mine at my touch and, at my words, that very engaging grin lit up her elfin face. 'Did you?' she replied — and was there a hint of an in-

51

vitation in her eyes?

I did not have any clear idea of the direction this encounter could take but some inner instinct convinced me that a new and especially exciting experience awaited me. There was a similar hollowness in my belly to that I had felt before Maria's spanking, only this time it was stronger. Our eyes were locked together as my hand left her hip and started a slow exploration of the shape of her buttocks, gliding down her flank and then laterally towards the centre and I could feel the separation of the twin globes, even though there were several layers of material in between. I thrilled to the roundness of her cheeks and to the way her flesh yielded to the pressure of my palm, even though the first impression was one of firmness. I searched her expression for the least sign of discomfiture as my caresses grew in urgency and intensity. There was nothing more than a shy smile which spoke only of a welcome. My hand rested in the very centre of her bottom while I absorbed the messages being sent through my eyes. As I have said, she had an elfin look to her: small, neat features. Her hair was shorter and less fair than my own and hung freely down to her shoulders; her brown eyes were wide apart (and wide open) and were glistening with what I hoped was a similar excitement to mine; her mouth was also wide, with a subtly charming curve to her rosy lips.

Slowly, she turned until she was facing me, our eyes and mouths almost exactly level as we were of similar height. Of its own accord, my left hand moved up until it rested on her right breast and, if the thrill of this contact was not quite the equal of the previous first touch on her bottom, the immediate realisation that it was bare under her blouse was gratifying to say the least. I noticed that her dear little face was filling more and more of my vision, that her mouth was changing shape, from a soft smile to an inviting pout. She wanted me to kiss her. And at once, I felt the strongest desire to do just that. Our lips touched. Their softness came as no real surprise, for I had kissed before. What was a new and delectable experience was the way her moist, stiff tongue flickered against my lips, gently eased its way between them and then somehow drew the tip of mine to meet it. We breathed in each other's breath; tasted each other's saliva. My right hand tightened its hold on her bottom and pulled her even closer to me; her hand returned the compliment and the feel of it at the sensitive meeting of my mounds added an extra spice to the kiss.

Eventually we drew apart and gazed smilingly at each other. I saw that her lips were glistening from the attentions of my tongue, so bent forward and kissed them dry — which took an age, because mine were just as moist! Then we gradually came back down to earth. With a last affectionate squeeze my hands slipped away from her bottom.

'Somebody might come in . . . Perhaps we could see each other later . . . When you are free?'

She looked at me, no longer smiling but with her mouth slightly open. 'I can be free now. We would be safe in your room . . . if you would like to.' At that her mischievous grin reappeared.

I felt a resurgence of that hollow-bellied excitement at that prospect of prolonging our dalliance but, even more, a new sense of power. Elspeth was a dear girl whom I found both companionable and attractive. If I had begun to enjoy the strange pleasures of submission to Aunt Grace, I suddenly wanted to savour the other side of the coin. And by this stage I had learned just enough to be able to recognise an opportunity — and to take advantage of it.

'That was an extremely forward suggestion,' I whispered. 'I cannot allow such provocation to go unpunished. We shall go to my room and, on the way, I shall

53

bend my mind to finding a suitable, appropriate and effective way of punishing you.'

She fell into her part with ease. 'Oh Madam, I offer my most humble and sincere apologies. I must, of course, be punished, but I beg you please, please do not spank me. It would be too shaming.'

'Do not try to prejudice me, Elspeth. Now come along.' We set off with measured haste. 'Now, I had been thinking of some sort of imposition, such as a hundred lines, but the idea of spanking you does have a certain appeal.'

'Oh please, I'll do two hundred lines, but . . .'

'Silence! Your protestations have persuaded me that there could not possibly be a better way of teaching you the error of your ways than by smacking your bottom.'

'If you insist, Madam. But I beg you to preserve my modesty — I have a light skirt on and my drawers are the thinnest I have, so they will do little to stop me feeling the smacks.'

By this time we had reached my room and there was a slight pause while I opened the door and led her in, giving me a little time to choose my words. 'I have never heard such craven nonsense in my life! If you seriously consider that I would waste my efforts by beating the dust from your clothing, you will have to think again. The only way that I can ensure that you feel my displeasure, my girl, is to raise your skirt, lower your drawers — right down to your knees so that your bottom is completely bare — and administer the spanks directly onto your naked skin!'

Aunt Grace had told me not to let my mind be shuttered. This apparently trivial little episode was already widening the aperture to the inner recesses of my mind just a bit further. On our walk to my room, the headiness of the initial excitement had settled somewhat, leaving me in a calmer, more rational frame of mind and far more

54

in control then if we had continued in the kitchen. I was, therefore able to appreciate the joys of anticipation, to savour the prospect of spanking a girl for the very first time, and not to diminish the experience by rushing at it.

It would be wrong not to acknowledge Elspeth's part in making what had already happened, and what was about to take place, so important in the development of the sensual side of my nature. Had she not assumed the role of the modest maiden, it would have been far harder to have slipped into the complementary role of the stern mistress. It is very probable that I would have been much too diffident and would not have learned so much so quickly. As it was, I looked into her face and there was a distinct air of suppressed excitement in her expression. Her blue eyes were shining, her wide mouth was slightly open and I could feel the warmth of her breath as she exhaled.

I began to revel in the sense of power: this lovely girl was mine to command. The knowledge that she must have been spanked — it had never occurred to me that Maria's experience was unique — and the way that she had guided us into the roles which were proving so comfortable, did not lessen this feeling of power. In fact, I am sure that I would not at that stage have had the necessary confidence to dominate an unwilling partner. But with her help, this crucial step in my complex voyage of discovery was made easy.

I suddenly realised that I had enjoyed 'passing sentence' on her. The fact that some of the words involved were not those commonly used in polite society added noticeable spice to the situation. They re-echoed in my mind. Instinctively I took a second helping.

'Yes, Elspeth. Your naughtiness will be paid for in the way you obviously favour least. I am going to give you a sound spanking. I shall place you across my knees, bare your impudent bottom and smack it until it is as red as a ripe cherry.'

She clearly shared my intoxication with the spoken word — well, these words, anyway.

'Oh Madam, does it really have to be on my bare bottom?' Like me, she put a breathy emphasis on those last two words.

'We shall not discuss the matter any further, Elspeth. I am going to spank you, I am going to do it on your naked bottom and I am going to do it now. Move the chair by the dressing table over there — under the window. The light is better there so that I shall have an even clearer view of your bottom.'

'Yes, Madam,' she said in a totally convincing quaver.

What followed was every bit as exciting in actuality as it had been in prospect. To this very day I can close my eyes and vividly recall the variety of sensations. There was the soft, warm weight of her body on my thighs; the sight of her rounded globe thrusting against the seat of her skirt and the feel of curving and yielding flesh under my palm as I gave her bottom a few exploratory squeezes. There was the shifting of her weight as I tugged her skirt up to her waist and the sharp thrill as her drawers came into view, the slit stretched open by her posture so that several inches of tight bottom-cleft were exposed. I savoured the contrast between smooth cotton and silken skin as I smoothed my right hand over her seat; the visual delight when I eventually gazed down on her completely bared bottom spread out right before me, a firm, beautifully rounded, clefted globe, ending in two delightful little folds at the point where her buttocks and thighs met. Then there was the satisfying feel of her. I spent some time stroking her naked flesh, marvelling at the smoothness of her skin and the surprising way the firmness of her flesh yielded under the slightest pressure of my fingers. Then, when I finally got round to spanking her, three of my senses

56

were stimulated at the same time. The feel of my hand sinking stingingly into her; the sight of her buttocks wobbling and reddening as the steady rain of sharp smacks took effect; the delightful ringing sound of the spanks and the gasps and squeaks that grew slowly in frequency and intensity as the smart spread through her.

Perhaps the most significant aspect was that, even though this was such a new experience to me, I never lost sight of the fact that it was dear Elspeth whom I was spanking. For all the undeniable charm of her naked parts, I was always aware of her as a person — she never faded from my consciousness to become no more than a compliant bottom laid out simply for my pleasure. For example, after I had spent a delicious few moments administering a series of quite sound spanks, which made her cheeks bounce and wobble in a most abandoned manner, I eased off to avoid causing her to suffer anything more than sharp pleasure. It was very important to me that she should gain the same sort of fulfilment that I was achieving — and that I had received when I was in her position over Aunt Grace's generous lap.

I stopped after a few minutes. But only to stroke her and let her flesh cool down a little before starting again. In that way I could prolong the 'punishment' further, to my immediate satisfaction and eventually, when a fourth sense, that of smell, told me that her love nest was in the same moistly throbbing state as my own, I knew that it was to hers as well.

When her whole bottom resembled a glowing sunset, I told her that it was over. The need for the roles had disappeared the moment she had laid herself across my thighs and we became what we were — two friends with a strong attraction for each other. After a long stroking session, I helped her up and, unbidden, she sat carefully on my lap, taking her weight on her thighs and with her rump projecting comfortably clear. She rested her head on my shoulder with a movingly deep sigh of contentment and we sat there, rocking gently in silent contemplation of shared pleasure. Our lips clamped together and the passion began to surge simultaneously through us both. I slipped a hand underneath her, onto cool soft thigh, from there to hot soft buttock, with the tips of my fingers edging onto the moister skin of her cleft. As they drifted on to the wrinkled skin around her bottom-hole, her gasp nearly drew all the breath out of my lungs and she started to bob up and down. I moved my forefinger until it rested on the tight little hole itself and felt it jerk at my touch. Somehow she seemed to draw me inside her and although I at first felt a flare of slight distaste at the contact with this most personal and intimate orifice, the memory of Aunt Grace's touch on mine, together with the exciting way my finger was gripped in its tight, hot embrace, restored my equilibrium. As she squirmed with increasing fervour, I thrust my tongue into her mouth and wriggled my middle finger into the opening of her gaping sex. A moment later, her whole body went rigid, I could feel the ring of muscle spasm against my forefinger and my middle one slipped as far as it could go into a hot tunnel that had gone from moist to wet in an instant.

As her climax faded away, she sagged and I had to remove my hand from its two exciting little prisons so that I could support her.

My right hand was still smarting from the spanking. My wrist ached from the angle I had forced it to assume to stimulate her two openings. Her weight had rendered my legs almost numb. But I was supremely happy. Probably sensing my discomfort, she stood up and, putting her arms round my shoulders, she kissed me gently and smiled softly.

'Thank you, Annie.'

'I cannot imagine that you enjoyed it even half as much as I did,' I replied.

'In that case, my happiness is doubled. I should go now, but will you kiss my bottom better before I do?'

'Well, as I do not seem to have any pressing engagements at this time, I suppose I may just be able to accommodate you! Turn round and raise your skirts.'

She did so with a merry little laugh and I treated myself to a long look at my handiwork before granting her request. Her bottom was still very red but had turned rather blotchy, which was less attractive than the even glow which Aunt Grace had produced on Maria's flesh. Her right buttock was considerably more discoloured than the left one and there were clear impressions of my fingertips on it. I immediately realised that I needed a considerable degree of practice before I could match Aunt Grace's standards! I had time to appreciate the tight roundness of her bottom before saluting it, and her, with a gentle series of kisses, all of which gave me a vivid reminder of the soft smoothness of her skin while I inhaled the lingering scent of excited girl, which had wafted up over her buttocks from the secret recess between her thighs. I then reluctantly raised and refastened her drawers for her and sent her on her way with a final loving pat.

Afterwards, I felt curiously listless. All I wanted to do was to lie on my bed and re-savour what I had just experienced, something made considerably easier by the lingering reminders: her taste in my mouth, her scent in my nostrils and the tingling warmth in the palm of my right hand. It *had* been a richly rewarding episode and there was a surge of affection, perhaps even love, in my heart for the girl who had been so much more than a willing participant. I certainly know that I determined to go further along that particular road whenever the opportunity presented itself. I wanted to see more than just her bottom . . . the memory of what her furry little love-nest had felt like made me long to see it . . . Were her breasts as firm and tightly rounded as her buttocks? I wanted to know . . . Was the silkiness of her skin typical or unique? How could I find out? Maria's bottom was bigger, broader and her cheeks less tightly separated than Elspeth's — yet my impressions were not as clear as I would have liked, presumably because in both cases, my mind was in something of a whirl.

In short, I was beginning to put Aunt Grace's words of advice into practice — 'Look, observe, learn . . . the knowledge can only come from within you', she had said. I had learned a great deal. But from the innermost recesses of my mind came the realisation that I had only taken a few, tentative steps along the way.

After lunch, Aunt Grace told me to report to her drawing room in half an hour, time which I spent in another contemplation of my marble Goddess. I could now make a far more considered judgement of her figure and my attraction to her curves was no less than when I had first studied them. She was undoubtedly plumper than Elspeth and shapelier than Maria and yet there was something recognisably familiar about the formation of her rear end. It was only when I was on my way to my meeting with my mentor that it occurred to me that it was the mirrored reflection of my own naked charms which had caused the sense of familiarity. One more brick had been added to the wall of confidence within me.

Aunt Grace opened our discussion by informing me that there was to be another of her special dinner parties that evening, so could I please arrange with Cook to provide me with a supper tray in my room. This time I was much more curious as to the nature of these mysterious parties and, at the same time, slightly hurt at my exclusion. But

I did not feel that I could ask directly for an explanation and I trusted her sufficiently to feel that she would tell me when the time was right.

She then drove all such thoughts from my mind. 'Elspeth tells me that you spanked her with surprising competence. Did you find it a satisfying experience?'

I felt the prickling of a profound blush spread across my face and my bottom tingled apprehensively. For a brief moment I felt betrayed by a girl I had considered an intimate friend, but then I sensed that it was unworthy of me and did my best to present a calm, studied front.

'It was nothing more than a little romp, Aunt Grace. I was not trying to assume any special authority. And I freely confess that I enjoyed it immensely.'

'Excellent.' This comment came as both a surprise and relief. 'I wondered when your curiosity would lead you to confirm that it is better to give than to receive! I only hope that what you discovered does not lessen your interest in receiving, however. As I said to you some time ago, Annie, you showed the glimmer of great promise from the beginning and the thirst you have shown for further knowledge does you great credit. Never forget that there is always something to learn. Never accept the superficial. Now go and give Cook your supper order and then go and help Uncle George in the library.

We smiled at each other and I took my leave, trying to lock her words securely in my mind so that I could recall them and weigh up their meanings at appropriate times, while also thinking of what I could ask Cook to prepare for me. I was, therefore, a little preoccupied when I entered the kitchen. The door was open and so my entrance was silent and Cook was bending over the range, her back towards me presenting a stunning vista of feminine breadth! It was irresistible! I tip-toed up to her and whisked her voluminous skirt right up to her waist, with the firm intention of giving her a few hearty whacks on the seat of her drawers, in part settlement of those she had given me on my arrival. When I was confronted with an impressively large and dramatically rounded area of naked, deeply divided bottom, I was halted in my tracks, whereupon she straightened up and whirled round to confront her assailant. At the time, I was too confused to notice that the ferocity of her expression immediately softened as she saw me.

'Oh Cook, I *am* sorry. I thought you would be wearing drawers . . . I was just going to give you a little smack across them . . . I wouldn't have done such a thing if I had known you were all bare underneath . . . Please forgive me.'

She burst out laughing. 'Well then, my dear, you'll just have to give me a little smack across my bare bottom then, won't you?'

Without a moment's hesitation, she swept her skirts back up and bent over again, treating me to a tantalising glimpse of the way her bottom changed its shape as she did so. Laughing with her, I awarded each large buttock a hearty smack and we quickly concluded the business of the moment.

I then joined Uncle George in the library and we worked happily away until late afternoon, by which time the preparations for the evening's entertainment were well under way, so I slipped up to my room. The mellow sunlight pouring in lit the elegant furnishings with a warm glow and provided me with a perfect atmosphere to collect my thoughts. I first turned to the mystery of the dinner. I had now been excluded twice; yet we had had guests on other occasions and I had been made to feel almost 'one of the family'. I racked my brains for a plausible explanation, before giving up and turning to easier matters. Elspeth provided an obvious and delightful subject for happy reminiscence.

My mouth formed a happy little smile as I recalled the events of the morning. If seeing and spanking her bare bottom had been a richly rewarding experience, the most pleasing aspect had been the way she and I had immediately acted in concert and had turned what could well have been an awkward, fumbling exercise into a graceful act where the pleasure had definitely been mutual.

Then it occurred to me that the episode in the kitchen was in some ways even more significant, especially after what Aunt Grace had said to me. 'Never accept the superficial'. Was there more to Cook's reaction than girlish playfulness? After all, she was a mature woman of probably some 35 years and, although probably not well educated, was intelligent and had absorbed many of the principles of good and gracious living, so for her to proffer her naked buttocks to me in the way that she did could hardly be described as conventional!

When Connie, a maid whom I had not yet really got to know, came in with my supper tray, I had not reached any conclusion — other than to do what I had been told and observe and learn. I watched Connie as she moved round the room lighting the lamps and by now could hazard some sort of guess at the shape of the contours which rounded out the seat of her skirt.

I also felt quietly confident that I would be able to find out whether the reality bore any relation to my imaginings!

Cook had provided a cold game pie which proved absolutely delicious and a bottle of Uncle George's best Champagne which accompanied it to perfection. Replete and more than a little light-headed, I lay on the haven of my bed and tried again to unravel the mystery of the strange dinner party. There was something in the atmosphere — perhaps a suppressed excitement — which hinted that these occasions involved more than good food, fine wines and challenging conversation.

After a few moments spent in fruitless speculation, I gave up, undressed and, without putting on my night attire, made my preparations for bed. Before putting out the lights, I stood naked before the full-length glass, studying my image, both back and front. In the soft light, my bottom looked even fuller and more richly curved. It was considerably bigger than Elspeth's. A pumpkin to her apple and yet the central cleft almost matched hers for tightness. I then remembered the brief glimpse of Cook's as she had bent over, so I slowly copied her, awkwardly watching the changing shape and aspect, the opening of the cleft and of the deep folds at the top of my thighs as I did so. I gave myself a couple of firm smacks, noting the way my tightened cheeks quivered enticingly. I recalled Aunt Grace's examination of my anus — and the feel of Elspeth's — and it struck me that I had not the slightest idea of what this obviously sensitive part looked like. I moved nearer to my reflected image, bent down again and slowly parted my buttocks. In that position and in that light, detailed examination was all but impossible, but what I could observe — a neat, pinky-brown little centrepiece to my yawning bottom — was certainly enough to make me wish that I had separated Elspeth's buttocks so that I could study hers.

It did not seem worth putting on my nightdress and I slipped between the cool sheets stark-naked. Apart from the pleasing sensations resulting from this action, it allowed my restless hands unfettered access to those parts of my nude body most anxious for their touch!

CHAPTER 5

A few days later I was sitting listlessly in front of my statue. It was one of those infuriating summer days when the heavy clouds seem to reflect the heat of the day straight back at the ground, the air is leaden, the simple act of breathing is full of effort, one's skin is sticky and uncomfortable and there is little joy in life. I had come down into the garden for solitude, as Aunt Grace and Uncle George had gone to visit friends, and I had found being inside especially oppressive. At least the steady tinkling of the fountain cooled the atmosphere and the gleaming white nudity of my marble friend made me feel noticeably fresher. As I have mentioned, the garden could not be overlooked by any of the neighbouring houses and this, coupled with the reasonable assumption that the maids and Cook would be busy in the house, encouraged me to put into practice the inspired thought that the sight of the clear spray from the fountain had sparked off.

As I was wearing the minimum amount of clothing — no more than a blouse, skirt and stockings — it took but a moment or two to strip myself stark naked, and even less time to step into the base of the fountain. The simultaneous impact of cool water on my feet and even cooler drops on my body was sheer bliss. After a little squeak at the initial chill, I groaned aloud in relief. This was probably my undoing. Very soon afterwards, when I was standing there with my arms raised to the heavens in unconscious mimicry of the statue's pose, I became aware that I was no longer alone! With my heart fluttering, I whirled round, blinked the water from my eyes and there in a row, were all six maids and Cook, wide-eyed, red-faced and with mouths open. My hands immediately flew to my bosom and middle in an instinctive reversion to my previous, modest self, and for an embarrasing moment or two, we stared at each other. Before I could protest at the invasion of what had been a private moment, Elspeth suddenly raised her right hand, the forefinger extended and rapped out: 'Hands Up!'

I was evidently not thinking very clearly, perhaps influenced by a lingering childhood memory of tales of highwaymen holding up stagecoaches near our Leicestershire farm, for I immediately flung my arms above my head and seven pairs of eyes feasted themselves on the features revealed. We all burst out laughing and, in every sense, the atmosphere was lightened. I began to enjoy the frank appraisal and struck up a number of provocative poses, laying emphasis on my breasts, belly and the little triangle of fair hair, beneath which a familiar and always welcome tingle was starting to manifest itself. I shook my bosom at them; turned and pointed my bottom in their direction, stuck it out and pulled it in, before shaking it in the same way that I had done with my breasts; I danced, clumsily because of the drag of the ankle-deep water. They applauded. I was by then fast recovering my good spirits but even so, I remember hoping that my display would satisfy them and that they would then leave me to commune with my statue in naked solitude.

They did no such thing. Perhaps typically, it was my dear Elspeth who took the lead. While the clapping died slowly away, she began to remove her clothing and as soon as the others saw what she was up to, they followed suit with indecent haste. In no time, I had been joined by six squealing, stark-naked girls. My disbelieving eyes were filled by a kaleidoscope of white flesh, with highlights of tautening nipples, deep belly buttons, love nests covered by furry triangles of surprisingly varied hues and tight, deep bottom-clefts.

All my irritation fled and I felt a happy surge of pleasure. I splashed Connie and was splashed by Agatha in turn, whereupon Bridget soaked her and before long we had almost drained the base of the fountain, at which point we all stopped to catch our breath. While all this had been going on, Cook had obviously decided to join in and had been disrobing with the stately decorum appropriate to her years and position. Our cavortings had lasted long enough for her to have donned Eve's costume and she was ready to take the cooling waters — or what was left of them. Fortunately, the fountain's copious output was sufficient to restore an adequate level fairly rapidly, so that when she stepped in, there was easily enough to cover her feet. We all watched her avidly. I saw the slow smile of blissful relief spread across her handsome face before my attention was drawn to the more private features. She was a big woman and a splendid sight to behold. Her bosoms were large, but pleasingly shaped and had retained much of their youthful firmness. Even without the help of her corsets, there was a noticeable narrowing of her waist, which threw the bounteous bosoms above and the flaring hips and rounded belly below into eye-catching prominence. Her thighs and legs were in splendid proportion to the rest of her. Finally, and most prominent of all, was the large bush of jet-black hair at the junction of her thighs.

Our silence proclaimed our admiration of her opulent femininity as she walked slowly into the centre, then squatted down and with her hands placed on the floor of the fountain behind her, very slowly lowered her big bottom into the water. I watched the smile on her face change to an 'Ooooh' of pleasure and decided to copy her action.

I have often maintained that the simple pleasures are often the most rewarding, and slowly dipping one's hot, naked bottom into cool water is an admirable example. It must be done slowly. As one squats down the tight, almost pointed crowns of one's buttocks are the first part to touch the water and then the cooling balm creeps deliciously into the open cleft, on to the actual bottom-hole, around and into the love-nest until the whole bottom is blissfully covered.

The maids watched me with interest and obviously the expression on my face was as inspiring to them as Cook's had been to me, because in short order, six spread posteriors were inching their way downwards. We all sat comfortably for quite a long time. For my part, the easy atmosphere was gently spiced by the array of naked breasts around me — and the pleasing contrast between the softness of my bottom and the rough, wet stone on which it rested — so it was therefore hardly surprising that the conversation soon became based on the physical!

Even less surprisingly, it was the impish Elspeth who first guided it in this direction.

'Bridget, I could swear that your bosoms are getting bigger. Turn this way a bit so that I can see.' Bridget, a slender girl of about my age and with startlingly beautiful red hair, obeyed, squinting down at the twin globes under discussion. 'Yes,' continued Elspeth, 'they're definitely plumper. Have you been feeding her up behind our backs, Cook?'

'Of course I have. There was nothing to her when she first came. All skin and bone. Stand up, Bridget, so we can have a proper look at you.'

I was sitting opposite Cook and Elspeth, so when she stood up, I was facing her bottom rather than her front and took full advantage of the opportunity for an unhurried appraisal. She lacked Elspeth's tightly rounded pertness and was some way removed from Maria's womanly breadth, but I certainly found the view utterly charming. Her most striking feature was the pure whiteness of her skin, which was so fine that each cheek of her bottom clearly bore a pink patch on the part which had borne her weight. As I gazed, I tried to remember how Elspeth had looked in a standing posture. Obviously, I had spent the majority of the time looking at her bent over my thighs and had seen her erect only when I had kissed her as a final salute. I felt that her buttocks nestled together more closely than Bridget's, but there was a lack of certainty in my recollection. I had been too excited to make the effort to lock the variety of images in my mind.

After a while, Cook asked her to turn round and show them her bottom, which she did without a trace of inhibition and, when she had moved, our eyes met and she smiled with becoming shyness at me. I smiled back and then let my eyes travel slowly over her front. Her bosoms were a good deal smaller than mine and her nipples were of the palest shade of pink. She had slim hips and thighs and a delicate triangle of beautiful red hair at the bottom of her belly, which was so sparse at its base that the tight slit of her cunny was clearly visible. A charming little figure, perfectly matching her neatly featured little face. Once again, Elspeth's voice broke into the silence.

'And there's much more to your bottom now, Bridget. I remember when I first saw you bending over, I could see your hole. Come on, down you go and let's see if it shows now.'

Again the girl belied her apparent shyness by obeying without hesitation and those maids not in a position to see for themselves, moved to where they could. I stayed. Perhaps because I had not yet lost all the attributes of the old Annie and found this public examination of her most secret part embarrassing. And yet, as I studied her, her damp mass of gloriously red hair hanging down over her face, the rising plane of her back, glistening white and with the bones of her spine standing out, the rounded hips, I felt an urge to move round and add my face to those staring intently at her. Trying not to draw too much attention to myself in case my presence would be considered intrusive, I rose from my watery seat, moved round the base of the fountain and perched on the little stone wall surrounding it. After a moment's concentration on the unexpectedly pleasing sensation of the slightly rough, warm stone on my smooth, slightly chilled bottom, I fixed my attention on the sight before me.

I could not see her bottom-hole. Obviously she had plumped up nicely since her arrival. Slightly relieved, I quietly enjoyed the view of her tight, round buttocks, gleaming in the dull light and charmingly separated by a division which was emphasised by a pinkish tint in its depths. Even to my untutored eye, it was a beautifully feminine vista, made even more so by the diamond-shaped portion of her little cunny which protruded shyly between the slim thighs, the light covering of dark red hair bringing it into sharp focus against the whiteness of her skin.

Suddenly I felt an overwhelming urge to touch her. To stroke that silken skin, to squeeze the evident softness of her breasts and buttocks, to kiss her smiling mouth in the greedy way Elspeth and I had kissed, to finger her bottom-hole and love-nest as I had fingered Elspeth's after I had spanked her and to kiss her freshly-spanked cheeks. For the first time in my life, I felt the hot surge of pure lust — and rejoiced wholeheartedly as the chains of propriety fell away. For ever. And my desires gave voice to themselves:

'I do not believe that she is trying as hard as she could, girls. She gives me the distinct impression that she is tucking her bottom in and so preventing us from seeing her little hole. I consider that rather naughty of her!'

My bold statement was greeted with clear approval by the rest of the audience and with a giggle, Bridget moved her feet apart and then slowly bent her knees forward and as she did so, her bottom tightened, the cleft opened and the first bottom-hole I had seen, other than my own, popped into our view. All I could see from my relatively distant viewpoint was that it was neat, small and a lovely pink in colour and, after some time spent studying this delightfully unconventional pose, with her most private orifices now sufficiently exposed to make her buttocks fade into relative insignificance, I wanted to examine her closely.

'That's better,' I announced. 'But my curiosity cannot be fully satisfied from here.' To a smattering of applause, I rose, waded up to her and squatted down behind her, with my bottom dipping gratefully into the cool water. As I did so, I felt the excitement deep within me surge, because she pushed her rear end even further out, which increased the level of exposure even more. If the beginnings of sensual curiosity had made me momentarily regret not seeing Aunt Grace's back view in her revealing drawers; if I had actively looked forward to spanking Elspeth because I was drawn to her and had tickled her bottom-hole (because I knew how thrilling such a caress could be) and wished to please her, I now examined Bridget purely out of a strengthening desire to acquaint my various senses with the most intimate details of her body. So I drank in the sight of her distended buttocks, the fascinating bottom-hole and cunny. I felt the tight silkiness of her skin and watched the tip of my right forefinger as it trickled over the wrinkled pink surround of her bottom-hole, on to the tight little opening itself, down the little ridge of skin which led to her cunny, now with its plump lips slight-

71

ly apart, revealing the glistening pinkness of the inside of the slit. I tasted the sweetness of her flesh by running my tongue over her buttocks and into the upper part of her gaping cleft, where it lingered on the so soft skin stretched tightly over her little tail-bone. My panting inhalations filled my nostrils with the heady musk of her growing excitement.

I eased my questing finger into the clinging moistness of her sex and marvelled at the yielding tightness that closed around it. I moved my left hand from her buttock and reached between her parted thighs until it could take hold of one soft bosom.

I squeezed, stroked with both hands, while her gasps intensified to become inarticulate little cries, her rump bobbed and weaved until it suddenly stilled and I watched with fascination as her bottom-hole twitched as the hot thrill of her climax surged through her. I removed my hands, stood up and kissed her gently before putting my arms round her and holding her close. Had it been Elspeth rather than Bridget, I know that I would have felt a glow in my heart to complement the one flooding my body at the feel of her soft nakedness pressed tightly against mine, the way our breasts squashed together and the feel of her bare bottom under my hands. Nevertheless, I did feel a nice tenderness towards her. I felt grateful to her for the willingness with which she had offered herself to me — and a new sense of inner strength.

Soon her breathing had returned to normal and I led her back to the others. 'You *can* see her bottom-hole when she bends over properly, so keep feeding her up, Cook.'

Their laughter was encouraging. I began to feel as though I belonged, and actually led the ensuing discussion, which began with comments on Bridget's body, moved to bodies in general and then to specific aspects of our bodies. For example, the considered opinion was that men liked women with a prominence to front and rear, although none of us felt that the clumsy bustle would ever return to fashion. It was agreed that a narrow waist was the best way of giving emphasis to the upper and lower protrusions and Cook said that she had heard of women who had had their lower ribs surgically removed to achieve maximum effect. We agreed that it was absurd to go to such lengths. We were all sitting either in the water or on the little wall and so while we were talking I was able to openly study their naked bosoms, marvelling at the variety of shape, size and type of nipple. Cook's were clearly the biggest and her big brown nipples were in keeping with the rest. Maria's were delightfully plump, Connie's and Elspeth's like little apples with particularly pink and neat nipples; Bridget's were probably the smallest of all, but had their own sweetness — the others were sitting to my side and so were less easily discernible. With sudden inspiration, I envisaged the delights of having them all standing in a line before me, allowing me to judge their likenesses and differences at one and the same time, instead of looking at one body and trying to dredge a vague picture of another from the recesses of my memory to make a comparison. It suddenly occurred to me that I would gain enormous amusement — and further my education — if I could study them all together.

'Now that I have been able to study Bridget in some detail,' I said rather tentatively, 'it seems a shame not to seize the opportunity to put her undoubted charms into proper perspective. Would you all be agreeable to standing alongside each other so that I can get to know you all better?'

They stared at me. For a second or two my heart sank at the thought that I had overstepped the bounds of their propriety, even though I already knew that these bounds were far distant from those that I had previously recognised. Then each face broke simultaneously into a delightful smile, they stood up and placed themselves a yard or two in front of me, a proud parade of stark-naked feminity. I sat still and marvelled at the sheer variety. I had already been struck by the differences in the bosoms I had been able to study and I was now able to note that there were significant variations, not only in their individual shape and size, but also in their proportions in relation to the supporting chest. Agatha, for example, had smaller breasts than Cook, but they dominated her front to a far greater extent. Similarly, while I already knew that a girl's cunny hair was more or less the same colour as that on her head, I was now able to ascertain that there was little consistency in thickness, shape and size of the triangle itself.

I am sure that I could have stared for much longer than I eventually dared to but, even though there was no evidence of boredom or impatience on any of the seven faces, I did not want to try their tolerance. I did, however, keenly desire to study their bottoms, the part which had first sparked off my interest in the body. I asked if they would turn around. They did, with pleasing alacrity, and as I watched the quivering buttocks settle after the movements of their owners' turning had ceased, I heard myself give a deep sigh of contentment and the tendrils of pleasure began to seep outwards from the centre of my body.

At that moment, any lingering doubts I held on the attraction of this part of a girl's anatomy fled forever. The white curves; the weighty, firm softness; the so very exciting, deep divisions; the charming folds which marked the top of the thighs. All seemed to me to provide a logical explanation for the instinct which Aunt Grace had brought into my consciousness the moment she had touched me there.

Again, it struck me that if all of them shared the common elements, the differences in the forms and proportions were quite remarkable. Silently I studied, trying to memorise as much as I could so that I could afterwards recall the scene and savour it again and again. The way that they had all so willingly obliged my desire to see them 'en masse' also gave me encouragement. I began to feel confident that any one of them would happily act as partner in the sort of romp I had so enjoyed with Elspeth. My heart swelled with affection for this bizarre but happy band.

I knew that it would be wrong to indulge my pleasure for much longer but was loth to take any action which would bring the proceedings to an end. Not surprisingly, it was dear Elspeth who solved my dilemma. 'Wouldn't we all like to have a look at Annie?'

There was not a single sign of disagreement and in no time at all, they turned and I was standing up to face them, watching their expressions as their eyes travelled over my front and then turning excitedly so that they could study my back.

I seemed to slip slowly into a trance. The skin of my bottom tingled as though it could actually feel the intensity of their gaze, and even more notably when I clearly heard awe-filled whispers of approval of the richness of its curves and the whiteness of its skin. Then they did what had not occurred to me to do to them. They came up to me. I heard the splashing as they approached and then a soft hand rested gently on the undercurve of my right buttock, hefting its weight and squeezing it with delectable authority. I closed my eyes as another hand stroked the other cheek. Soon I was being handled all over, and a soft sweet mouth closed over mine, which opened in breathless ecstasy, and any resistance I may have harboured was sucked out, as a hot moist tongue slipped between my lips and tasted me. Hands and mouths teased my aching nipples, hands parted my quivering buttocks to let questing fingers tickle the hidden entrance, and again I was amazed at the strength of the pleasure that caresses to this most secret of places produced. Strong arms supported me as my legs grew weak. A palm moved up the inside of my thigh and cupped my mound, moved the softness around until I could feel the wetness flow in welcome. A fingertip slipped into the tight slit, on to the pleasure button, flickering rhythmically until my climactic cries rang in my ears.

They held me lovingly until I recovered something of my poise and smiled with sympathetic happiness at my pleasure. I kissed and hugged them in turn, enjoying the softness of their bodies but mostly revelling in the way they had given me so much pleasure, had made me feel welcome, had opened the shutters even further and had done all this in an atmosphere of innocent, affectionate gaiety.

I may have been sated but was reluctant to hide our nudity and bring the fun to a close. If seeing them all bare no longer excited my quietened love nest, I still found the sight exceedingly pleasing to the eye. I then rembered that the croquet hoops were in place.

'Who's for a game of croquet?.' I called out. My suggestion was greeted with enthusiasm and in the blinking of an eye, I was treated to the unforgettable sight of six naked maids plus Cook trotting through the gap in the hedge. The tantalising glimpse of their bare bottoms wiggling, swaying, twinkling, quivering out of my sight suddenly made me reconsider and I opened my mouth to suggest that we should get dressed before beginning the game, but by the time I found my voice they had gone. I hurried after them. My worries were twofold. Firstly, that the lawn was far less sheltered from view than the fountain and secondly that our naked bodies would be adversely affected by the rays of the sun. We were not even wearing hats to protect our faces! However, as I trotted after them, I reassured myself that only a determined spy would be able to see us and that the sun was so obscured by the thick clouds that the whiteness of our skins would not be spoilt.

By the time I arrived, they were emerging from the summerhouse with armfuls of mallets and handfuls of balls and we began to organise our little tournament. With eight of us all told, it was simple enough. Elspeth and I challenged Cook and Maria, and Bridget paired up with Connie against Agatha and Vera. We let them start first and settled down on a rug spread on the grass to watch an event which quite probably would have made history — had the details been made available to an historian!

It was a time of supreme contentment. If the novelty of our nudity had worn off, the pleasure had not. My senses drifted idly from one stimulus to another. I savoured the feel of the rug's woollen fibres under my bottom. When emphasising a conversational point to Cook it was natural to rest a hand on her thigh and satisfying to be able to enjoy both the intimacy of the contact and the softness of skin and flesh. My eyes continually watched the movements of the four players as they moved without inhibition about their game and I could note the subtle alterations in the posture of the bodies in general and bottoms in particular as they stood waiting for their turn or crouched with rapt attention over their mallets. I found the movements as they walked away from me especially attractive and again, the differences struck me most forcibly. For example, Bridget's apple-tight little rump twinkled far more noticeably then Agatha's considerably more ample one. But the latter's buttocks definitely wobbled, which Bridget's did not.

Two little incidents proved especially memorable. The first was when Vera was carefully placing her ball alongside one of her opponents' in order to croquet her, and so that she could achieve the most perfect angle, knelt right down to place her eye at the exact level of the two balls. Her back was towards us and there was a reverential silence as her delightfully large bottom loomed up into the air, broadening and opening as it did so, exposing almost the full length of her dark, hairy cunny and an anus which was both bigger and browner than Bridget's (up to that point, my only basis for comparison). It was a most lascivious display of her fundamental feminity but was done in such a natural circumstance that it caused not a trace of discomfiture.

The second occurred a little later. Bridget and Connie were losing badly and Connie made yet another careless shot, at which Bridget feigned annoyance and told her partner that unless she showed a marked and immediate improvement she would get her bottom smacked. My interest in the game quickened and to my delight, the improvement requested was not delivered. Bridget marched purposefully up to her, whereupon she assumed a most convincing woebegone expression, turned her back on us and slowly bent over. Until then, I had not really noticed her. She was undeniably pretty, with lovely black hair, a pleasingly chubby figure and a complexion which was as white as any, but there was little about her that was outstanding on early acquaintance. However, as she stuck her bottom out and engaged my full attention for the first time, I suddenly appreciated the subtlety of her attraction. She had a beautifully formed pair of buttocks, a particularly soft looking cleft and in all, presented such a mouth-watering target to Bridget that the trembling waves from my middle began to seep through me again. She had not bent down as far as Bridget had earlier — she had placed her hands approximately halfway between her knees and ankles, with her legs straight, so that her bottom was

78

plumply rounded rather than taut and wide.

Bridget came up alongside her willing victim, placed her left arm round her waist and leaning slightly forward to obtain a better and closer view of her target, ran her hand over the fleshly mounds and then raised it and brought it firmly down onto the exact centre of the right buttock. Even in its relatively tightened state, it quivered visibly and a hand-shaped red blotch appeared instantaneously on the snow-white skin. Five further blows spread a bright pink blush over the lower half of the guilty bottom and the impact of each one had as profound an effect on my rising excitement as it did on her naked flesh.

It was over far too soon — and Connie's game improved out of all recognition thereafter!

Then it was our turn and I freely admit that I was fully aware of being in Eve's state, and even though this was in many ways a distraction and probably caused me to miss several opportunities to demonstrate my more devious shots, it did nothing to mar the enjoyment. I relished anew the caress of the air on my skin; I was happily aware of the gentle bouncing of my unfettered breasts; I knew that the others would be observing the movements of my bare bottom. I could not resist kneeling down with my rear thrust lewdly upwards to line up the balls whenever I had the opportunity to croquet one of our opponents. At the same time, I could relax and watch the movements and actions of the other three — plump bosoms swaying; round bottom-cheeks quivering, dimpling, tightening.

Elspeth and I eventually triumphed and we rejoined the others. By this time the blood was flowing through my veins and although I knew that we had been playing truant for some little time, I could not bear the thought of bringing the entertainment to an end. If the little waves from my love-nest were pulsing rather than throbbing, I still had not had my fill of the sight of my companion's nudity, nor had I tired of my own. The heaviness of the air had been pleasantly relieved by a light breeze and whether this sparked off my inspiration or whether it was just the burgeoning imp of sensuality within me, I do not know. It may have been the memory of the girls trotting off to the croquet lawn.

'Ladies, I feel that some more strenuous exercise would provide an ideal ending to our sporting afternoon. Let's race each other — up to the top of the lawn and back would provide a fair test of our abilities. Come on, who will take me on?'

Elspeth was the first to accept my challenge and we soon agreed on what rules were necessary, namely that we had to touch the hedge at the far end, turn outwards to reduce the likelihood of a collision, and the winner was the first to touch the oak tree beyond the summerhouse, which would also serve as the starting point. After a short delay while our enthusiastic comrades settled down behind us, we crouched down, Cook said, 'Ready — go', and we raced down the lawn. To be honest, the word 'raced' is an exaggeration. After but a few strides, I realised that it takes a little time to accustom oneself to the peculiar problems of running naked, especially when there is not only the distraction of an equally bare competitor immediately alongside and whose bouncing curves are discernible out of the corner of one's eye, but also the full knowledge that the violent movements of one's rear portions are being closely watched by an experienced audience. As a child, I had often had to run home from the outer reaches of my father's farm in a desperate attempt to avoid mother's displeasure at my usual tardiness and so was, I thought, fairly fleet of foot. Nevertheless, Elspeth beat me handsomely. We soon recovered from our exertions and Bridget and Vera settled on their marks. I do not think that I drew breath until they had both finished

— with Bridget the victor. If the sight of a naked girl walking away is a combination of grace and a sensual vulnerability, then watching one run in the same direction is pure lasciviousness! Even though I had been very conscious that my bottom wobbled impressively, I had vaguely attributed this to its generous proportions, but watching open-mouthed as the much more slender Bridget showed that she moved in an equally magnificent way, taught me a little more of the fascination of the feminine physique.

We took turns in running with each other and it was more than simple weariness which caused the pace of each contest to diminish. We all enjoyed the novel sensation and were all happy to please the others by concentrating on fleshly agitation as opposed to speed. At last, we could run no more and sank onto the rugs, limbs outstretched, our bosoms rising and falling as we panted in the scented summer air.

With returning energy, came renewed sensuality. Surprisingly, it was the quiet Vera who, as she lay on her belly having her buttocks idly stroked and patted by Cook, provided the most exciting diversion. Claiming that the sight of me on all fours lining up the balls for the perfect croquet had been 'wickedly beautiful', she suggested another series of races, this time pushing a ball up the lawn — with our noses! It certainly took me a moment or two to appreciate the implications and then the outrageous nature of the idea almost shocked me. I watched the first two rivals: Cook (who had proved the slowest but bounciest runner and who greeted this event with some avidity, stating that it obviously involved a more suitable pace for one of her years and figure) and Maria. As they slowly knelt down and placed their noses on the balls, my gaze fixed unblinkingly on the gradual spreading and opening of their bottoms until the tight, pink and brown bottom-holes were fully exposed to view, with two darkly furred cunnies below, both slightly agape and revealing tantalising hints of moist pinkness inside.

The fact that progress was slow made the role of spectator even more enjoyable and, by the luck of the draw, Vera and I were the last to compete, so by the time I stood up to move to the starting point, my bottom-hole and love-nest were tingling delightfully. As I slowly positioned myself, I mused on the good fortune which had allowed my nature to derive almost equal pleasure from both viewing other girls' bodies and displaying my own. The caress of the cooling air on my skin as I knelt was a clear indicator of the increasing exposure of the inner recesses of my bottom-cleft. I sensed the hot gaze of the others on me. The skin of my drum-tight buttocks felt alive. I looked across to my opponent and the sight of her in profile was, if not as exciting as it would have been if seen 'end-on', nonetheless beautiful. Her breasts hung down with her protruding nipples brushing the grass, the steep, slightly curved slope of her back ending in the almost pointed arc of her bottom, with a tuft of dark hair delineating the junction of her thighs.

With a thudding heart, I addressed my nose to my ball and, on the command, 'Go!' I set off, my concentration veering between the surprisingly difficult task of steering the stubborn sphere and the restricted movements of my bottom. Obviously I was completely absorbed because it was not until two pairs of boots, one with just the toes visible below the hem of an elegant skirt and the other in full view below a familiar pair of trousers, swam into the outer reaches of my vision, that I had the slightest inkling that our sophisticated romp had been rudely interrupted . . . Uncle George and Aunt Grace had returned.

In less than the blinking of an eye, I changed from nudity to nakedness. I instantly felt the range of emotions that

Eve must have done when cast out of the Garden of Eden. I clambered to my feet, blushing like a peony, my heart thudding even more frantically, a very unpleasant hollow feeling in my belly and a throat suddenly dry as dust. My eyes flickered up to meet theirs, noted the thunderous brows and immediately sought the relative comfort of the grass at my feet. I knew that retribution would be swift, painful — and well earned. My bottom felt embarrassingly naked rather than beautifully bare. I was ashamed, ridden with guilt. And very afraid of the consequences of my actions — which proved to be as painful as I had feared. But, perhaps more importantly, further opened the shutters and shed more light on the hidden pastures of my soul.

We were taken into the main drawing room. Aunt Grace sat on the end of the chaise longue, with Uncle George standing quietly by the wall, unobtrusive but somehow dominating the room with his presence. Instinctively we formed a line facing our 'executioner'. We were then spanked in turn. Hard. All of us. Even Cook's majestic buttocks were turned up and reddened as effectively as the rest. I had done my best to convince Aunt Grace that I was responsible for their dereliction of duty but my speech had been cut short in the most peremptory manner. I was the last to be treated, and so in addition to my very vivid apprehensions as to my own punishment, I had to watch my new-found friends march in turn up to the solid lap awaiting them, prostrate themselves over it in that humbling but effective posture and proffer their tender flesh for the two dozen ringing spanks which Aunt Grace had deemed to be a just penalty.

I was too dazed to note anything of the first chastisements and it was only as my turn approached that my awareness increased to the extent that I began to approach a state of normality. The physical symptoms of my fear intensified. To the dry, constricted throat and thudding heart, were added a marked weakness in my knees and a heightened awareness of my own bottom: I could feel it trembling; it felt even larger than usual; its naked skin seemed to be crawling; it felt soft and vulnerable, yet at the same time, massive and almost solid. Maria moved forward as Cook rejoined the penitent line. I watched the quivering sway of her buttocks and saw the changes in their formation as she bent over — but without really seeing. My eyes followed the slow upward sweep of Aunt Grace's right arm and then the fast downward move until her right palm sank visibly into the plumpness of the right cheek before her. My ears heard the loudness of the impact and my buttocks tightened in nervous sympathy. I saw the red stain spread dramatically over Maria's once-white bottom, heard the growing intensity of her cries of pain and then watched her clamber back to her feet and stagger back to her position. I noted the sparkling diamonds of her tears and her face screwed up as the burning smart was intensified by the agitation caused by the simple act of walking. By the time Elspeth's pertly plump curves had been reduced to an equally vivid hue and it was my turn, I was audibly whimpering as my nerves approached breaking point.

On legs that would hardly support me, I moved forward, eyes fixed on the broad spread of waiting lap, warmed by the bellies, thighs and cunnies of my partners in crime. But something made me look up at Aunt Grace's face. She smiled at me. Only a little smile, but enough to eliminate the most shaming element of the fear that had been draining my small reserves of strength. *She was not really angry with me!* At once, my feelings altered. No longer afraid that the delicate shoots of love that I had found so important had been killed off by my intemperate behaviour, I knew that I could proffer my bare bottom to this extraordinary woman to be beaten as bottoms should be beaten — with as much concern lovingly to correct waywardness as pleasure at the sight, feel and sounds that are such a vital part of the complex pleasures of spanking.

Slowly I laid my quivering body across her lap, and just as carefully cocked the now willing flesh to offer her the easiest and most pliant target.

'Three dozen for you, Annie.' Her voice floated towards me from miles above and miles behind.

And three dozen of the firmest, crispest, snappiest spanks imaginable sent my rounded globes into blazing motion. I was sobbing before even half of them had landed. And crying like a baby by the end. But my tears were as much caused by gratitude as by the agonising pain. Gratitude because, having lost my family, I was no longer in danger of losing what had become more than a replacement for it.

When my punishment was finished, we stood in our line while both Aunt Grace and Uncle George inspected our red bottoms and were then sent to collect our clothes and go about our business. Not surprisingly, once we had gained the shelter of the fountain, there was a rapid but passionate examination of our afflicted areas, which were soothingly dipped into the water, stroked and kissed better (I was flattered that my bottom seemed to be the first choice by all the others for soothing caresses!) and then we hurriedly made ourselves decent and went our separate ways.

Once I had regained the sanctity of my comfortable room, I again resumed Eve's costume and lay wearily on my bed, face down to let the still sultry air play over my throbbing buttocks.

Elspeth woke me some time later with three of the softest possible kisses — one on each cheek and the third on the division between them. As I came to, she was just disappearing, having lit the lamps and left a tray of food and a bedewed bottle of Champagne by my bed.

I ate and drank in a daze, then slept till the morning's rising sun bade me to join it.

CHAPTER 6

The events of the previous day had left me bewildered. I slowly arose, drew the curtains to let the rays of a bright sun flood the room with welcome light and, having moved the appropriate mirrors into position, lifted my nightdress up to my waist and examined my bottom. It was quite a sorry sight, still blotchy and red with small circular bruises dotted over both sides, memories of Aunt Grace's fingertips. After a lingering bath and a leisurely breakfast, I slipped quietly into the garden to revisit the fountain. Once again I walked slowly round my statue, looking at her with newly opened eyes. Understandably, the sculptor had sought both physical and artistic perfection and it was therefore invidious to compare her with any of my companions. Nor did I wish to. If the Goddess gained by virtue of the absolute purity of form, the girls' soft, warm living flesh had given them a desirability that marble could never match. Even Cook's mature figure had stirred me, arousing within me a yearning to stroke and squeeze her ample flesh. I summoned up the memory of her rounded bottom bent over Aunt Grace's lap for her spanking and my breasts tightened as I closed my eyes and brought the vision to the forefront of my mind. I relived the events of the day and selected some of the more vivid and most treasured sights and sounds. I was standing there in a state close to rapture when Connie interrupted to inform me that Aunt Grace wished to see me in her drawing room.

I went at once, shaking my head to clear it of the recalled delights and to compose my thoughts in readiness for the meeting with my mentor. It did not come as a complete surprise to me when she wanted to examine my afflicted bottom and I obediently — and quite willingly — settled myself comfortably across her lovely thighs with my folded arms resting on the seat of the chaise longue providing an adequate pillow for my head. She laid me bare with a pleasing lack of haste and as by now I was completely at ease having my naked curves put on display, I could lie there and enjoy the slow spreading of the warm glow of sensual pleasure. The visual examination lasted several minutes and was followed by an even longer period of manual stimulation, throughout which I lay, breathing deeply and with my eyes closed, concentrating purely on the quite delicious feeling of her admiring palm on my bare skin. Finally I felt a hand on each buttock and then a slowly increasing pressure as she prised them apart to open up the cleft in between. The thrill as I felt the relatively cool air kiss my exposed bottom-hole was sufficient to stop me breathing altogether and I found that I was biting my hand in an attempt to stifle the groan which was threatening to well out and disturb the reverent silence. Now that I knew for myself how exciting a girl's bottom-hole was, there was no longer the slightest trace of embarrassment in having my own looked at so purposefully.

Eventually she let go of my buttocks and let them slap together into their normal posture.

'Did you enjoy your afternoon, Annie?' she suddenly asked.

'Oh yes, Aunt Grace.'

'How did it start?'

I explained, haltingly at first but with growing assurance as I realised that she was curious and had no apparent intention of chiding me. I am sure that by then I would have been taken aback had her attitude been anything else because even I had absorbed enough to know that she was an extraordinarily sensuous woman. It was also easier to be completely honest in describing my emotions while lying across her lap with my bare bottom protruding blatantly into the air! I told her how I had felt flattered at the attention they had paid to my body. I tried to explain to her that there was a special little flutter in my heart, belly and cunny at the sight of their bottoms. I confessed that I had approached the opportunity to view Bridget's anus with a certain trepidation, not knowing whether I would find it distasteful. I described the incident of Bridget spanking Connie for playing badly and said that, on reflection, I had found it the most stirring of all . . .

' . . . it is very difficult to find the right words, Aunt Grace. Obviously if one enjoys looking at a girl's naked buttocks, a spanking is likely to be an appealing spectacle. But when I knew that Bridget was intent on smacking Connie's bottom, my insides began to churn in a very special way . . . and my natural curiosity to witness a spanking had been satisfied when you let me watch Maria being punished, so it was not just a novel experience. Nor was it that Connie posed her bottom so prettily — although she certainly did that. Her cheeks quivered and wobbled delightfully; they were a delicious pink by the end . . . I found myself envying Bridget and her close view of that lovely naked flesh . . . I also found my own bottom tingling at the thought of her spanking me . . . I'm sorry, I cannot explain at any better.'

Aunt Grace laughed. 'Could you explain the subtle flavour of a fine Champagne to someone who only has the taste for Claret? I doubt it . . . So you will understand that I feel an urgent desire to spank you now?'

There was no need for a reply. I giggled, clenched my

buttocks as tightly as possible, relaxed them and then slowly cocked my hips upwards in invitation. If the spanking she had given me the previous evening had been a punishment in its most effective form, this one was purely an exercise in loving sensuality. The spanks were crisp enough to produce a noticeable wobble in my yearning cheeks but no more. The glow spread slowly and I was able to derive full enjoyment from my position, the feel and sound of her hand, the simple pleasure of being bare-bottomed and of knowing that I was giving as much pleasure as I was receiving. She did not stop until I was tingling all over and I was bobbing happily up and down on the firmly elastic flesh of her thighs. After a long pause while she stroked my glowing buttocks, she resumed our conversation:

'Annie, I have said to you on several occasions that I felt you had exceptional promise. I now feel sure that I was not mistaken. You certainly have the most beautiful bottom of all, and the way that you have taken my words to heart and have not shut your mind to events and attitudes which must have seemed exceedingly strange, does you nothing but credit. I feel that the time has now come to welcome you fully into our little secret society.' The warm lassitude I had been feeling disappeared in a trice. My heart began to pound again, with a mixture of excitement and trepidation.

In my innocence, I had not been suspicious of an atmosphere that had been a complete mystery to me — and had only at first found the various assaults and investigations to my person beyond comprehension. It had been the romp with the maids which had given me a glimpse of the fact that pleasures of the flesh were not regarded as heinous sins — and I had not had the time since then to ponder. Perhaps if Aunt Grace and Uncle George had not returned and if we therefore had not been spanked like

90

the naughty girls I had presumed we were, then I may have given further consideration to the strangeness of the establishment. Now that I was about to be enlightened I focused on the underlying mystery for the first time.

'You have just told me of the special emotions you felt when Connie spanked Bridget,' she continued.

'Bridget spanked Connie,' I interrupted.

'It doesn't matter.' She administered a sharp little spank to the very middle of my bottom by way of emphasis. 'The point is, my dearest Annie, that you are by no means the only one who gets special feelings about spanking. Let me explain more clearly what I meant when I said that you had exceptional promise. Cook was the first to test you and the way that you accepted her little punishment without demur was the first indication. Then, even though you were clearly discomfited at the thought of exposing your body to the eyes of a complete stranger, you only protested silently at my examinations. The outstanding beauty which held my eye — especially your bottom — made my hopes for you even stronger. You have done as I asked. You have kept your eyes and mind opened and unshuttered; you have not allowed the normal rules to pull you back from experiencing new sensations and that is good. Even better is the way you have used each lesson to project yourself towards another, more difficult one. You enjoyed the way Mrs Savage and I enjoyed seeing you naked and I could see in your eyes the conflict within you when you saw me virtually naked — at first you were moved to turn away but before long you were looking and seeing. You wanted to watch as dear Maria was spanked. You offered your bottom with willingness and curiosity. You enjoyed Elspeth in exactly the way I do. And then yesterday you led the maids and Cook into realms of pleasure which I think came as a surprise even to them. You have fulfilled all the promise which I suspected was there and have done it much more quickly than I thought possible.'

All the while she was speaking, the glow in my heart waxed. As I have said, neither of my parents was generous in their praise of me and so my opinion of my own virtues had not been of the highest. I may well have been fortunate in my looks but it was always made clear to me that these were no more than a gift of nature, and therefore of little account. It was only later that I realised that had mother been able to have more children and especially the son that they both craved, then it is possible that they would have been more proud of me. But then I would never have come to the attentions of Aunt Grace and Uncle George!

'So, my dear,' she continued, 'I was saying that there are many others in this world in whom the sight of a naked bottom, especially the female one, incites great excitement and enthusiasm and, as you tried to explain, spanking brings on notably strong emotions to those of us with this inclination. Now I used the phrase "secret society" earlier; it is not a Secret Society, with vows and private ceremonials. We have a number of friends and acquaintances, who we refer to as our "guests", all of whom share our tastes. Every now and then we entertain them — there have been two such occasions since your arrival, as you know. We dine well and then after the gentlemen have had their port and cigars we go down to the cellar, which we have turned into what we refer to as our theatre, and we put on some sort of play. These are quite simple, involving no more than some of the maids being suitably punished for some real or imaginary crime. There are other aspects, but that is all you need to know for the moment. Now I have made arrangements for a dinner for the day after tomorrow and you and all the maids will be publicly chastised for the activities yesterday afternoon. I know that I have already spanked you for that but I am sure you will agree that yesterday's punishment did not fit the crime. I let you off lightly.'

Thoughts raced through my mind. Even the soothing reassurance of her hand stroking my naked flesh was not enough to ease the immediate stab of fear which pierced my heart. If yesterday's spanking had been a light one, my buttocks cringed at the prospect of a proper one. Then there was the natural concern at being dealt with in front of an audience, however sympathetic, although yesterday's treatment had at least made me accustomed to the presence of witnesses. (It was at that moment that I remembered that Uncle George had been watching. A man! I had obviously been too full of other thoughts at the time for this unpalatable fact to strike home!) While I was preoccupied with these cares, Aunt Grace was silently fingering my naked bottom and gradually the sensual feelings began to ease my apprehensions. Until she spoke again:

'Yours is the most beautiful bottom of all, Annie, and I do not think that the gentle introduction I would usually insist on for a new maid would be worthy of it or you. You will take the main role. You will be spanked, of course, and you will be first to be treated but you will also provide the grand finale. When the maids have been dealt with, you will be birched.'

If I had felt nervous on previous occasions since I joined her household, her casual comment reduced me to a state far beyond that. I almost believe that my heart stopped for a beat. I had not spent more than a year or so at school (my education had been entrusted for the most part to a governess) but while I was there, the threat of the rod had been the most effective encouragement to good behaviour. Only one girl had received it and vivid descriptions of her ravaged buttocks had spread like wildfire. Presumably I had clenched my nether cheeks in a spasmodic reaction to my terror because Aunt Grace immediately continued the heavy kneading of the bounteous flesh there.

'Do not panic, Annie. The joy of the birch as an implement of punishment is that it can so easily be tailored to suit the circumstances. A wanton criminal sentenced to a judicial whipping would feel the weight of a rod specially made to make her howl as though the devil himself had stuck his pitchfork into her bottom, whereas the tender and relatively innocent rear end of a young girl merits no more than the lightest of twigs, which would deliver no more than hot, chiding kisses. You are not a little girl and you are blessed with a bottom perfectly made for the birch. It will sting. But neither I nor any of our guests love cruelty for its own sake. As I have said to you, do not close your mind and pre-judge the unknown.'

Her words helped. But not a great deal. After a few final strokes, she dismissed me. I clambered down from her lap, adjusted my clothing and wandered off seeking for some diversion which would act as solace for my confusion. Cook was out, the maids were busy about their duties, I suddenly found the prospect of joining Uncle George in the library awkward – he had not only seen me in a state of total nudity but had also watched me being spanked, which was even worse. Not even my bewitching statue could provide a great deal in the way of comfort. I did my best to make myself think sensibly. After all, I had had several spankings and had found them not only tolerable, but capable of inflaming my senses in a way beyond my comprehension. And the last one had been before an audience, one of whom had been a male – undoubtedly the first one ever to have seen my private parts. Yet all were known to me; all bar Uncle George had seen me bare on occasions when I had been quite happy for them to do so. Then there was the underlying fear of the effects of the birch on my tender skin. I knew that this particular implement was always applied to the bare flesh and so I did not have even the vaguest hope that I would have the protection of my drawers. Despite Aunt Grace's reassuring words, I was extremely frightened.

The days crawled; the hours sped. At last the time to start the preparations had come. I was bidden to act as a maid for the dinner and the barely suppressed giggling when the others rehearsed me in my duties and I kept getting things wrong did a great deal to raise my spirits.

Then I was taken into Cook's sitting room to try on my costume. If to be told to strip naked no longer came as any surprise to me, the uniform most assuredly did! It consisted if a tight bodice and the sort of tights that are apparently worn by circus performers. They both fitted like a second skin and, even worse, were made of a fine net so that when I was taken before a looking-glass to survey the effect, I gasped aloud. The sheen on my skin gave the slightest pink tinge to the pure whiteness of the material; my nipples and the triangle of hair at the base of my belly were clearly discernible. I instinctively turned to view the area which would without doubt be the centre of attention. The swell of my bottom stretched the mesh and so the tight cleft down the middle was made all the more eye-catching.

My first reaction was a flaring of my tautened nerves as the evidence of the display I would be offering was so conspicuous, but as I stared at my shimmering reflection, I began to see it as though through the eyes of a spectator and my knotted muscles eased noticeably. And when I had donned the knee-length boots and grown accustomed to their high heels and could walk with something approaching a normal gait, the beginnings of that welcome sensual excitement reduced the worried lines that had furrowed my brow for the last two days. The tights were, as I have said, like a second skin, and yet one which was not fully attached, so that the rolling movements of my buttocks, exaggerated by the boots, caused tiny slithering movements of the material against my real skin. That I was sensitive enough to notice this is the best possible testimony to the heightened state of my senses, which did not bode well for the physical ordeal of Aunt Grace's birch!

After I had bathed, dabbed myself with lavender water and attended to my golden hair with special care, I walked downstairs and reached the hall just as the clattering of hooves announced the arrival of the first carriage of the evening.

Sensibly, my duties at the dinner were in keeping with my inexperience, namely clearing away plates and glasses at the end of each course. I made a mental note to find who had been responsible for making my earlier training session so arduous. Her bare bottom would certainly smart for teasing me so effectively. I had few distractions to take my mind off my immediate problems, which were, in ascending order of magnitude: walking in the strange boots; trying to keep the wanton movements of my buttocks in some semblance of control; doing my best not to blush like a silly little schoolgirl whenever I saw the guests' eyes fixed on my bobbing breasts and cunny hair and not letting my mind dwell on the entertainment to come. As the dinner progressed, I obviously became more accustomed to my circumstances because slowly but surely the trepidation lessened and I began to take a perverse pleasure in the extraordinary atmosphere.

I started to notice with increasing interest the other maids as they bustled about, taking every chance to gaze openly at their barely concealed charms. More surreptitiously, I took note of the guests themselves. Women were in the majority, which came as some surprise to me at first because I would have expected it to be a predominantly male gathering. Then it occurred to me that had I been in the position of being offered the chance to be a guest and watch near-naked and very pretty girls flitting around the dinner table, with the certain knowledge that afterwards I would be watching them receive corporal punishment, then I would have had no hesitation in accepting. Even though I was one of the attractions, I was still able to see myself — and the rest of us — from the guests' point of view. Had I not been able to do this, then I am sure that I would have benefitted less from the lessons that awaited me.

As soon as the ladies had been settled in the drawing room and the gentlemen served with a decanter of Uncle George's best port and a box of Havana Coronas (this was my responsibility and resulted in the first ever male hand on my bottom, which was lasciviously and delightfully squeezed by a very handsome young cavalry officer as I leant over to place an ashtray in front of him) we maids scurried into the kitchen to prepare for the entertainment.

Under Cook's direction, we stripped off our serving uniforms and donned the clothes appropriate to the forthcoming chastisement, which consisted of tight blouses, stockings, drawers — some with the traditional split, others all of a piece, but all close-fitting and of the finest silk, so that our buttocks were wrapped like the most precious of gifts — and short skirts which reached no further than our knees and our usual ankle boots. I caught assorted glimpses of naked breasts bobbing; bare buttocks trembling; furry feminine mounds; tense faces. They meant nothing to me. My first serious test was fast approaching and I was more frightened than ever.

As soon as we were all ready, Cook led us through a door off the hall and down a short corridor, then down a staircase and into the cellar. My mouth dropped open in amazement. The whole area was brilliantly lit by a profusion of gas lamps. Immediately before us were two rows of comfortably padded chairs, the second one raised well above the one in front, presumably to allow the occupants an unrestricted view of the events taking place on the 'stage' before them. There could be no mistaking that this was the execution area. The furniture left no possible doubt. In the centre was a chaise longue (obviously Aunt Grace's favourite type of seat when she was belabouring a girl's bottom), its flat end towards the audience to provide them with the best possible view of the bottom being belaboured. Behind it was a strange construction, which took me several moments to identify. A whipping block! My heart thudded as I studied it. Obviously considerable thought had been devoted to its construction — if at this point in my life, I was inexperienced in these matters, I seemed to be able to compensate for this lack of knowledge with an enthusiastic imagination — because I could see immediately how it would hold the victim firmly with her target area properly poised for the whipping. The main section was some two feet in width and long enough to provide support for the head, with a gentle downward slope to increase the angle between the upper body and the thighs. The kneeling part was slightly wider, presumably to allow a splaying of the legs for increased exposure. The whole edifice was well padded and covered in a rich blue material which appeared to be velvet. It was exceedingly ominous, not least due to the several visible straps designed to prevent any shifting of the position.

Immediately, all the symptoms of fear returned. My blood pounded through my veins, my breathing was reduced to shallow little pants, my bottom tingled and seemed to swell, my saliva flooded into my mouth, causing me to swallow convulsively, before it dried up almost completely. Elspeth moved alongside me and put a gentle arm around my waist, a kind and loving little gesture that nearly brought the pent-up tears pouring out, before I regained sufficient control and, on trembling limbs, tottered with the rest onto the stage. Cook lined us up with our backs to the still-empty seats and well to the right of the chaise longue and instructed us on the required procedure — mainly for my benefit, of course.

'Right, we're all to be spanked in turn, with you first Annie to give your bottom more time to recover before you are birched.' At that, Elspeth reached round and gave my right buttock a reassuring little squeeze. 'When you are summoned,' she continued to me, 'walk smartly up to Madam. She will bare your bottom and spank you. When she has finished, stand up, take your drawers right off and, holding them in your left hand, walk back to the other end of the line — next to me. Elspeth will have moved up as soon as you leave, so there will be plenty of room. Your skirts will be pinned up so that our guests will be able to look at your bottom if they wish. You will *not* rub or soothe it in any way. When Elspeth moves up for her spanking, Bridget will move into her place and we will all move up with her, leaving room for Elspeth to move back on your right. Understand?'

I nodded, incapable of speech, rational or otherwise. Luckily we did not have much longer to bear the suspense. We heard footsteps above us, murmuring voices, getting closer and louder until they filled the confined space. Far too rapidly, they had settled down, Aunt Grace had seated herself on the chaise longue and she began to address the guests:

'My husband and I spent Thursday afternoon visiting friends in town and returned to find the house deserted and little of the day's work complete. We eventually moved into the garden and found all the maids, Cook and Annie romping on the croquet lawn. As if that was not enough, they were all stark-naked. I accept that it was a particularly

99

sultry day and I freely confess that foremost in my mind was the desire to remove my clothes and sink into a refreshing bath. However, I would not have considered for one moment disporting myself in the open. They will all now receive the due punishment they so richly deserve. I shall spank them all, soundly, and on their bare bottoms. I am therefore especially grateful for your presence as witnesses because I am sure that this will add immeasurably to the effectiveness of their punishment. After all, it is humiliating enough to have to present what is one of the most private of bodily parts to be stripped naked, to have to proffer such tender and intimate flesh so close to another's gaze, as I am sure that the ladies here will fully understand. So, how much more shaming is it to be for them knowing that ten complete strangers will be seeing their bare bottoms, will be watching every little quiver and wobble, will be noting the spreading red stain as the chastisement progresses?'

Oh the power of the spoken word! Her voice, though soft, lashed me like a whip. My mind had been trying to avoid lingering on the audience and to shy away from my imminent fate but Aunt Grace's speech brought my attention very rapidly back to the essentials. It was not just what she had said. Her intonation, especially of that delicious phrase 'bare bottom', had been full of threatening relish. She continued: 'Annie, come here to have your bare bottom soundly spanked!'

I had just enough control to take in a deep breath and then, on legs that were shaking uncontrollably, I tottered across the stage to her and as I did so, she swivelled round on her seat so that she was facing the guests. Instinctively, I stood facing her and with my back to those about to bear witness. She went about the preparations with an unhurried care which must have delighted everyone else and certainly extended my suffering. First of all, she carefully selected two pins from a box on the floor, rolled up the front of my skirt and pinned it securely well above my waist. I was then turned round and the same thing was done to the rear. I couldn't face the sight of the staring, watching eyes, so held mine tightly closed, trying to shut out the intrusion and keep the prolonged humiliation purely to myself. I knew that there was a long stretch of naked thigh visible between my stockings and drawers and that the latter were so tight and small that a large proportion of my furry triangle was protruding through the slit. By the same token, when she turned me back again, I was horribly conscious that the middle of my bottom was sticking rudely out of the rear part of the central slit. Not that I had much time to consider this exposure, for her next action was to untie the drawstrings of my remaining protection and lower it down to my ankles.

I could feel the multitude of eyes boring into the revealed curves and I knew that my face was scarlet with mortification. Aunt Grace took full advantage of the situation by giving me a quiet lecture on responsibility and general decency, although I confess that my attention was far more on my nakedness than on her words, to the extent that when she finally reached out for my left hand to guide me across her knees, it came as almost a relief! Once again, there was no urgency in her actions. She smoothed her hands over my bottom, squeezed the plump flesh to assess its pliability, made minor adjustments to my position until she was satisfied with both the shape and resilience of my buttocks. Then she began. It was virtually a replica of the spanking she had given me three days before — two dozen really crisp smacks, each one of which jolted me against the yielding flesh of her thighs and every one stinging like the devil. I almost forgot all about the guests in my efforts to contain myself with some decorum but before the halfway point was reached, my poor bottom was smarting too much. I began to kick my legs, jerk my hips about and when she announced that there were still six more to come, I lowered my head onto my folded arms and gave way to the sobs which had until then been dammed up by what courage I possessed. I was dimly aware that the combination of these actions had taken all the tenseness from my body and I was lying limply over her lap. I certainly could feel the final half dozen make my cheeks wobble even more frantically.

At last it was over. Her hand was resting on my thigh and the pain was no longer increasing. I pulled myself together as quickly as I could, clambered back to my feet and followed Cook's instructions to the letter, removed my drawers completely, very conscious that in so doing, I was treating the guests to a splendid view of my bent rear end, and rejoined the opposite end of the line. There was an appreciable pause, presumably to allow the guests time for a lingering study of my red, bare, bottom. By the time Elspeth started to move forward, I was recovering with gratifying rapidity. Presumably the flesh of my bottom was already becoming accustomed to the special pain inflicted by an experienced and enthusiastic hand because the smart soon changed to a prickling, burning feeling, which was quite tolerable and then that receded to a hot glow, which was distinctly pleasant. I could therefore watch my friends receiving their medicine with more attention than I had managed last time. Even the fact that our viewpoint was to the side rather than 'full-face' did little to mar my growing enjoyment of the sight of their varied bottoms wobbling their way to the scarlet climax which so brightly signalled the effectiveness of the penalty we were all having to pay.

I was even able to appreciate things from the guests' point of view. In between the spankings, they were able to look to their right and see an increasing line of red bare bottoms, the slightly sideways view giving added emphasis to the inwards curve of the cheeks.

When Cook strode up as the last in line, I could feel the glow from my bottom spread forwards and upwards and I was again affected by those sensations to which I was beginning to become addicted. Forgetting what awaited me, I watched with bated breath as this loveable and handsome woman had her massive buttocks laid bare, placed herself with surprising grace across the waiting lap and took her punishment with a fortitude that put the rest of us to shame. Admittedly Aunt Grace had a larger target on which to distribute her spanks but she seemed to compensate for this by using considerably more force. Certainly by the conclusion, Cook's bottom glowed as brightly as any other and Aunt Grace was breathing heavily and immediately began to massage the palm of her right hand, evidence that she had not escaped unscathed.

When we were all back in our original line, there was another appreciable pause, which I assumed was to allow Aunt Grace to make a complete recovery from her labours and to let the guests enjoy a prolonged look at the display before them. It also gave me ample time to contemplate the next stage in the proceedings, namely my birching. I would not be telling the truth if I claimed that I was anything but extremely anxious. Standing there with a bare and gently throbbing bottom, even though there were seven others in the same state to keep me company, was no reassurance whatsoever, but the spankings had served one purpose in that I was in far better control of my feelings than I would have been if I had been the first and only attraction. I had grown accustomed to exposing myself to strangers and the pain of the smacks had warmed up my flesh. I did not feel that my behaviour under punishment had been any less brave than the maids. Only Cook's remarkable stoicism could be used to chide me and she was obviously very much more experienced than the rest of us. I held my head up, tried to breathe evenly, kept my bottom and legs from trembling and awaited the next move.

'Put your drawers back on, Annie,' Aunt Grace said to me before turning to face the guests. 'Now, dear friends, we come to the finale. Annie, whom none of you have met before this evening, was the prime instigator of the events for which they have all been punished. For this reason, I have decided that a simple spanking is not sufficient a penance and so I will now administer a sharp little whipping. Now I understand that the traditional birch rod is becoming less fashionable in our educational establishments and the cane is replacing it. Apparently the main reason is that the twigs are only truly effective when applied to the bare skin, whereas the cane is almost as effective if there is a layer of clothing to protect the erring girl's modesty. I am sure that you will all agree with me when I state that this is quite absurd. As I have already declared, being made to expose her buttocks is a vital part of the punishment for any well-bred and modest girl. If it were a simple matter of pure affliction of pain, there are any number of ways of achieving this, but none would have the same chastening effect on her; none would correct her and leave her as genuinely penitent as a properly conducted chastisement on her naked bottom. I shall birch Annie on her bare buttocks; I shall do so firmly enough to render them crimson and she will not be able to sit comfortably for some time. But I shall also do it with love. Because in the short time that she has been in my house, I have grown to love her dearly.'

She paused to let everyone weigh up her words. I could sense an air of suppressed excitement pervade the cellar, not just among the guests but also from the maids. For myself, her lecture stiffened my resolve in a remarkable fashion. The fear of the unknown pain was still very evident but was no longer of the nature which weakens the heart, mind and limbs. I stood firmly upright, very aware of the fact that the central part of my posterior was thrusting nakedly through the slit of my tight little drawers but I was no longer trying to banish that awareness from my conscious mind. My time was nigh and I again resolved to meet the challenge by matching Aunt Grace's declaration of love by co-operating to the best of my ability.

'Elspeth, will you unpin Annie's skirts, please.' Her nimble fingers soon achieved the requested covering of my charms. 'Maria and Bridget, please move the chaise longue to the back of the stage and place the block in its place.' I was able to obtain some enjoyment from the glimpses of their red bottoms as they moved about their task.

'Now, Annie, please stand before the block.'

I obeyed, staring sightlessly at the far wall while Aunt Grace carefully rolled up the front part of my skirts and pinned them securely to my blouse, leaving even my belly button exposed. With her guidance and support, I then knelt on the lower part of the block and slowly placed my torso along the upper, sinking comfortably into the deeply upholstered surface. Aunt Grace took each of my wrists in turn and strapped them fairly tightly to the sides, enabling me to take stock of my position. It was surprisingly comfortable. My weight was evenly supported by my knees and my chest; the downward slope of the main part of the block was sufficient to raise my hips to greater prominence but not so steep that the blood rushed to my head. The outward and upward thrust of my rear end had pushed my buttocks even further through the slit in my drawers and I was very conscious of the way the silken material of my skirts caressed them at every slight movement of my body.

Having fastened my hands, she placed another strap about my waist, adjusting it until it held me firmly but by no means uncomfortably. Her hands then passed slowly and questingly over my bottom, the fingertips pressing firmly into the flesh, then moving to the backs of my knees to encourage them further inwards to tighten the curves just a little bit more. They moved back upwards to assess the effect and then she probed the gaping cleft between my cheeks, encouraged my knees a few inches further apart, checked the division again and then, finally satisfied, fastened the last straps about my thighs.

Nervously I awaited the baring of my bottom. Even though it had already been publicly displayed, there was no escaping the nervousness that I am sure would have afflicted any young girl in these circumstances, especially after Aunt Grace's speech on the subject and with the prospect of it becoming very much the centre of attention. She did it with tantalising slowness, inching my skirts upwards, so that I could feel those expert eyes boring into each inch of naked flesh as it was revealed — my thighs first, then the material slithered over my half-naked buttocks until it could be folded neatly around my waist. She paused yet again, presumably to let the guests have a clear view. Then she explored my bottom once again, and once again I thrilled to the feel of her hand sliding across the taut silk, onto naked skin, across the great divide and back onto silk until she reached my right hip bone.

She was building up the anticipation with consummate skill and I could feel myself quivering uncontrollably with the tension, so that when I at last felt her fingers on the drawstring of my drawers I heard myself give out a soft, low moan. The upthrust posture I was in prevented my last protection slipping down of its own accord and Aunt Grace added to my ordeal by stretching the waistband and dragging it down over my buttocks so that I was in no

106

doubt as to the exact extent of my exposure. When she reached the tops of my stockings she let go and my drawers slumped around my knees like a flag of surrender.

My bottom was now completely bare and she once again stood by my left side, leaving a clear view for all concerned. By now my head was swimming with the combination of fear and excitement. In spite of the hot atmosphere, my exposed skin felt cold and clammy — except for the palms of my hands, which were hot and moist. Half of me silently begged her to start the whipping; the other half dreaded the onset of the pain.

Her hand moved across my naked flesh for what was to be the last time. If my skin had been sensitive beforehand, her touch sent the nerves alight. Then I sensed movement from her, so turned my head to my left and saw her reaching down under the block, pulling out a bucket and extracting the rod. I watched with open eyes and mouth as she shook it and droplets of liquid flew around, some landing on my bottom, making me gasp in surprise. It was far less frightening than I had feared: perhaps a foot and a half in length, slender and seemingly consisting of fine twigs, as opposed to the bushy branch my fevered imagination had envisaged. I watched her measure it against my helpless bottom, felt the cool touch against my overheated skin and buried my head between my arms with a half-stifled sob.

I heard a faint whistling sound; then a 'thwick' as it landed; then I felt it. Immediately the tensison seemed to flow out of my pinioned body, my pent-up breath sighed gustily out of my lungs and I melted into the soft embrace of the padded block. It had not hurt. It had been a great deal less stringent than a spank from her hand. It did sting. But pleasantly. I was able to feel the several twigs individually as they bit into me, noting that the stinging band was distinctly broader on my right buttock than on the left but that only the tips caused any real sting. She waited much longer in between strokes than she had done between spanks. I realised that I had instinctively tucked my bottom in to receive the first stroke and managed to relax it in time for the second, which landed just below the warm strip left by the first. Again, the initial flaring smart died away almost immediately to a pleasing warm glow. I sighed with what was nearly pleasure — and would have been perhaps if I had not been aware of the strange eyes fixed on my naked flesh, in spite of all my efforts to obliterate the audience from my consciousness.

It was not until some dozen or so strokes had landed that I began to appreciate that the pain from the birch had a peculiar accumulative nature, compared with that from the palm of the hand. Suddenly each visitation was not only increasingly full of a burning smart in its own right but was also re-igniting the fires left by previous ones. I could no longer keep still and began to writhe gently against my bonds and, as I did so, Aunt Grace left an appreciably longer interval between her blows, for which I was initially grateful, as I could then keep myself under better control. Having already found that curiosity was a reasonable antidote to the pain of a well-smacked bottom, I craned my head round to my left and watched her as she beat me. She was frowning slightly, with concentration rather than anger, I surmised, and her eyes were as firmly fixed on my bare bottom as I assumed were those of the guests. I noted that she put very little effort into each stroke, applying the rod with little more than a smooth sweep of her arm. As soon as it had landed, she leant some way to her right, the better to observe the effect, then made little adjustments to her position before eventually lining her weapon up against the part of my bottom she wished to assail and delivering the next stroke. Being able — for a fairly short time, I must confess — to observe both her actions and their effect on my person, allowed me to learn something about the skills required to make the best use of what I was rapidly discovering to be a most sophisticated implement. I worked out that the reason for here adjustments was simply to ensure that the tips of the twigs did not fall on the same area of buttock. By moving backwards and forwards, she could direct them from the more obvious further reaches of my right cheek, onto the equivalent part of the left one and anywhere in between. Including into the gaping division, where their sting was especially noteworthy!

Not surprisingly, my interest was soon overcome by the mounting torment. I buried my face between my arms again and let the pain wash through me. My world slowly contracted until it seemed to consist of little more than my naked bottom, the skin of which felt so hotly stretched that I began to wonder if it would split. It was like being enveloped by a rising tide of molten lava. My breath whooshed from my lungs; flames flickered in my closed eyes; the steady 'thwick' of the birch landing sounded like thunder in my pounding ears, for some inexplicable reason sounding louder than the low moans which I could do nothing to prevent.

I was vaguely aware that my hips were moving to and fro within the confines allowed by the straps. My bottom was burning. I began to cry out.

Then, suddenly, the feelings changed. I felt a strange languor creeping through my helpless body and then a tingling flame burst through my cunny, in spite of the overwhelming fire in the tightened globes above it. My bottom bucked and weaved in tune with the rod; my cries grew more piercing; the pain was suddenly a friend to be welcomed and no longer an enemy to be fought. Once again, I was near to a complete faint and it took some time before I was fully aware that she had stopped. I knelt there, in my restraining bonds, and my sobs died away while the pain in my poor bottom took over the whole of my being. I was vaguely conscious of Aunt Grace asking if any of the guests would like to examine me closely. Murmuring voices swam distantly in and out of my consciousness; gentle touches on my afflicted flesh relit the fires; then, towards the end, a hand eased its way between my legs and squeezed my love-nest, sending flames of a different sort into my vitals.

Still near swooning, I was eventually taken by Elspeth and Maria to my room, where I was tenderly stripped stark-naked and laid on my belly. A blissfully cooling lotion was applied to my buttocks and rubbed in with the gentlest possible touch. The pain began to ebb away. I was given a glass of milk, which I gulped down with the rampant haste of a thirsty child and which must have contained some kind of opiate, because I fell asleep very quickly. Not for long, however. Not being used to sleeping on my belly, I must have turned to a more natural position in due course and this brought the whipped part of me into contact with the sheets and the resurgence of the pain woke me. But it mattered not, for on perhaps the second occasion I realised that there was someone else in the bed with me.

Struggling through the mists which enveloped my mind, I first identified her as my beloved Elspeth and second realised that she had been bold enough to discard her night attire and was, like me, as naked as the day she had been born. Suddenly my cunny caught fire with lustful desire, as though the flames which had been devouring my buttocks had spread to its delicate interior. I gave a little cry of delight and clasped her hungrily to my bosom. Our mouths met, crushing each other's lips painfully and our tongues slithered joyfully in and out of our panting mouths. She gripped one of my breasts and squeezed it; I returned the compliment and thrilled to its firm, yielding softness, highlighted by the stiffly pointed nipple. She pulled me on top of her so that my bottom was free of any painful contact. With one hand on my back holding our hot bodies closely together, she moved the other on to my yearning cunny and slipped a finger between the lips until it had found the spot and my swirling mind could lose itself completely in a shuddering 'little death'.

I slept again. Soundly now. Until the delicate threads of dawn's early waking penetrated the room and woke me with them. My bottom was throbbing but in a different way. I felt completely refreshed and joy, happiness and sensuality flooded through the whole of my being. I turned to Elspeth and kissed her soft, wide mouth with infinite tenderness. She awoke and we lay for a long moment, smiling at each other, before she rose and walked over to the windows to pull back the curtains and I watched the white gleam of her naked body and the startlingly visible dark line of her bottom cleft. My love-nest joined me in my wakened state as I knelt on the bed and as she returned, her now fully visible nipples and furry triangle made me catch my breath.

'How is your bottom?'

'Much better. It is still throbbing and aching. I cannot imagine that I will be sitting with any comfort for quite a while. But it is a strange feeling . . . Oh, dearest Elspeth . . . I *like* it . . . It makes me feel restless . . . I want to feel you pressed hard against me again.

'I know . . . Lie down and let me have a good look at it.'

I obeyed, thrilling at the prospect of her closely studying my bare bottom. I heard her light a candle to make her examination more effective and while I waited, I wriggled my front against the rumpled silk beneath me until she was kneeling on the floor at the side of the bed, with the candle poised close to the area under scrutiny.

The feel of her eyes on my nudity was very exciting and my hands stole to my aching bosoms and clasped them in an embrace which, though less welcome than it would have been with her hands there, was still more than enough to keep the pleasure waves rolling.

'It's very red, Annie. But the little weals and dots are standing out through the flush, so you are beginning to recover.'

At this point I felt the first, butterfly wing touch of her lips on my bottom. When I had kissed hers after I had spanked her, it had been no more than a perfunctory few pecks. She kissed mine with her heart and cunny as involved as her mouth was, trailing the soft wetness of her tongue over the hot flesh and then blowing gently on the moistened area. It was quite delicious. I began to pant my lust into the cool morning air. Her tongue pressed into the tops of the cleft. It eased into and along the folds at the top of my thighs. A hand rested on each cheek and gently — and only slightly painfully — drew them apart until I could feel the fresh air on my stretched little anus. I shivered at the invasive thrill. Then I screamed aloud as that most intimate place was flooded with a hot wetness which sent a surge of unimaginable pleasure straight into the very core of my being. Had my buttocks not been so tender, I may well have clamped them together in shock. As it was, I was momentarily petrified. Then the thrill took over completely and I surrendered myself to this new delight, lying liquidly spread-eagled as my delicate little bottom-hole savoured the attention it was being so expertly and lovingly given.

I then found that I was kneeling up in the most abandoned and wanton manner, with my throbbing buttocks splayed wide open. Her stiffened tongue pushed past the tightness of my opening and into the passage itself, which was, to my amazement, even more sensational. I felt her hand on my cunny and that was all I needed to send me over the brink and into the throes again.

I must have slept for at least another hour, for I awoke to see the full morning sun streaming into my room and Aunt Grace's presence adding further to the warmth and light. Once again my bare bottom was closely examined and again I was reassured as to its powers of recovery. It was once more gently soothed with cooling ointment. I dozed again, overtaken by a gentle languor, woken at intervals by all the maids in turn, all of whom wanted to see my bottom, to add yet another layer of balm, to kiss it.

Eventually I stirred myself sufficiently to look at it myself and stiffly rose to adjust the looking glasses appropriately. I gasped at the state of my flesh. It looked red, swollen and the fine tracery of purple weals and dots covered every inch. I was so amazed that, when I had recovered from the shock of my appearance and sat down on the edge of the bed, it was several moments before I realised that it was still sore and leapt back to my feet!

However by dinner-time I was feeling little more than stiff with a gentle aching throb, which caused no more than mild discomfort.

As apparently was the custom, we all dined together, maids, Cook, Aunt Grace and Uncle George. It was a sparkling happy time and my sense of intoxication had nothing to do with the generous supply of wine which accompanied the food.

I knew that I had passed the real test. I had been accepted.

I was home.

CHAPTER 7

During the ensuing months, my education in the techniques of sensual enjoyment proceeded apace. My bottom soon recovered from its introduction to the sharp joys of the rod and I was able to make love more uninhibitedly to Elspeth by the fourth day. I shall never forget the simple pleasure of drifting into sleep with the yielding firmness of her silk-skinned body snuggling up against mine. Nor the less simple excitement I felt when I first held her buttocks wide apart, gazed long and closely at her neat, pinky-brown little bottom-hole and, taking a deep breath, lowered my mouth onto it to kiss her in the same way that she had kissed me. None of my apprehensions that it would be a distasteful thing to do were realised. The scent of excited girl from just below made my nostrils flare with matching excitement and the intimacy of the taste made my mouth water. Perhaps the greatest source of satisfaction to me was the stream of gasping squeaks from the other end! Her very evident pleasure, added to the feeling of being wrapped up in her delicious bottom, made me really want to force my tongue as far as the tight ring of muscle would allow.

Slightly to my surprise, when she told me that the maids often shared a bed and caressed each other in the same way that we did, I felt only the merest flicker of jealousy. I am sure that this was a sign of the growing confidence I was feeling about my position in the household because from then on, I felt free to indulge my growing taste for naked female flesh whenever possible.

Cook was the first target. The memories of her statuesque curves kept prodding me and the desire to bury myself in her fleshly opulence grew until I could endure it no longer. Inspiration came to me one hot afternoon. I found her in the kitchen preparing a cold collation for supper and asked her if she would be so kind as to take her supper with me in my room. Her broad and happy smile was all the reward I needed. Uncle George had graciously permitted me to take a bottle of champagne up with me and it was suitably chilled by the time she entered, accompanied by a mischievously smiling Connie bearing a laden tray. Although the room was well enough lit by the sinking sun, I had taken the precaution of lighting several candles, not only for better illumination but also to increase the temperature of the room!

She had taken great care with her appearance (as had I). Her dark hair was drawn up elegantly, leaving her long neck bare. She was wearing silk gloves of the purest white, a tight blouse showing a delightful décolletage and a full-length silk skirt which flowed round her limbs and clung to the curves of her hips and bottom in the most enticing way. It was obvious that she was wearing neither shift nor petticoat.

I opened the champagne and we had a glass before starting on the food, during which time we talked with the fluent ease of old and good friends, gradually moving from the general to the sensual.

'Do you ever spank the maids?' I asked casually, as we placed the empty plates back on the tray and I refilled our glasses.

'Of course I do,' she replied.

'Properly, I mean. As a punishment. Or do you report them to Aunt Grace so that she can do it before our guests.'

115

'It depends. If there's an entertainment in the offing, I might well tell her about it in case she needs another maid for punishment but they are all so good that it is very seldom that they need to be punished. No, I enjoy it. So do they — as long as it isn't too hard of course. Apart from anything else, putting one of them across my lap for ten minutes or so gives us both a good chance to take the weight off our feet!' We both laughed.

'Do you let any of them spank you?'

She laughed out loud. 'If I want to have my bottom warmed up a bit, then yes. But only if Aunt Grace is not free. She does most to keep it under control.'

I took a deep breath. 'Well, Cook my dear. I have not forgotten my introduction to this house and I now feel that the time is right for me to pay you back. You will lay yourself across my lap, I will slowly — and with great pleasure — lay your magnificent bottom completely bare. I shall indulge myself fully in feeling, stroking, pinching and patting it so that I am totally cognisant of its texture and consistency, then I shall spank it until it is scarlet. When I am satisfied that it has been well and soundly spanked, I shall kiss it better. If, that is, you have conducted yourself with due courage and decorum. After that, I shall strip you stark-naked and play with whatever part of your body takes my fancy. Understand?'

As I spoke, she looked at me with a yearning which was extremely flattering and, at the end of my little speech, her mouth was open and her large brown eyes shining with anticipation. In as stately a manner as I could manage in my excitement, I moved an armless chair into the centre of the room where the light was at its best, sat down and beckoned her to me. Even though I had by then spanked all the maids, this was certainly the most thrilling preparation I had experienced. I knew that she was blessed with a splendidly large and well-shaped posterior and as she bent herself across my trembling thighs and shifted herself into a comfortable position, with her weight evenly distributed between her hands and feet on the floor and her rounded belly on my lap, I could clearly see the bounteous flesh under her skirt wobbling gently as she shifted about.

Determined to savour everything for as long as possible, I lingered over each stage, staring at the roundness thrusting against the seat of her skirt, feeling it and pressing my hand right into the yielding flesh, slowly pulling up her skirt and relishing the gradual exposure of her magnificent full thighs, the naked areas between her stockings and drawers gleaming in the mellow light. I ran my hand up and down both naked columns; prodded the large area covered by the tightly stretched seat of her drawers; untied the strings and lowered them slowly, enjoying the way her bare bottom gradually loomed into view. I played with her buttocks, enjoying the amplitude of the flesh and the warm satin of her skin; I pulled them apart and marvelled at the rich brown colour of her bottom-hole, big like the rest of her. I spanked her quite hard so that her whole bottom wobbled like a blancmange and slowly assumed a brilliant hue which contrasted dramatically with the whiteness of her thighs and the small of her back. I spanked her until she was sighing with emotion and my palm was blazing.

Then, after she had lain quietly over my knee while I rubbed her and we both recovered, I stripped her with increasing haste, gasping as her tremendous breasts sprang quiveringly free from the confines of her blouse. I kissed her delectable softness. I took a stiff, brown nipple in my mouth and sucked, gently then hard, and she groaned. I buried my face between them, enveloping myself in her sweet-scented flesh. I tore her drawers and stockings off, and I gasped at the first close view of the profuse bush

117

of dark hair at the base of her belly. I leaned forward to kiss it and thrilled to the feel of the crisp hair and the musky scent.

I stood up, clasped her tightly to me and we kissed with a hard and fiery passion.

'Oh Annie, let me strip you naked,' she breathed into my mouth.

I was shortly as bare as she and our hug was even more pleasing as our bareness melted together, softness against softness. Our hands reached simultaneously to our buttocks, clawing into the flesh, hers hot and red, mine white and cool, pulling our middles even more tightly together so the hairs on our gaping cunnies mingled and intertwined.

We fell onto the bed and our mouths and hands roved freely over each other. At one stage, Cook rolled me onto my back and raised my legs until my knees were almost touching my bosom. I could see my cunny, the fair hairs darkened by the moisture seeping from within and, above it, the lower curves of my widely separated buttocks. Her face loomed above my exposed intimacies, mouth open in panting ecstasy, eyes gleaming softly as they fixed their steady gaze on my avidly pouting anus, which was already tingling madly in expectation. I could just watch her lower her head onto me, her tongue already protuding and then my whole bottom passage thrilled as it touched the opening. Then she moved onto my cunny and her tongue found my spot; she seemed to suck the surrounding flesh right into her mouth; I screamed my delight to the quietly approving walls of my room. And passed right away as the sensations overcame me.

I returned the compliment later, for the first time separating the lips of a woman's cunny and gazing with awe at the moist, convoluted pinkness inside, and her cries were even louder than mine. Spent, we slept together. She pillowed my weary head against her big soft bosom and

I slept like a child.

My friendship with Aunt Grace (although I was now certain that there was no kinship between us, it seemed wrong to address her in any other way) also flourished. My enthusiasm for being beaten in public had waxed as the marks left by the fiery kisses of her rod had waned, and our conversations usually started on my impressions of being the main attraction at the last such occasion. For fairly obvious reasons, these talks seemed to be best conducted with me lying across her lap with my bare bottom providing inspiration to us both. She had, by the way, already complimented me very prettily on my demeanour at the entertainment and had given me half a guinea as a present, plus a very smart money box to keep it in.

On one such occasion we were discussing the various 'plays' which were put on for the guests' amusement when a childhood memory flashed through my mind. During my time at school it had been a regular practice to have a spelling bee, for which we had all stood in a line and the Mistress had tested our vocabulary by asking us to spell the words out loud. If one was successful, one moved up a place — and vice versa. Obviously the purpose was to reach the top of the line and stay there until the end, for there was always a pleasant little reward for the victor. In contrast, the girl at the other end was given a smacking, albeit a light-hearted one administered on the seat of her skirts with a ruler. I remembered seeing the shining eyes of the loser on one of these tests as she rubbed her bottom and rather wishing that I had less of a talent for spelling! Her excitement had been very plain to see. I therefore described this to Aunt Grace.

'That could provide the basis for a very entertaining evening, Annie. Now let's think. We shall need some appropriate furniture — that should present no problem.

Naturally we shall have to change the procedure somewhat!'

'Well, it would obviously be a very strict establishment,' I replied. 'Every mistake would be punished by some good smacks as well as a move down the line.'

'And a birching for the loser.'

'Good idea, Aunt Grace. In fact the last three could receive a punishment. Perhaps a spanking each, then say six, twelve and eighteen strokes.'

'And of course your bottoms would be bared all ready before the test began.'

'Yes. Oh, Aunt Grace, I really think the guests will enjoy it. A row of bare-bottomed girls not knowing which one will be getting spanked — or when. And then a truly exciting climax. You would play the Mistress, I assume.'

'Of course.'

'And you could announce the rules at the beginning. Including the penalties for the last three pupils. In fact, we could pretend that this is a completely new test. In fact, you should be a new Mistress, disgusted at the lack of discipline in the school.'

'Excellent, Annie. I know, we could start from the beginning of my first class. You could be the mischievous one and I could give you a formal spanking in front of the class as a declaration of my serious intentions.'

'That would be nice. Should I also play a stupid girl who qualifies for a multitude of spanks and the rod?' At that, she laughed and smacked my provocatively posed bare bottom.

'Don't be greedy, my dear. No, you have far too intelligent an expression for that role to be convincing . . . Wait. I have it. You do well during the test. We shall select three others to be the dunces — perhaps Elspeth, Agatha and Vera would provide the best variety of bottom — but your behaviour during their punishment — too gleeful perhaps? — suggests a finale of you being birched to humble you.'

'Oh Aunt Grace . . . please spank me now . . . hard.'

And on that note, our entertainments assumed a new and very successful dimension. The scenario was exhilarating to take part in and proved immensely popular with our guests. Afterwards, Aunt Grace presented me with a guinea for my box as a token of appreciation.

I also furthered my education in other directions. In another of our little conversations, Aunt Grace had been instructing me on some of the finer points of administering a spanking. For example, to lessen the sting of a spank without being too obvious, the best way is to curl one's hand to match the curve of the buttock being assaulted. Conversely, a stiff palm delivers a greater sting. She took advantage of this topic to inform me that she was beginning to see me as her 'Lieutenant', alongside Cook in order of priority and, at the same time, lectured me on the responsibilities of my position. I was, for example, fully entitled to give any of the maids a punishment spanking but she then went on to lecture me on the dangers of abusing my power by forcing them into doing something against their will.

'Not that I can imagine,' she continued, 'that anything you might want them to do would be disasteful to any one of the dear girls, but it is something to bear in mind, Annie.'

It was shortly after this that my chance to exercise these powers came to me. I caught Vera helping herself to some cake which we both knew was Uncle George's especial favourite and was therefore reserved for his exclusive use. I cleared my throat, she whirled round and for a long moment we stared at each other, she guiltily and I with a stern expression deliberately assumed to disguise my mounting excitement. There was no need to explain her crime to her, nor to make any excuse for my instant decision to deal with her myself.

'Come with me up to my room, Vera. You know that I am about to spank you and you know full well that you thoroughly deserve it.'

I took her trembling hand and led her up the stairs, where I moved my armless chair into the middle of the room and sat down. She offered no resistance as I helped her across my knees — not that I would have been less than amazed if she had done so — and raised her hips to allow me to pull her skirt and petticoat up to her waist.

My actions had been brisk up to this point but the moment her drawers were exposed to me, I relaxed and began to appreciate this new experience — no, I should be honest and admit that I was enjoying it. All the spankings I had so far delivered had been first and foremost sensual ones, with the straightforward object of laying bare one of my friends' bottoms and warming it up as far as her pleasure and satisfaction allowed. Now, I was about to punish. It resulted in a different kind of tenseness and hollowness but it was no less a pleasing sensation for that.

I stared down at the well-filled seat of her plain, thick, one-piece drawers. They had moulded themselves pleasingly to her big rump and had got slightly caught up in the cleft so that the twin globes were outlined. I patted her quite firmly and from the feel of her flesh under my hand and the way it quivered, I confidently expected a particularly soft bottom to spank. Apart from seeing her all bare during our romp in the fountain and on the croquet lawn, I had had few dealings with her. I was therefore glad of the chance to know her better.

'I am going to pull your drawers down and spank you on your bare bottom, Vera. You understand that, don't you?'

'Yes, of course, Annie.' And she again raised herself

to help me. I was careful not to touch her skin while I was baring her so that I could assess her without having my first impression influenced by the feel of her. I looked down, with my excitement both controlled and increased by the need for a disciplined approach. It was a different bottom to the two which I had studied in the same position, namely Elspeth's and Cook's. As I have said, she was easily the quietest and most self-effacing of the maids and her bottom seemed to reflect her personality. It certainly looked beautifully soft, with very smooth white skin and the flesh clearly lacked the massive solidity of Cook and the tightness of Elspeth, for her buttocks were spread out to the extent that I could just discern the dark beginnings of her anus. While this would normally have been a source of excitement to me, on this occasion I felt that I should only be aware of her bare buttocks. I studied her pose and then instructed her to move a little further forward and also to straighten her legs. She did so with due alacrity and the result was a distinct improvement. With the reduction in the angle her body had assumed, her cleft closed up enough to hide her bottom-hole and the folds at the junction of buttock and thigh reappeared. I was now faced with a proper target.

I could not resist a further manual assessment. She certainly was the proud possessor of the softest bottom I had ever touched. Her skin was silken smooth and my fingers sank into her flesh at the slightest pressure. It was a bottom which cried out to be properly spanked and so, without further ado, I made my final preparations. I pushed her skirts up a bit higher, rolled up my sleeves and then laid my left arm across her naked loins and gripped her right hip. This not only held her down effectively but also brought the soft skin on the inside of my forearm against the even softer skin of her lower back. Quite delicious. Finally I raised my right arm and brought my stiffened palm down firmly onto — and into — the yielding flesh of her left cheek.

The ringing sound of flesh on flesh was music in my ears. The instant impression of softness on my hand; the way her weight jolted against my thighs; her sharp little gasp at the sting — all moved me deeply. I revelled in the next few moments as passion flooded through my being and I delivered a wild series of spanks before I drew breath, paused for a moment and then went about my business in a more methodical manner. My first impression as I gazed pantingly down at her was how amazingly rapidly her bottom had reddened. My wild assult had resulted in her right buttock receiving far more attention than its twin but both were brilliantly discoloured. Poor Vera was rocking and gasping at the obvious pain and her flesh was quivering constantly.

Drawing a deep, steadying breath, I started anew, with the deliberate intention of evening up the redness. My smacks were now somewhat less forceful but I added a flick of the wrist at the moment of impact, so although there was considerably less noise, each one made her whole bottom wobble in a delightful, almost liquid manner and her body jerked sharply against the restraints of my thighs and my left arm. It took perhaps two minutes to make both cheeks uniformly red.

I paused again. This time I devoted some of my attention to her, as opposed to just her bottom. She was panting hard and rapidly but was not crying and, in fact, I had not been aware of even the tiniest squeak from her. And yet her skin was bright red and, to my inexperienced eyes, suggested that its owner had been very adequately spanked. I then realised that I was learning another lesson — one cannot judge the effectiveness of a spanking purely from the speed and degree of the reddening of the buttocks.

I focussed my full attention back to her naughty big bottom and proceeded, this time adapting a regular rhythm, beginning at the very top of her left cheek, moving to the same part of the other one, then back to the left and smacking below the place where the previous blow had landed and so on until I had reached the tops of her plump thighs. Then, using just the ends of my fingers, I moved down the soft warmth of her bottom cleft. As a finale to the 'round', I administered a rapid volley to the fattest part of each cheek. After a brief pause to study the effect, I started again. Halfway through the third round she was crying out; by the end of the fifth, she was sobbing quietly. As I began the eighth, she broke down and her cries of pain echoed through the room. I completed it and stopped, running my hand gently over the trembling flesh until she had quietened a little. Her whole bottom was the colour of a ripe cherry — more purple than red, and must have been burning like a furnace. I was breathing very heavily from my exertions and I suddenly became aware that my right hand was stinging and extremely warm. But the joy of power still gripped me.

'Vera, you have taken your punishment very well. It is now almost over. I shall give you six more. Right on this part — where you sit — so that you will be reminded for a while longer that stealing will not be tolerated. Understand?'

'Yes, Annie. I am sorry. I won't do it again. I promise.'

'I am pleased to hear it. Right, lift your bottom up a little more and spread your legs. Hold yourself as still as you can. Good girl.'

Slowly but steadily she obeyed. Her cleft opened sufficiently to expose the beginnings of her anus and separating her thighs resulted in a few wisps of the dark hair on her cunny coming into view. This time I did not mind. In fact I surmised that the further exposure of her little secret places might add something to the effectiveness of the final spanks. I gave them to her hard and with a long interval between each. Two to the base of each buttock and the last two across both, low down and sinking deliciously into the open cleft. Each made her howl and each added to the warm glow in my belly. I then sat back and watched with amused fascination as she flung her hands back and frantically rubbed her burning bottom, making it wobble even more violently than any of my efforts had done.

I had found it a deeply satisfying experience, although very different to the other spankings I had previously administered. I did not feel the urge for further sensuality, which was in no sense a criticism of her naked charms. What I did want to do, and what I did as soon as she had recovered some of her composure, was to hold her in my arms and comfort her. Before that I made her rise and turn her back to me so that I could replace her drawers. She obediently held her skirts above her waist and so I was able to make a reflective study of the damage. The relative looseness of her buttocks was evident from the way that in the standing position, the top few inches of her bottom were more or less untouched, apart from the odd blotch which had presumably been inflicted during the first part of the spanking when I was not aiming the smacks properly. The rest of it was a deep, even red and I felt I could be reasonably proud of my efforts. I kissed her tenderly on each side, relishing the soft heat of her skin against my lips, buttoned her up and then folded her in my arms.

She began to cry again. Softly and quietly. I held her tightly and murmured soothingly, while a glow of warm affection for this shy and very sweet girl spread through me. I realised that I wanted to know her better, so some time later I asked her if she would like to spend the night with me. She looked at me and a shy smile lit up her pretty little face. Tears sprang out of her reddened eyes and she could do no more than nod her acceptance.

'How about tomorrow,' I suggested. 'Your bottom should have recovered by then.'

'I'll make sure it has.'

We both laughed and she trotted off, obviously and flatteringly pleased at the prospect.

I enjoyed her very much. She came in her night attire — a white nightdress, which clung tightly to the soft curves of her full bosom before falling straight down to her feet, modestly hiding the curves of her hips. Her dark hair was unpinned and flowed over her shoulders framing her face, which was wearing an even more anxious expression than usual. I poured two glasses of wine and beckoned her to sit with me on the bed where we sat and talked about little of any consequence until she had relaxed.

Then, giving her my empty glass, I asked her to put them both on the tray by the window, while I watched the barely discernible sway of her bottom under the nightdress. On her return, I signalled her to halt some three paces away from me and I again felt the pleasure of power.

'Show me your cunny,' I said.

Blushing very prettily, she slowly raised the robe until the neat little furry triangle was exposed.

'A bit higher — I want to see your bellybutton.' Very nice it was. 'Now your bosom . . . Good girl.'

I stared at her virtually naked form with undisguised pleasure. She really did have the most lovely complexion. Purest white and the soft smoothness of her skin was obvious. Her breasts lacked the firm jut which made Elspeth's so desirable and did not have the classic proportions of my statue, but were nicely full, with neat brown nipples. I nodded and she let her clothing drop, looking slightly puzzled as she did so.

'Turn round,' I instructed. She did so and as she had

not let go of her dress, it was held more tightly against her body and the twin globes of her most important feature were outlined. I kept her waiting for several minutes.

'Let me see your bottom, Vera.'

Inch by nervous inch the hem rose, revealing bare legs, plumply naked white thighs, two wide and deep folds indicating the beginning of that exciting upward curve of buttock. She paused for a moment at the juncture, her hands trembling visibly as they clutched the folds of cloth as she steeled herself to make the final exposure. I did not bid her to hurry. I was enjoying both what was already on view and the anticipation of the further delights to come. The folded edge of material eventually, and with tantalising slowness, crept upwards and more and more curved, white flesh, so beautifully divided, was revealed. I satisfied my visual desire and then told her to strip naked, which she did with no hesitation and stood there while I examined her complete rear view, noting that her bottom looked quite a lot larger when it was no longer topped by the voluminous folds of her nightgown.

By then my hands were positively yearning to feel her soft skin and yielding flesh, so I told her to step back until she was within easy reach. She did so clumsily, the awkward movement causing her buttocks to quiver and shake most temptingly and I took great pleasure in putting my right hand on the lower part of her bottom and flapping it about, which caused the most dramatic agitation of her mounds. I then spent several moments on an investigation into which part − of those easily accessible to me − was covered in the softest skin. I found the choice lay between the inside of her thighs and her bottom-cleft and eventually found it impossible to make a firm decision. It then occurred to me that her breasts and belly would also present considerable rivalry, so turned her around and checked. Both parts were truly delightful but I eventually settled on the inside of her cleft, an inch or so from its top, as the winner.

I stood up. Our eyes met and she blushed again with that charming shyness. I put my arms round her and held her closely but gently to me, our cheeks nestling comfortably together and both my hands on the lovely flesh of her naked bottom. By this time my little love-nest was tingling most insistently and I was debating to myself whether to continue with my exploration of her body and to look at her bottom-hole and cunny in greater detail than I had so far done with either Cook or Elspeth, or whether to yield immediately to my growing desire to have her hands on my body. She suddenly offered a third alternative: 'Would you like to smack my bottom, Annie?'

The simple answer was, of course, 'yes', but having spanked her so comprehensively only a day or so before, I thought that I would rather save that treat for later in the night. 'Of course I would like to, Vera — is it fully recovered, by the way?'

'Completely. It wasn't a really hard spanking and it does seem to get better very quickly.'

'Good. I certainly did not notice any bruising when I was looking at it. But I don't think I will do it now. Not yet. No, I am going to lie down and I want you to bare my bottom and kiss it. All over. Understand?'

'Oh Annie. I would love to.'

I drew my head back to see her face and, once again, I was moved and flattered at the obvious delight and enthusiasm which she was making no attempt to conceal. I kissed her. Our tongues briefly flickered against each other and I savoured the hot sweetness of her breath before breaking away from our embrace and flinging myself face down on my bed. Quite deliberately I had decided to revert to earlier days in my choice of apparel and was wearing my favourite negligee over a silk nightgown on which Mrs

Savage had lavished special care, with stockings and satin drawers underneath. These were in one piece with no slit and fitted deliciously tightly. I turned my head so that I could watch her. She stared at me for a while, her brown eyes wide and gleaming and her mouth slightly open. Then she ran the tip of her tongue over her lips and moved to the side of the bed, where she knelt down and began to lay my bottom bare as instructed. I saw the subtle jiggling and swaying of her bosoms as she raised the negligee become even more noticeable as she had to tug the nightdress upwards. As she reached the swell of my buttocks, the pleasures of being bared demanded my full concentration, so I rested my head between my outstretched arms, closed my eyes and surrendered to her attentions. To my pleasant surprise, her inherent shyness did not prevent her from giving full rein to her sensuality, for she went about her task with a skill and keenness which suffered nothing in comparison with Cook and Elspeth. Her hands were as deft, her lips as soft and after she had covered every inch of my buttocks with slitheringly moist kisses, she prised them apart and bent to address my yawning cleft in the most gratifying way.

I made her follow Cook's example and lay on my back with my legs pulled right back and widely parted and watched avidly as she sent those incredible thrills right into the depths of my bottom with her tongue. She even produced a novel sensation, by running her soft but fully extended tongue from the end of my tail bone right round to my 'spot' in one sweeping movement. It was so delightful that I gasped at her to repeat it. Many times. The tinglings had by then turned to the most urgent throbbings but I did not want it to end. I wanted to save my trip to heaven for later and, with some help from her, stripped all my clothes off, pushed her down on the bed and lay on top of her. Our softnesses united. Bosom to bosom;

belly to belly; cunny to cunny and thigh to thigh. I crushed my mouth to hers on a surge of passion and immediately tasted the lingering scent of my own love juices on her. At first this took me aback but then it suddenly seemed wildly exciting and I drew her lips, then her tongue right into my mouth to suck the last drop from her. We thrashed all around the large bed, gasping, panting, kissing, sucking, nibbling, biting and licking. Her stiff nipples made the inside of my mouth tingle. Her anus was moist and very slightly salty. Her love-nest was slippery and musky and within moments of my drawing the part surrounding her 'spot' into my mouth, she bucked and squealed and then stiffened as the spasms overtook her.

My own passion eased as I moved to cuddle her hot and flushed little face to my aching breasts. In fact I welcomed the chance to gather my energies for a rather less hectic exploration, to mull over the variety of sensations of which I was aware and to decide on those I most wished to savour. I eventually told her to kneel over me with her bottom over my face and use her finger and tongue on my cunny. In seconds the waves were again flooding through my whole being and the sight of her rounded bare buttocks, neat brown anus and the glistening pink slit of her love-nest, with its protective surround of matted hair, all looming over me, added a most welcome variation.

We both slept exceedingly well and I saw her out in the morning feeling a genuine fondness for her. But I had to admit that the satisfaction from the night's activities had come primarily from the new feeling of being in control, of the freedom to bid her to do whatever pleased me — even if what pleased me had been thrilling her — as opposed to the way I had loved before, when I had (quite happily) fallen in with my partner's desires. Then I remembered that I had omitted to smack her bottom and began to anticipate the next tryst!

131

Before I could arrange that, my sensual education was advanced significantly. A day or so after my night with Vera, I was with Aunt Grace in her drawing room and after we had had our tea, she sat back in her chair and studied me thoughtfully. I sensed that something of importance was in the offing and tensed accordingly.

'My dearest Annie. As I have said before, you have exceeded my wildest expectations. You will not, I am sure, be surprised to learn that I have had a long talk with Vera about the spanking you gave her and the night you spent with her and everything I learnt has further increased my respect for you. You remember that I said it was time to introduce you to our rather secret little ''society'' and your reaction to, and behaviour during, our entertainments has been excellent. I hope, by the way, that you have put your rewards in your money box? Good. Now, there are other services that we offer our guests and I think it is now time to lead you towards them. Please take all your clothes off.'

Not for the first time, my heart started beating faster and louder. The difference was that since my first public whipping, I no longer felt any real fear about Aunt Grace's schemes. I was certainly apprehensive at whatever lay in store for me but as even the blazing smart of her birch had eventually led me to strange and unimagined pleasures, I approached my immediate future with some equanimity. I undressed without frivolous delay and soon stood before her, by now completely at ease with my nudity. She rose, took my hand and led me to the chaise longue but instead of putting me across her lap as usual, she made me kneel on the end. I was told to rest my head on the seat, to move my knees further apart and to arch my back downwards, and as I obeyed, I could feel my buttocks stretch and spread to their limit and was certain that both secret openings were in view. My whole bottom tingled with the uncertainty and I closed my eyes and gathered

132

my courage to withstand the pain of whatever new method or implement Aunt Grace planned to introduce me to. Nothing happened. Opening my eyes, I turned round and saw her walking towards me carrying a low footstool, which she placed immediately behind me, and seated herself on it, her face only inches from my gaping bottom.

'I have already told you that your bottom is perfect, Annie, but I do not think I have referred to the charms of your hole. So petite. Such a delicate pink. So deeply hidden. And both Cook and Vera have told me that it seems especially sensitive to caresses.' She then gently stroked it with the tip of a finger and my loud gasps and sighs were answer enough.

A few moments later, she reached down and drew out a small leather case from its hiding place under the chaise longue, which she placed on her lap and opened. I was mystified.

'Face your front, Annie. And stick your bottom out as far as you can.'

I did so. And waited. The position was more comfortable than I would have expected and I did obtain a certain pleasure from knowing that she was studying my most personal parts so closely. Then I felt her finger touch my bottom-hole again, this time on the tight little opening itself. It felt different. Cooler. Slippery. Before I could think of a reason for this, I gasped again as I felt it nuzzle against the tight ring of muscle and then force its way further in, until I could actually feel it inside my bottom. She wriggled it gently and suddenly it no longer felt strange but very pleasing indeed. The tingling spread upwards from the opening and combined with the fullness in my passage to send tremors all over. I began to wriggle my bottom, to tighten and relax the hole and then I felt her move her finger about in me and the excitement was such that I felt real dismay when she removed it. I wanted to turn round again but did not dare, so knelt with my rear thrust out to its fullest extent, hoping that there were more thrills to come.

I was not disappointed. I had just identified a strange smell as being that of the scented oil which we were occasionally allowed to add to our baths and had realised that she had coated her finger with it so that it would slip more easily into my bottom, when I felt another object nuzzling at the entrance, this one harder, colder and much larger. There was a similar feeling of discomfort as she pushed it in — only significantly more intense — but again, this soon gave way to even more intense pleasure. Whatever it was seemed to fill my bottom completely and then I could feel her push it further and further up me. Once she had inserted it to the hilt, she paused and I began to relax the tightness of my muscle, which changed the prickling ache into a much more comfortable throb. Of its own accord, my bottom began to move slowly backwards and forwards and I knew that she was moving it in and out in time with my movements because when I felt most filled with the object, I could feel her fingers brush against the inside of my cleft.

This strangest — and most unexpected — of pleasures actually brought me to a sort of climax. It was not like the ones I had experienced from the stimulation of my 'spot', but it was easily enough to bring about a warm flood of pleasure. She slowly withdrew the peculiar implement, leaving me with a throbbing and gently aching rectum. And several questions, none of which I had the courage to ask. In silence, she wiped my slippery hole with a deliciously damp, cool cloth, patted each of my drum-tight buttocks and told me to get up and dress myself again, closing the case before I had the chance to see the contents.

We then returned to our original seats and resumed our

conversation, which soon made me forget the delightful ache in the very depths of my bottom.

'Now Annie. You seemed to find what I have just done to you quite pleasant.' I nodded. 'Good. As I said earlier, we offer our guests more than the entertainments with which you are now familiar. Some like more personal and secluded pleasures. One such friend is visiting us tonight and wishes to be birched. Soundly. But not as a public display as you were. I shall be assuming the role of strict governess and the guest has specifically asked if you could play my assistant. You, more than most I think, will be sympathetic and it will also be an important part of your education. Are you willing to participate?'

'Of course, Aunt Grace. I would love to. What will be required of me?'

'Do not worry. I will instruct you in your duties as part of the scenario, so to speak. Just be subtly enthusiastic. Wear that tight black skirt and a white bodies, stockings of course, and . . . let me think . . . no drawers at all. Yes, the unencumbered movements of your bottom under that skirt will certainly add to the pleasure. Be ready at six o'clock.'

'Where?'

'In the main part of the cellar. We shall be administering the punishment in a small room on the other side and I will fetch you at the appropriate moment.'

I found the prospect exceedingly exciting and was dressed, with my hair drawn back in an unnaturally severe style, at least half an hour before the appointed time. I then waited impatiently in the now dimly lit cellar, gazing at the stage and recalling the delightful torment I had already experienced there. At last, Aunt Grace appeared, summoned me and led me further down the corridor to a heavy oak door, dark with age, its gloomy appearance full of foreboding of the probable fate awaiting any miscreant

135

having to pass through. She opened it and led me through. Two severe shocks awaited me. The first was the small room itself. Lit by only a few candles, it had a suitably ominous gloom, which was made more threatening by the sparse furnishings, an upholstered ladder fastened at a reasonably gentle angle to the opposite wall, and a rack beside it on which hung a terrifying array of birches, straps and whips. My own unthreatened bottom prickled at the sight of them. The other surprise was the guest waiting patiently before the ladder. It was a man! My thoughts immediately went into a frantic whirl. The idea of girls being spanked and beaten was by now part of the natural order of things — I had overheard Cook say that if the Good Lord had not intended that to be so, He would not have given us such fleshy and receptive bottoms — but apart from criminals being flogged in the past and, of course, schoolboys, it seemed contrary to man's position to accept such punishment, even for pleasure. Then I suddenly realised that I would be seeing his bottom all bare and the prospect filled me with anticipation.

I then started to look at him properly, although with only his back view facing me, any judgement was, of necessity, incomplete. He was of middle height, seemed to be clean-shaven, had nice, thick, dark-brown hair and was dressed in a plain jacket and grey trousers. I assumed him to be beyond late youth. Perhaps twenty-one or so.

Aunt Grace had been standing beside me while I was recovering my composure, presumably watching me and waiting until I had done so.

'So this is the naughty, wicked boy who is in such need of a sound whipping!' I heard him give out a little gasp and he bowed his head. In assumed shame? In genuine trepidation? 'Well,' she continued, 'whip him soundly we shall, Annie. On his bottom. His *bare* bottom.' He quivered and I could see that his ears had reddened. 'That is how naughty boys should be treated. Turn round, you villainous little scamp.'

Now that I could study his face, I realised that he was considerably older than I had thought. Certainly over thirty. He was also quite handsome, in spite of his naughty woebegone expression. We both glared at him; he stared at the floor until Aunt Grace's stern voice again broke the silence:

'It is time for your punishment, my boy. Remove your jacket then lay yourself on the ladder.' With trembling hands he obeyed the first part of the order, hung it on a hook conveniently situated on the wall, then turned and positioned himself, his feet on the outside of the base and his arms stretched up to grasp the top rung. 'Now, Annie, truss him up tightly.'

The apparatus was well equipped with straps and it did not take me long to fasten his wrists and ankles. Aunt Grace then passed me a long belt and told me to tie it firmly round his waist. I stepped back beside her and we both stared at the tightened seat of his trousers. I found myself keenly awaiting the moment when they would be taken down but had already learned enough to know that prolonging the anticipation of that deliciously humiliating action added enormously to the resulting emotions.

'Right, young man, we are now going to take down your trousers and bare your impudent bottom for you. Annie, please proceed.'

My heart leapt. I turned to her with my mouth open in surprise but only for a second. 'Certainly, Madam,' I replied briskly and stepped up to the quivering and helpless victim. I bent down behind him and reached forwards round the sides of the ladder to find the buttons, suffering a moment of slight panic when I realised that I had no idea how a man's trousers were fastened! Fortunately my natural feminine adeptness came to my rescue and with

137

only an excusable degree of fumblilng, I had them completely undone and was able to tug them down to his knees, catching just a brief glimpse of the lower portions of his rump before his shirt slipped down to cover him again. Taking a deep breath, I grasped this last protective item and slowly rolled it upwards, folding it neatly and securely under his belly. I then felt free to look at my first male bare bottom. My initial reaction was one of disappointment. While his skin was passing white and the cheeks quite nice and chubby, it did not match the aesthetic appeal of any of the female posteriors I had seen. It lacked that series of delightful curves from the waist and loins; there was none of that impression of yielding softness that even Elspeth's tight little roundness displayed; the cleft lacked the sharp definition, probably I surmised, because the growth of dark hair blurred its outline.

Notwithstanding all this, as I stepped back alongside Aunt Grace, my eyes remained fixed on his buttocks, my heart beating with great speed and vigour and my mouth again open — and dry. And I could not deny that there was a special little throb in my love-nest.

Once again, Aunt Grace demonstrated how the right choice of words could add so significantly to the ceremony.

'He has a nice bottom, has he not, Annie? Note the plumpness of his buttocks and the whiteness of his skin. I think a long slender rod will be best for it. It will wrap itself nicely round those curves and as we are in no hurry, I can make up for the lack of bite by giving him many more strokes. We shall have him howling before we finish, my dear, and his whole bottom will be as red as a sunset. He will not sit down comfortably for several days and every time he does, he will be conveniently reminded of the penalties of misbehaviour. Now, you wicked boy, how are you feeling? It is not particularly pleasant having your trousers let down and your bottom bared in front of two members of the weaker sex, is it? Oh well may you clench your naked cheeks together! I am delighted to see such evidence of your shame. Annie, I think we should remind ourselves of the feel of a boy's naked flesh. Come and we shall examine him more closely . . . relax your buttocks, boy . . . that's better.'

My hands confirmed the impressions that my eyes had given me. Neither his skin nor his flesh beneath had the smoothness or the yielding softness to which I had grown accustomed and which I found so sensual. I patted the fullest part of his right cheek and, while it quivered quite satisfactorily, it did not wobble in the almost liquid way that is characteristic of the flesh of a female bottom. And when Aunt Grace told me to separate his buttocks 'so that we can look at his hole', the growth of hair in that area was less pleasing than the near-nakedness of the girls that I had examined.

I was, however, impressed by the muscular strength he displayed when he clenched up in an initial attempt to resist this humiliating invasion! And the fact of his masculinity, and the subtle difference in his scent, moved me in a new and different way.

While I was finishing my studies, Aunt Grace selected the birch and was ready to commence and judging from the panting and trembling from our victim, so was he. She birched him in the same manner that she had dealt with me. Almost leisurely strokes, with long intervals between them and always making small adjustments to her position so as to alter the point of impact.

I watched, completely absorbed and fascinated, moving my own position from time to time to see the display from differing viewpoints. But I always returned to where I could achieve the closest possible sight of his bare bottom and could see the dramatic fashion in which the tiny weals imparted by the whippy little twigs appeared so suddenly on his skin, even when the whipping was sufficiently advanced that his buttocks were a glowing red.

His fortitude was impressive. For the first dozen or so, the only reaction was the firm quiver of his flesh. Then I could hear a little gasp of pain as each stroke 'thwicked' onto his bottom. But, with the knowledge gained from having my own bottom dealt with, I knew that the accumulative nature of the birch rod's unique bite would soon cause even a grown man to lose some control. And, as the strokes began to fall on areas of his bottom which had already been whipped more than once, the evidence of his pain was increasingly manifest. At first, he drew his muscular buttocks tightly together as the rod fell away and his breath hissed through his teeth. Then his moans grew louder and his hips began to jerk rhythmically and in time with the swooping impacts of the supple implement which was torturing him so beautifully.

I was mesmerised. I stood back, so that I could absorb both participants. His bare bottom, bright scarlet at that stage, was bobbing and weaving, the little folds marking the base of his buttocks opening as he pushed out to meet the rod and forming again as he pressed against the ladder. Aunt Grace, her lovely face serene as she concentrated on the task, her gleaming eyes fixed on the quivering flesh at her disposal, swept her arm with majestic grace and with much shorter intervals between the blows. At last it was over and we stood beside each other gazing at his well-whipped bottom. As a final surprise, Aunt Grace led me round to the front of the ladder and raised his shirt to reveal a thrilling length of stiff manhood. Unbidden, I reached out and touched it nervously, marvelling at the feel of the skin on the swollen end before Aunt Grace grasped my wrist and whispered that it was time for me to leave.

As I did so, I had the thought that I must be fortunate

indeed if I could still savour the delights of feminine flesh while at the same time finding at least an equal fascination in the male of our wondrous species.

CHAPTER 8

After Elspeth had left me the following morning, I lay in my usual scented bath and took stock. I had learnt to appreciate that the female body, both my own and others, could provide a wide variety of sensual delights, specially the area used normally to sit on! I had discovered a natural affinity for the subtly painful art of punishing for pleasure. I was fully aware of my own good looks but had learnt not to use them as a device to bend others to my will. I had seen and touched proud manhood and sensed that Aunt Grace was leading me to further involvement with men. That prospect pleased and excited. On the other hand, the enjoyment I had felt the night before when I had parted my dear Elspeth's sweet buttocks and laved her deliciously pink little bottom-hole with my eager tongue proved that my brush with the most intimate details of a member of the male sex had not diminished my love of my own. I rose, pink and gently steaming, ready to accept anything that Aunt Grace put before me with open arms, a welcoming mind — and inevitably a moistly tingling cunny.

At that point, she came into the bathroom, took up my towel and dried me, at the same time asking me if I had enjoyed the previous evening's diversion. She had smiled at my eager confirmation.

'Good. Now I want to exercise your bottom-hole again, Annie. Finish your toilette and come to my drawing room as soon as you can.'

I did not even bother to dress but carelessly trotted stark-naked through the house, attracting happy grins from Connie and Maria when I passed them in a corridor. The free movements of my bare bottom as I walked helped to alleviate the slight uncertainty that I felt about the imminent prospect of having my back passage plugged by her mysterious implement. It had been strangely pleasant but the initial feelings of being uncomfortably stretched had lingered. I should have known better.

As I walked unashamedly into her room, her lovely face broke into the warmest of smiles.

'Oh you wicked and wanton girl. You will corrupt the poor innocent maids. I shall have to spank you. Come here and bend over my lap. Oh, you are all pink and glowing . . . and so soft and warm . . . Quite exquisite . . . Now take that, you naughty girl . . . and that.'

So when I eventually assumed the kneeling posture on the end of the chaise longue, her oiled finger slipped easily into a passage that was tinglingly ready to receive it. And the larger, harder, implement which followed caused virtually no discomfort before the pleasure made me move my bottom lasciviously in time with her smooth and gentle thrusts. Again I experienced that peculiarly different climax.

Then she revealed the contents of the case. There was a phial containing the oil and no fewer than six beautifully crafted wooden replicas of the manhood I had touched the previous evening, each slightly longer and thicker than the other. The smallest was glistening with the residue of the oil and I stared at it in amazement, wondering how my tight little bottom had accommodated it with such apparent ease. An odd thought then struck me.

'Aunt Grace . . . er, does this mean that men will want to put their er . . . things in my bottom? I thought that . . .

143

well, I am not absolutely certain, but isn't my love-nest for . . . well, that?'

She laughed. 'Sit down, my dear. Yes, it is. But one day you will meet a man whom you will love as much as I love Uncle George and you must save your maidenhead for him. Until then — and only if you wish it — some of our guests would love to, as you said, "put their things in your bottom". In fact, I was going to discuss the matter with you anyway.' With my buttocks still glowing from her little spanking and the central hole quietly throbbing, I listened enthralled as she described her ideas.

In essence, apparently the guests had commented most favourably on me and most had requested the opportunity to enjoy my company alone . . .

'The ladies will mostly want to give you a spanking, Annie, although some of them will also wish to make further explorations of your person — and have you do the same to them. The men seem generally to wish to use your bottom in the way I have with my dildo. It goes without saying that there is no question of you being compelled to see any of them, but I should add that I am sure that they will be happy to present you with a guinea or so as a mark of their appreciation. You have exceptional talent in the sensual, and it is only fair that this should be rewarded appropriately.'

Some time later, I walked back to my room in a happy daze, although sufficiently aware to appreciate that walking along bare-bottom was noticeably more exciting when the traces of Aunt Grace's oil still clung to the inner surfaces of my buttocks, so that they slid together as I walked with a delightful slipperiness. I dressed and decided that on such a lovely morning, another visit to my statue was called for.

Her unchanging beauty still charmed, even though all the questions which she had posed at first had now been answered. I sat on the little wall surrounding the fountain, gazing up at her glistening bottom and in my heart, deep contentment mingled happily with the keen anticipation of new adventures.

The first came the following day. Aunt Grace had told me to come to her to have my bottom plugged each morning after my bath and I had dutifully reported to her room, fully clothed this time, to find Uncle George with her. I was somewhat taken aback at his presence although I assumed that he would soon be leaving us as, though I felt much more at ease in the presence of the male sex, especially since I had assisted in the birching of our guest, the thought of proffering my naked bottom to be plugged in front of him was, to say the least, disconcerting. I then noticed an unusual air of tenseness about him and when he showed no sign of departing, I began to experience the first signs of real trepidation. I had probably put the full implications of having a male guest insert his manhood into my bottom into the inner recesses of my mind and with the growing certainty that he was going to witness my plugging, I felt childishly coy and awkward. I was, however, already well disciplined and I knew that my discomfiture must not be made obvious, so when he gave me a smile I was able to return it.

'Strip naked please, Annie,' Aunt Grace ordered.

I did so without demur but with no coquettishness and soon was standing mother-naked before them, and if my nerves made my posture verge on the rigid, I at least had the wit not to try and cover any part of my body with my hands. Side by side they stood and openly appraised my nudity — while I stared at the wall behind them, doing my utmost not to blush.

'Could you turn round, please?' That was Uncle George. I obeyed immediately and found the more familiar sensation of having my bare buttocks stared at far less embarrassing — possibly because I could not see those who were doing the staring. Eventually, Aunt Grace asked me to assume my usual position on the end of the chaise longue and with only the occasional gulp as a sign of my nervousness, I did so. Perhaps even in those days there was a basic flirtatiousness in my character. On the previous occasions I had bent over for a plugging, I had just thrust my bottom upwards and outwards as quickly as I could. But knowing that Uncle George was watching — and having observed the hungry gleam in his eyes when he had been studying my naked front, I had no doubts that he was keenly anticipating the display — I assumed the required position with slow deliberation. First I knelt, then parted my legs, then bent the upper half of my body forward and supported it on straight arms before lowering them and finally pressing my suddenly excited bosoms into the welcoming upholstery and, as I did so, feeling the division between my buttocks open out. A gentle zephyr of summer air confirmed that my little bottom-hole was bare for all to see. I could not resist craning my head round in the hope of seeing approval on his face and, although my view was somewhat obscured by my own naked limbs. I was left in no doubt that my most secret parts were pleasing to him. Relieved (but honesty bids me to admit that I was not altogether surprised), I cushioned my head on my hands, drew my knees a little further up to widen the cleft still more, and waited.

Hands smoothed their way over my tight cheeks; I could actually feel warm breath on my skin as they peered closely at me. My anus started to tingle in expectation; I had to make myself draw deep, even breaths. The pleasure tendrils slowly spread from my bottom, outwards and upwards, then surged through me when gentle fingertips stroked first the wrinkled surround and then the opening itself. When I felt the steady intrusion of Aunt Grace's oiled finger, I welcomed it with a heartfelt sight. It worked away inside, further and further up the passage; then it withdrew and after a short interval, slipped even more easily into the readied orifice. With firmly closed eyes, I squeezed my bottom round it until it was again removed. I had already grown to love this special invasion of my person and so waited for the second stage. My bottom felt deliciously naked. I hoped that she would use one of the bigger implements. I knew I could accept it. I vaguely heard strange rustling movements behind me but took no notice of them. Then, at last, something was nuzzling at my bottom-hole. I groaned with a combination of relief and reaction to the sharp, prickling pain that was the tight ring of muscle's reaction to the sudden stretching. I arched my back even further downwards and pushed my bottom against the invader, panting hard as I did so. Then I realised that there was something very different happening. The implement felt unlike the sculpted wood to which I had been accustomed. It was warm, not cool. It was smoother. It was living. It was Uncle George.

I whipped round to see if I was correct and in so doing, must have moved my bottom because he slipped out and I saw it thrusting out of the front of his trousers, red, glistening — and frighteningly large. Before I could say anything, Aunt Grace stepped forward between us, slapped both buttocks firmly but without ire and then came and sat by my head.

'Come now, Annie stiffen your resolve. I promise that you will find it far more pleasing than my dildo and I assure you that for my husband to want to do this to you — and for me to be happy for him to do it — is a true mark of our respect and affection for you. Now stick that delectable bottom out again . . . Good girl . . . Right, George, gently now . . . breathe deeply, Annie . . . He will just get the end in and wait for a while until you grow accustomed to it . . . There, that's better . . .'

It was. The pricking ache began to subside and the pleasure wave started. I felt his hands on my buttocks, pulling them even wider apart. She wriggled round and laid my head on that ample lap, reaching underneath me to stroke and squeeze my cunny. It began to exchange pleasing sensations with its sister orifice. I tentatively tightened my bottom-hole round his thing. I could feel it slide in a bit further. He moved it back out and for an instant I felt a flare of disappointment that it should be over so quickly. Then he pushed again and it filled me up a bit more.

Aunt Grace's hands, one on my love-nest, the other stroking my back, soothed and encouraged. I felt his hands move onto my hips, clasping them firmly and then he must have thrust himself all the way in because despite being flooded by an overwhelming sensation, I could feel the rough cloth of his trousers against my buttocks. Again he paused and the breath 'aaaahed' from my lungs. I tried to expand the passage. But couldn't. I must have tightened it instead for I heard him groan softly. I feared that I had caused him pain at first.

'Oh Annie, you are exquisite . . . Your bottom grips like a velvet vice . . . so hot and tight.'

Instinctively I straightened my arms, my hands sinking delightfully into the yielding flesh of Aunt Grace's thighs. Her hands moved onto my dangling breasts and her soft mouth closed on mine, inhaling my pantings, tasting my saliva as I tasted her and breathed the heady scent of her perfume.

I ground my splayed-out buttocks against Uncle George's trousers and the touch inflamed my burgeoning desires even more. Of its own accord, my bottom started to pump in and out, slowly. I felt the clingingness of my inner flesh against him. My cheeks moved free of the tickling embrace of good Scottish tweed and his thing slipped backwards towards my straining little anus until only the knob-like end was within me. Then he thrust forward and my ever-slipperier passage welcomed him anew. Aunt Grace then cradled my head against her ample bosom and I lost myself in the multitude of sensations as his thrusts grew quicker and longer, my bottom felt more and more naked and seemed to take me over until I was all bottom — and my bottom was all there was of me.

After either a few seconds or a hundred years, I felt as though some hot liquid jets were being pumped into my depths. But I cared not what they were. Only that Uncle George's groans had reached a crescendo and then he had slumped across my back. To my surprise, I could hardly feel his thing inside me. Then he straightened up and I was vaguely aware of something soft slipping out of my anus. My back and legs were aching. My bottom-hole was throbbing and aching, and prickling, and rather sore. But I nestled my head in Aunt Grace generous lap and began to weep. I knew not why, except that it was not from either pain nor unhappiness. She held me to her, murmuring nothings but with infinite tenderness until my tears dried up and I clambered stiffly to my feet. I was dismayed to find that Uncle George had slipped away, because I wanted to hug and kiss him. I could not explain it, but I knew that he had led me up yet another steep slope on the journey to knowledge.

From that moment onwards, my desire for each and every sensual experience consumed me. I looked forward eagerly to participating in the entertainments. My initial fears at the thought of exposing myself to an audience of complete strangers and at the prospect of the pain of being beaten were exchanged for a keen sense of anticipation of the feeling of being bare-bottomed and I had soon learned to let the pain wash through me until it overwhelmed my senses.

It was during one such session that somebody who was to influence my future profoundly first appeared. My idea of the school-room scenario had proved very popular with the guests and we were enacting one of the happier variations on this theme. Mrs Savage had made us a collection of most authentic uniforms — short skirts, flared for easier raising, tight across the bosom to disguise our womanly curves, short stockings and loose, split drawers made out of rather coarse linen. We also took care to ensure that other aspects of our appearance were in keeping. We tied our hair with pretty ribbons and applied rouge skilfully to suggest rose-cheeked youth.

All six maids and myself were playing an unruly class under Cook as an ineffective Mistress. The scene opened with her bellowing for silence and order while we, the pupils, made merry, talking to each other, throwing screwed up paper across the room, pinching each other's bottoms and so forth. Just as everything was degenerating into complete chaos, Aunt Grace as the Headmistress walked into the classroom, restored order with one of her sternest glances and silently beckoned Cook to come with her. With judicious use of curtains and by lowering and raising the brightness of some of the gas lamps, the scene changed to the Headmistress's office, where Cook was given a lecture on her incompetence, advice on how to enforce discipline in her class and then a practical demonstration in the form of a really sound spanking on her bare bottom. A subtly effective touch was that we had powdered her hair with flour to make her seem considerably older than Aunt Grace, and so being humiliatingly punished by an apparently younger woman added delightful piquancy to the scene.

Having reversed the position of the curtain and readjusted the lighting, we were back in the classroom, where our Mistress, her own bottom smarting, established her authority in no uncertain manner. We were all spanked. More than once. And in a pleasing variety of positions — across her lap, bending over her desk, touching our toes, kneeling on the seat of a chair. And, of course, with out bottoms properly bared.

I was enjoying my third such treatment, bending right over with my hands gripping my parted ankles and my knees bent inwards so that I was presenting a nicely tightened pair of stark-naked buttocks to the audience. In that position it was easy and natural to peer back between my legs at the guests and I was slowly absorbing the two rows of rapt faces when my gaze was held by one of them: a young woman, approximately the same age as myself, leaning forward with her elbows on her knees and her face supported by her cupped hands, watching Cook's right hand smacking my exposed flesh with even more obvious enthusiasm than the others. It was not her attentiveness that kept my eyes on her. It was something indefinable about her. She was, from my limited viewpoint, exceedingly lovely, but then all the women and girls around me had aspects which were beautiful. There was something about her which simply captured my heart and I was so enraptured that I forgot about my smarting bottom. I omitted to act the part of a punished schoolgirl for several minutes until I managed to collect my wits and resume my role.

'Oh Madam, please, no more,' I wailed at last. 'I am sorry. Ooooh my bottom . . . it is really smarting . . . Owww . . . Ohhhh . . . Please, Madam . . . I didn't do it . . .and I won't do it again, I promise . . . *Owwww* . . . my poor, bare bottom . . .*Owwwwwwww!*'

Relieved, I think, that I had rejoined the scene, Cook responded accordingly.

'I am delighted to hear that it's smarting, my girl' . . .

Smack, smack, smack. 'Maybe these will make it smart enough to make you appreciate the consequences of being so naughty.' Smack, smack, smack.

'Oh no more, Madam, please, no more.'

'I — have — not — finished — with — your — fat — bottom — yet, Annie. Not — by — a — long — chalk. Take that. And that. Now let me have a look.' A rather welcome pause while she stood back to assess the redness. 'Six more, I think, young lady . . .'

And those six almost took my mind off the captivating guest. But not quite, because I 'asked for' one more spanking and during it, did all I could to point my bottom at her, so that she had the best possible view.

Following another of my suggestions, we took a theatrical 'bow' at the end of the performance, but not in the normal manner. With our bottoms still bare, we turned our backs to the audience and then bowed deeply, presenting them with a final and dramatic view of well-reddened buttocks, separated by the white flesh of the inner recesses of our clefts and, of course, the rear portions of our cunnies and our bottom-holes in the middle. This always elicited a hearty round of applause and watching the beautiful guest through my legs, I was very happy to note not only that she was clapping with more enthusiasm than any of the others but also that her eyes were fixed on me to the exclusion of the others.

I slept alone that night, and her face continually intruded into my fitful dreams.

Fortunately I was also increasingly active in the affairs of the household, which meant that my fascination with 'my' guest did not become the obsession it may otherwise have done. One morning Aunt Grace called me to her room and told me that one of the male guests had asked if he could have a private session with me.

'What exactly will this entail?' I asked. It transpired that he would want to spank me and then bugger me, which I discovered was the correct term for having one's bottom plugged by a man. I accepted immediately and it was only as the time approached that I began to have reservations. No longer would I have the comforting presence of the maids. When Uncle George had buggered me, Aunt Grace had been there to reassure me. This time I would be alone. I would not have a chaperone. The only other occasions I had been alone with a member of the male sex were when I had my various meetings with my lawyer after my parents' death and then the conversation had not strayed significantly from the professional matters in hand.

As I walked towards the cellar room set aside for our tryst, I was extremely nervous, if not genuinely frightened. Had it not been for my faith in Aunt Grace's love for me, I may well have turned tail and fled.

In the event, it was an unforgettable hour. The spanking was quite stimulating and I appreciated the difference between the muscularity of the male lap and the yielding softness of the female. And when I identified a strange protrusion thrusting against my belly as his 'thing', I found my excitement building up most satisfyingly. Although his hand was larger and harder than any of the others which had smacked my bare bottom, he did not pain it as much as I expected, mainly because no sooner had he built up a pleasing degree of warmth, than he spent an equal amount of time stroking, rubbing, squeezing and paddling it, seeming to find great delight in making the relaxed flesh wobble like two big blancmanges. I did not complain! And certainly by the time he bade me to rise to prepare myself for the agreed conclusion, I knew that I was rosy-cheeked at both ends.

I stripped slowly, first removing my skirt and petticoats, then my blouse, so that I was left in my chemise with my replaced drawers underneath. Smiling at him, I gradually slipped the former garment over my shoulders, exposing first one plump, stiffly-nippled breast and then the next, before standing with it rolled down as far as my waist to give him a leisurely look at my bosom, while my eyes were as firmly fixed on the prominent bulge distorting the front of his trousers. I then pushed it down, stepped out of it, turned my back on him and bared my red bottom for him in the same lascivious manner, leaving me in just my black stockings with their bright blue garters adding a dashing touch of colour. As I had done with Uncle George, I presented my rear (which Aunt Grace had previously oiled for me) with tantalising deliberation, ensuring that he had time to appreciate the changes in angle and perspective, the appearance of the diamond-shaped back of my cunny and finally, the small, delicately wrinkled pinkness of my anus. I had, of course, spent some time with my mirrors suitably placed, practising this action until I felt that I had reached a satisfactory level of expertise. I watched him as I did so and his reactions were a just reward for my efforts. A handsome man in his thirties, probably an officer in one of our better regiments judging by his general demeanour, he went red in the face as my naked bottom opened like some exotic flower. When I flashed my anus at him as a sign that I was ready for his penetration, he leapt into action with almost unseemly haste, unbuttoning his trousers, tearing them off (with some difficulty, for they were fashionably tight) and then burrowing his face between my widely spread cheeks with a piercing cry of 'Tally-Ho!'

I had by that stage had my bottom-hole kissed and licked by all the maids, Cook and Aunt Grace, so I could claim some experience in this most deliciously personal of all caresses. The first shock of having it done by a man was emphasised most strongly by the way his moustache tickled the sensitive skin between my cheeks. After that, his skill and enthusiasm carried me away no less effectively than any of the others had done, so by the time his mouth was replaced by the end of his cock, I was shuddering with desire. The combination of this, the extra slipperinesss provided by his saliva and the oil already in readiness, resulted in a penetration which was far less painful than previously and so the onset of the pleasure was even more rapid, especially when nice Bertie rested his weight on my willing back so that he could fondle my dangling bosoms with one hand and my love-button with the other.

All too soon for me I felt an uncontrolled urgency in his movements; he squeezed me yet more tightly, gasped, moaned, and then with a shuddering cry I felt the hot spurt deep in my bottom and he went limp on top of me.

It took him some little time to recover sufficiently, during which we lay on our backs. I gazed happily at the ceiling, enjoying the heavy throbbing in my anus and the lingering warmth which still infused my buttocks after his spanking, before I was overcome by an urge to see his thing, the source of so much bliss. Unsure of exactly how to ask his permission, I reverted to my natural feminine wiles, turned onto my side with my head on his broad chest and casually placed my arm on his belly, so that my open hand rested on it. I had to stifle a little gasp of amazement. Instead of the mighty fleshy lance which I had somehow expected, there was a soft little sausage which nestled comfortably in the palm of my delicate hand. It was still moist and slippery, presumably from the oil in my bottom and despite my initial disappointment, was delightful to hold.

It became even more delightful when I felt it stir in my grasp. It grew a little firmer. And longer. And thicker. With a squeak of excitement, I wriggled round so that I could watch this phenomenon at close quarters and, with the encouragement of a rising chorus of gasps and sighs from nice Bertie, started to play with it.

I squeezed it gently; I ran a fingertip all over it; I wiggled it around. It grew still firmer, longer and thicker. It then occurred to me that if the in and out movements inside my bottom had proved so exciting to it, perhaps I would be able to recreated this effect by curling my fingers round it to form a sort of tunnel or passage and was delighted to feel my theory proved correct almost instantly, especially when I added a little extra pressure to that most fascinating part towards the tip, where the folds of loose skin could be moved very easily. They had already retreated sufficiently to expose the smooth red skin of the knob-shaped swelling of the very end.

The increasing volume of his sighs and moans did not penetrate my consciousness, so great was my absorption with what was happening in front of me. I felt one of his hands grip one of my buttocks; I noticed his back stiffen and began to arch upwards; the handsome balls in their wrinkled, hairy bag moved up nearer his belly. And then he shuddered all over and spurts of thick, creamy liquid jetted out of the tiny hole in the end of his cock. With a cry of alarm, I jerked backwards, fortunately remembering to let go of him as I did so. Immediately, with a deep groan, he grasped it in his own hand, pumping away rapidly until the spurts stopped and he sank back, panting.

I apologised profusely, knowing that my childish reaction had been a disappointment to him and my heart warmed to him when he smiled at me, held me affectionately to his breast and told me that it did not matter.

'Have you never seen that before, Annie?' he asked.

'No,' I admitted. 'I have only seen a man's thing once before, and that was merely a brief glimpse. '

He laughed, and for the remainder of our time together, taught me all manner of things about men, their private parts and their basic functions, making love and the various aspects of women which attracted men — or, at least, attracted him, as he admitted that he could hardly speak for every man on earth! It interested me that most of the things which I had found so pleasing about a woman's body also appealed to him: the smooth, white softness of the skin; the yielding nature of the flesh of their breasts and buttocks; their special scents; the plumpness of their bottoms.

'And,' he added, 'their neat little bottom-holes, with little or no hair around them to distract the eye. Let me see yours again, Annie. No, kneel over me . . . with one knee on either side . . . further back so that your bottom is over my face . . . Oh, Annie, what a view . . . Squat down a bit . . . My word but your buttocks are so round and plump . . . I shall have to hold them open to see you properly . . . That's better, I fear my attentions have reddened it somewhat. Is it sore? Good . . . Oh yes, Annie, Ohhh *yes*!'

I had not been able to reply to his kind enquiry as to the health of my exposed anus, and had brought about the last exclamations for the simple reason that my novel position had brought his cock close to my mouth and I completely failed to resist the temptation to envelope it in another hot, wet passage. In return his tongue laved both my bottom-hole and the slit of my cunny, while his hands roved freely over my buttocks and the rapid swelling of his flesh in my straining mouth and his expert attentions to my other end, combined to send me into that so-loved near swoon, moments after I had managed — just — to swallow his final spend.

Strangely, this rapid advancement in my experience did nothing to lessen the delights of intimacy with members of my own sex. Two days after my loving time with Bertie, I asked Elspeth to spend an evening and night with me. She bounced in like a happy puppy, grinning broadly at the prospect, showing off her daring décolletage and cheerfully admitting that she was wearing only her 'sauciest drawers' underneath her skirts. Her mood matched mine exactly and I immediately berated her for being an impudent little baggage.

Her demeanour changed from puppy to crestfallen waif in a trice.

'Oh Madam, you are right. I should be punished for being so forward. Please will you treat me like the naughty little girl that I am, place me across your lap, raise my skirts, take my drawers right down and give me a really good spanking?'

'R-r-raise your skirts?' I stuttered, eyes wide-open in shock. 'Take your drawers down? But that would mean that I would see your bot—er, posteriors all ba—naked. It would be most unseemly.'

'Madam you know how much I respect your sensibilities but imagine the shame that I'll be feeling, knowing that such a private part of my body is laid out naked before your eyes. And how degrading it will be to feel your hand on my bare skin! It would not be the punishment I so richly deserve unless it was administered to my bare bottom, Madam. And, apart from that, I must be spanked until my bottom is a rich, deep red in colour. The redness of shame and pain. And how could you properly judge my condition unless I was appropriately stripped?'

I was rather taken aback at her poetic eloquence and could do no more than stutter feebly, trying at the same time to suppress the flood of happy giggles which was threatening to burst out.

'So, come on Madam, you must do your duty by me, however painful and strenuous it may be. Come over and sit on this chair. It is perfect for the purpose . . . Now, I will lay myself across your lap . . . Ooh, Madam, you *do* have beautifully firm thighs . . . Let me help you with my skirts . . . there. Are they well clear of my naughty little bottom? Good. Yes, Madam, I insist that my drawers are pulled right down to my knees . . . slowly, so that I can feel the humiliation as my intimate flesh is gradually revealed to you . . . let me lift my hips a little . . . Oh, the shame . . . the degradation of it all . . . Now, please I must feel the pain!'

What could I do but oblige her? My hand bounced off her naked, elastic buttocks with soaring enthusiasm, but without venom, so that those deliciously firm, tightly divided mounds quivered and pinkened rather than wobbled and reddened.

Then, after I deemed that enough was enough and had rubbed her better, we continued our play acting. She rose, looked at me smilingly and stripped completely, flaunting all her charms before my avid eyes and stood before me, arms akimbo and her adorable triangle of fluffy fair hair only inches from my face.

'Now, Madam. I tempted you and you have fallen. We both know that the Master is solely responsible for punishing me. You have proved that your will is weak and I am therefore going to spank you now. On your bare bottom. Stand up.'

I was in no way reluctant to be spanked by her and assuming the role she had suggested — 'Oh how terribly shaming,' and 'please do not open me up and look inside . . . *Ohhh*!' — added further to both the anticipation and the pleasure. One little surprise was how pleasingly different it was to be put across her bare thighs, although I must confess that it was but a short time before the warmth she was adding to my bottom drove all other emotions from my mind.

After that, we retired naked to my bed and became ourselves again, two bodies acting as one in a writhing tangle of glistening flesh until we were sated. We fell asleep curled up like two spoons, her bottom nestling comfortably against my thighs and belly and her breast filling my hand. The combination of physical satisfaction and the contentment from snuggling sleepily up to a close and dear friend, sent me off to sleep in a state of real happiness.

The following day provided yet another new and very sensual experience. It was Maria's birthday and it was apparently a tradition in the household that such an event should be celebrated in appropriate fashion. After a special luncheon in the main dining room and with the food and wines chosen by her, she was led away by Bridget and Connie while the rest of us began to clear away. When I arrived in the kitchen, my heart leapt with delighted surprise. A narrow couch had been set up in the centre of the room and Maria was lying on it, with silken bonds securing her feet and wrists. She was dressed only in a little bodice with buttons all the way down the front, a pair of very loose, split drawers — and a blindfold. From what I could see of her face, she was tense but not fearful. On reflection, it would have been a grave injustice if fear had been part of her celebrations! While I was endeavouring to find a reason for her position, Bridget entered through the other door and presumably did not see me in the shadow.

'Are you ready, Maria?' she asked.

'Yes.'

She stood contemplatively over the prone figure. I watched with bated breath, still as a mouse, puzzled, curious, and expectant. Suddenly she began to strip, quickly, until she was in just her stockings and the sight of her slender white body, with her red hair on head and belly providing such a beautiful contrast, made the blood flow through my veins. Then she perched on the edge of the bed and with calm deliberation unbuttoned Maria's little bodice and laid her big, soft bosoms bare. The brownish nipples

160

stiffened visibly at the pleasure of exposure and I could hear the heaviness of her breathing in the silence, despite the pounding of my own heart.

As her nice fat breasts were stroked, tweaked, kissed, licked and general stimulated, she seemed to relax, which I found surprising as similar attentions had always had quite the opposite effect on me! This state was less apparent when Bridget opened up the wide slit in the drawers, baring the generously mossed cunny, and began to play with it. When I saw her middle finger slip into the actual slit, her helpless accomplice finally reacted as expected and began to gasp aloud and buck and weave her hips uninhibitedly. Far too soon, the finger slid out, Bridget stood up and, treating me to a fine sight of her naked back with her neat little bottom drawing my eye, turned Maria over onto her stomach, before resuming her perch and opening the drawers to expose the broad cheeks beneath. These were then treated in a similar fashion to the sister mounds above and in front before being gently smacked.

As a finale, she knelt between Maria's spread thighs, spread her bottom-cheeks widely, looked down at the revealed pleasures, licked her lips and then bent down and applied her pink tongue to the appropriate spot and in the appropriate manner. Once again sighs became audible and the loosely tied body gently writhed as the waves spread. It was a delectable sight: Bridget's slender bottom as the pointed apex to her body; the recipient's distorted buttocks almost completely hidden by the red locks which flowed around them; the barely discernible slurping noises and the obvious ecstasy shown by both participants.

The inevitable climax brought the proceedings to a halt. Bridget got up, turned her partner over on her back again, kissed her, wished her a happy day, dressed and left. I was left wondering whether this was some private celebration or whether I could help myself to her exposed softness without causing offence. I had just decided to slip out and return later, when I heard footsteps behind me and just had time to close the door and pretend that I was about to enter. It was Agatha, who bustled past me.

'Has Maria been prepared for her treat yet? Yes she has. Goody.' Marching across to the couch, she stood in keen contemplation of the heavily breathing occupant, before turning to me.

'Would you like to got first, Annie?'

'To do what?' I asked with only partly feigned innocence.

'Oh, haven't you been told? Honestly! Well, on our birthdays, our treat is to be tied to the couch like this and all the others have to keep giving you nice feelings. Being blindfolded, you're never quite sure who's doing it to you — or exactly what they're going to do next. It's lovely! Shall I go first?'

'Yes do. I'd like to watch,' I replied with mounting excitement.

Mounting was the word. With great haste, Agatha undid her skirt, stripped off her drawers and clambered on top of Maria, facing her feet and with her bare bottom poised over the waiting face, before lowering her delightfully large buttocks until Maria was enveloped in soft flesh. This time I was free to move around and gaze on them from whichever angle took my fancy. I noted with particular interest a later action, when Maria had again been turned over onto her belly, her big bottom bared, and Agatha placed her even bigger one on it, providing for herself an extremely comfortable seat! Peering at the delightful mingle of squashy buttocks shifting around as their owners wriggled in pleasure made me even more impatient for my turn — and also to get to know Agatha's general curves a great deal better.

At last, I was free to enjoy what I had watched so keenly. At my insistence, Agatha did not restore Maria to her clothed and face-up position, so I started on her already bare bottom, which was anyway by far my favourite part of the female anatomy. I reacquainted myself with her nice broad and very soft buttocks, looked at, tickled and licked her bottom-hole and then slid my middle finger up it, relishing the way her anus seemed to draw my finger into the depths of her passage. Her bottom was clingingly hot, slightly moist and the way her big brown anus spasmed against the base of my finger sent all kinds of throbbings through my vitals! In the meantime I used my other hand to spank her lightly and, when her cheeks were duly reddened, I moved it onto her cunny and slipped its middle finger up inside that. It proved to be considerably moister, a little hotter and, if less tight, just as thrilling a tunnel. I especially enjoyed being able to feel one finger with the other: obviously the twin passages ran closely together and by turning the finger in her cunny, I could press both tips gently together. Her loud groans were definitely of pleasure and, as always, pleasing her added considerably to my pleasure.

It was clearly an occasion for experimentation. I followed Agatha's example, bared my bottom and sat on Maria's, which proved to be as nice as it had appeared. I held her buttocks wide apart and rubbed her hot little bottom-hole with my nipples. I squatted on her bottom with my knees well up and crushed my cunny into her soft flesh. I turned her over and did the same thing on her bosoms and thighs. Finally, I remembered that the idea was to please her rather than myself, so knelt on the floor in a good position to open the plump lips of her wet love-nest, ran my tongue around until it settled on the pleasure button and brought her to a shuddering climax.

I had enjoyed myself greatly. The fact that she had been bound and blindfolded had added to the excitement by em-

163

phasising the sense of power and control over her. Then I envisaged myself in her position — helplessly at the mercy of all who came along and who could help themselves to whatever private and personal part of one's anatomy that took their fancy.

I longed for my own birthday!

CHAPTER 9

I had never been as happy as I was then. I had found the maids and Cook to be the staunchest of friends; Aunt Grace and Uncle George provided the mature guidance that any young woman needs; all my basic requirements were exceedingly well catered-for. And as if this were not enough, there was the constant stimulation of sensual pleasures. The maids all seemed perfectly content to allow me to bare their bottoms if I felt like administering a playful little spanking, or to share my bed if I wanted the intimacy provided by snuggling off to sleep in the arms of a friend. If I needed the special emotional release best supplied by a sound but loving chastisement, Aunt Grace always seemed to sense the restlessness before even I was aware of it and dealt with my bottom appropriately — and the maids, especially Elspeth, were always on hand to kiss me better.

Adding rich spices to my life's excellent fare were the entertainments and my private sessions with selected guests. Apart from the welcome contributions to my money box, which was now satisfyingly heavy with coin, I found the variety of challenges involved increasingly rewarding. Apparently the guests favoured my posterior above all others and so I was spanked or whipped more frequently and with greater severity than the others. Far from upsetting me, I found that the nervousness before the ordeal not only added to the sensations I felt during it, but also notably increased the physical and spiritual glow I experienced for some time after. Nothing else provided the same flow of varied feelings and emotions than being positioned with my bottom bared and prominent, knowing that it was being stared at lasciviously by a number of strangers (although I was, of course, becoming acquainted with some of them through my private sessions) and waiting for the biting sting of Aunt Grace's birch to set my blood coursing through my body and to challenge my will and courage to the utmost.

The private sessions offered a different stimulus. My bottom-hole was now very used to being plugged and none of the guests birched me, so I was not called upon to face anything really painful. Even if most of the spankings I was given were severe enough to bring tears, the warm glow which always followed provided ample compensation. What I did find challenging was trying to anticipate and fulfil the real requirements of my visitor.

For example, a certain Mrs A came into the room dressed as a young schoolgirl which, as she was a well-built lady with greying hair, could have invoked nothing but impolite laughter, but I did not find her either funny or even ridiculous. I had, of course, been told to assume the role of a schoolmistress and fell easily into it.

'Now, Mary, why have you been sent to me?'

'Talking in class, Miss.'

'I see. So Miss Dickens wants me to punish you, does she?'

'Yes, Miss. Oh, Miss, I was by your window yesterday afternoon and I heard you giving Dorothy Higgins a spanking. Is that what you are going to do to me?'

'Well, it is either that or two hundred lines. Which would you prefer?'

'Oh dear. What do you do when you spank someone? Do you smack them on the hands?'

'Silly girl. Of course not. On the bottom.'

'The bottom? But . . . I mean . . . Why on the bottom, Miss?'

'Because it is the part of a girl's body best suited to it. It is sensitive enough to feel the smart, yet fleshy enough to suffer no damage. Besides, if I beat you on your hands, you would not be able to hold your slate and chalk properly, so your work would suffer whereas it matters little if you find sitting a trifle uncomfortable.'

I was watching her expression closely during the conversation and was gratified to see that I seemed to be pleasing her, for there were visible signs of rising sensual excitement in her demeanour.

'I understand, Miss. I shall take the spanking rather than the lines, if you please.'

'Excellent. Now come here so that I can pin your skirts up.'

'Oh! I did not realise that my person would be − er − uncovered.'

'Surely you cannot imagine that you would feel anything through those skirts and − what, two petticoats? Now come here and stand before me, facing the far wall.'

'I hope you don't find me offensive, Miss. I do have a rather large posterior.'

As I had the pins in my mouth at the time, so that both hands were free to fold up her garments, I did not respond until her bottom was nicely bare and posed literally inches in front of my face. I then waited a little longer while I inspected it carefully.

'I am, of course, here to smack it, not judge its beauty, but I have no hesitation in telling you that even if it is a big bottom, it is not in the least offensive, Mary. Of that I assure you.'

'Thank you, Miss,' she whispered.

I did not lie to her. She did have a massive pair of buttocks, which swelled proudly from her waist and loins;

167

they certainly lacked the firm shapeliness that characterised all the maids' bottoms; nor did they share the solidity of Cook's. But her skin was beautifully and flawlessly white, the long and deep folds at the tops of her thighs brought the eye naturally to the prominent overhang where her cheeks curved inwards, and the cleft between them was delightfully deep, long, soft and tight. If the dimples disturbed the overall smoothness of her flesh, I attributed them to her understandable nervousness. It was obvious from her dialogue that she was seeking appreciation more than anything else and as I gazed on the splendid hemispheres before me, I found that I was keenly anticipating the imminent spanking and at the same time, my sympathetic understanding of her needs encouraged me to prolong the introduction. Aunt Grace had only said to me that 'she will not thank you for being too rigorous', so I pushed my desire to start reddening that lovely white flesh to the back of my mind and continued with the reassurances.

'Yes, Mary, it is a pleasure to look at. Now I am going to feel it all over, to test the abundance and resilience of the flesh. This will help me determine the best position for you to adopt for your spanking. Mmmmm, what delightfully soft, smooth skin . . . and can you feel the way my hand sinks into this buttock? And the same with the other one? There is already a proper womanliness about you which is exceedingly attractive . . . and feel how I have to force my fingers into the division between your cheeks . . . it is so tight . . . and deep. Now will you please bend forward and place your hands on your knees? Good girl. Yes, excellent . . . now right over . . . your hands on your ankles . . . what a magnificent spread. Your stretched skin feels even smoother, my dear, although I would not have thought it possible. Stand up straight again, Mary, while I consider.'

168

Once again, the power of the spoken word was manifest. Her buttocks were now relaxed and the rather charming dimples had all but disappeared.

'You know, Mary, I think it would almost be an insult to your exquisite bare bottom to restrict ourselves to any one position. So, I shall administer the first part with you placed across my knee, which is of course the traditional way of placing a naughty little girl for a spanking — and you *have* been a naughty girl, haven't you, Mary?'

'Yes, Miss.'

'After that I shall make you lay yourself across my desk. This will spread your cheeks, they will wobble less, which is a disadvantage perhaps, but the cleft will be open enough to allow some choice spanks there. Finally I shall want you to kneel on the seat of this chair and to thrust your bare bottom as high and as far out as you are able. I want those buttocks as tight as twin drums. I want the division between them as wide open as you can manage. Do you understand, Mary?'

I then knew that I had been able to provide her with just the stimulation that she had been hoping for. Her nice blue eyes were shining with excitement and she looked at me with that entrancing expression which I now knew denoted the onset of those unique sensual tendrils. I patted my thighs and she carefully laid herself across them until her body formed a graceful curve from her feet resting on the floor to my right, down to her hands on my left. Her bottom formed a marvellous spread of succulent white flesh before me and it was almost impossible to resist the temptation to start spanking it immediately, but I again stroked and kneaded away until she was moaning quietly. Then, when I sensed that her apprehensions at the prospect of the pain had finally vanished, I began. Firm little slaps but carefully designed to bounce her bottom around rather than make it sting, because I now knew that the movements of the buttocks on impact sent fleshy waves to the even more sensitive areas between and below, which is one reason for the pain from a spank being subtly unlike any other — provided that one has attuned one's mind correctly.

I surmised that my partner probably had overheard a companion being spanked in her childhood and the desire to emulate her experience had lain dormant since. And that her husband was unlikely to be particularly sensual by nature, hence her need for admiration. I also concluded that she felt that by adopting the role in which she had come to me she could avoid the entanglements which reality would have brought with it.

So, in my understanding I could not only accede to her unspoken wishes but also eliminate all thoughts of the strangeness of the circumstances. As I did not think it ridiculous for a mature woman to be dressed as a young schoolgirl and to be lying across my knee having her bare bottom spanked, I could play my role with conviction. At the same time, I could also enjoy it all the more. If her bottom did not greatly appeal aesthetically, it was wondrously female, it wobbled more enticingly than any other I had spanked and the whiteness of her skin resulted in a rapid spreading of a lovely blush over the whole surface.

It developed into a gently sensual and lovely spanking. As she appreciated that hurting her was not part of my plan and she eased her mind towards accepting the novel sensations wholeheartedly and without apprehension, we began to act in better concert, my hand and her bare bottom giving and receiving nice feelings with equal measure. And my instinctive plan to place her in different positions proved pleasingly helpful to us both. I gauged the changes so that they were implemented at the moment when she was beginning to feel the hurt and thus gave her flesh a pause in which it could recover a little. I could also gain

pleasure from close study of her big behind from a variety of viewpoints and took the opportunity to make suitably
personal comments:

'Now straighten your legs, Mary, and move them apart
a little. That is perfect. Can you feel that your cheeks are
just a little tighter like this? And that lovely cleft between
them slightly more open? Good. Now let me have a good
look at you. My, you *are* a well-reared girl! Keep your
bottom nice and still, please . . . and don't try to clench
your buttocks − I want to see them wobbling properly
when I smack them . . . excellent . . . good girl . . . I
really do think that yours is the most satisfying bottom
I have ever spanked.'

And then the time came for the final position, which
demanded the full exposure of her bottom-hole and this
caused her to blush exactly like a shy and modest young
girl. Again, by telling her that what she was presenting
gave me great pleasure − and she did have a sweet little
hole − and by directing my spanks to give her the nicest
possible sensations, I overcame all her inhibitions by the
end and, with my tongue up her rear end and my finger
on her love button, she climaxed quickly and rigorously.

She was to become one of my regular visitors and I never
failed to enjoy seeing her. We advanced our 'scenario'
somewhat by including Aunt Grace who played the Headmistress of our school and entered my room just as I was
administering the last few spanks. She would then berate
me for exceeding my authority and smack my bare bottom 'in front of this innocent girl whom you have so
mistreated', while Mrs A avidly watched with her own
buttocks reminding her vividly of what I was experiencing. Then Aunt Grace would make the two of us bend over
the desk and spank us to a happy conclusion, while we
glued our adjacent mouths together and breathed in each
other's pain and pleasure. Then we would be left alone

for mutual commiseration and solace.

But increasingly often I would wake at night with the image of that other lady guest's face, with that lovely and loving expression of rapt concentration on my posterior charms, bright and clear on my mind. I did not dare to ask Aunt Grace to tell me more about her, but whenever I featured in one of the entertainments, I would look round in the hope that she had returned. I used to hide my disappointment by pretending that she was there. I would proffer my naked bottom with special care; accept my painful punishment with extra willingness, as though her eyes were on me and her heart was willing me to excite her more and more.

When one of our male guests was buggering me, I moved my bottom to the rhythm of his thrusts with exaggerated enthusiasm, because I was so hoping that the almost painful feeling of having my rear passage filled to bursting point by that miraculous masculinity would drive her face from my dreams.

Then, Aunt Grace told me (while I was lying in my normal position across her lap) that she wished me to entertain a lady guest that evening but would say no more about either the desires of the lady or what was expected of me. As the time approached, I bathed myself with special care, pouring an ample quantity of my scented oil into the water, put on my best undergarments, selected my most attractive dress — a tight-fitting wollen ensemble which hugged my curves most intimately — and asked Agatha to help me arrange my hair to best effect. Although I had always been aware of the need to look my best for all my visitors, some instinct propelled me to additional efforts. I was still taken aback when eventually *she* appeared in the doorway.

If I had thought her beautiful when seen peering backwards past my naked flank and surrounded by the other guests, the sight of her so much closer, clearer and alone, took my breath away completely. Her hair matched the golden hue of mine and fell in waves about her bare white shoulders. The unfashionably low cut of her dress gave evidence of deliciously plump and firm bosoms; her dress clung to a lusciously narrow waist before swelling out over cello-shaped hips and then falling straight to the floor, so I could only assume that her thighs matched the rounded nature of the visible parts of her form.

My swift glance assimilated all this in an instant, before returning to her lovely face. At the time — and ever since — I could not decide whether her big blue eyes were more striking than the full, red sweep of her mouth or vice versa. Both caught my attention simultaneously and equally and have presented the same conflict of selection to this day.

She was utterly lovely. And she was smiling at me in a way that eclipsed even one of Aunt Grace's special smiles. All the poise I had learned to display vanished as I stared at her, undoubtedly with my mouth agape and my cheeks blushing in confusion.

'Hello, Annie. May I come in?' she asked in a voice whose timbre thrilled me in the same way that her looks had just done.

I managed to gather my wits reasonably quickly, sat her down, poured her a glass of champagne and was bold enough to seat myself next to her on the sofa. Still smiling, she raised her glass to me and wished me, 'Health, wealth and happiness.' Smiling for the first time, and with my heartbeat gradually returning to normal, I returned her toast. We drank. Our eyes were locked into each others'. We did not speak, for there seemed to be no need. Our faces moved slowly closer; our lips parted; we kissed. Gently to start with. Mouths brushing against each other with the light touch of a butterfly's wing. We tasted our breath, breathed in scents and tasted tongues. Then her

173

hand stole softly down until it rested on my hip and she looked at me.

'What is your name?' I asked. For the first time with a visitor I really wanted to know.

'Lady Arabella C,' she replied. 'But we are friends already, I know we are. Please call me Arabella.'

I smiled happily at her, acknowledging the compliment. Her hand squeezed my hip and she gazed into my eyes with even greater intensity. Instinctively I knew what she wanted of me and rejoiced.

'I want to spank you, Annie. Twice I have watched you . . . ' Twice? I had only been aware of her presence on the one occasion!' . . . and it has taken until now for me to pluck up the courage to visit you alone. Are your agreeable?'

I looked at her. My eyes must have signalled all the yearning which was welling up inside me, for her smile suddenly moved from warmly appealing to dazzling.

'How would you like my bottom?' I asked simply.

'Over my lap please, my dear.'

She placed my spanking chair in the middle of the room and seated herself. I somehow floated over to her and settled myself in the time-honoured position, my senses whirling to the extent that my bottom had been bared before I was fully aware that the process had started. I jumped as I felt her hand on my naked flesh, so strong had been the desire to feel her touch. Then I lay still and my entire consciousness was devoted wholly to my bottom. I could be sympathetic to the pleasure she was receiving from my body and, at the same time, even though her hands had less experience or expertise than most of whose who had caressed me in like fashion, could regard her touch as the most welcome of my life.

She eventually began the spanking, and she smacked me as hard and for as long as I had ever been smacked.

Yet when she at last sat back, panting and breathless, I wanted to plead with her to continue, for the heat she had brought to my bottom was still no match for the heat of my desire. We gathered ourselves and she embraced me, holding me silently and tightly, her soft cheek lovely against mine and the scent of her golden hair sweet in my nostrils. We kissed and kissed until, with our mouths still closed fast to the other's, we found ourselves on my bed. Then the fever of loving lust broke upon us both together and suddenly clothing seemed a hindrance. She helped me to remove every stitch I had on, pushed me firmly onto my back and, making little mewing sounds in the back of her throat, she tried to touch as much of my heated flesh as she could at one and the same time, using both hands, her lips and tongue. Every so often she would pause and remove one of her own garments with almost frantic haste and with her eyes a-glitter as they roamed over my nakedness.

By the time she was reduced to just her chemise, drawers and stockings, her ardour had settled somewhat and she continued her caresses with a calmer purpose, which increased rather than lessened the pleasure I was deriving from them. She lingered on my bosoms until I thought the nipples would burst; she toyed with my little belly-button, dipping the hot, stiff point of her tongue right into it and providing a delicious foretaste of what I was sure would eventually follow. She stroked my furry triangle; she trickled the tips of her fingers up and down the inside of my thighs. She turned me over and gasped at the brilliant redness of my buttocks; she kissed them better before kneading the softened mounds, pulling them apart, pushing them together, running her fingers down the cleft and along the folds at the tops of my thighs. At last, she eased them apart and again gave out a small, sighing gasp as my anus popped into her view.

At that, I opened my eyes and peered back over my shoulder, consumed with curiosity, because her reaction had plainly suggested that she had never looked onto this intimate part before. Her beautiful face was flushed, her red lips slightly parted as she stared down into my yawning bottom-cleft. I pushed the muscle in and out at her and her mouth moved to form an 'O' of surprise. I saw that the area between her neck and bosom was blushing with her thrillings and the knowledge sent even greater waves through to the very core of my being. I buried my face in the coverlet again and pushed my bottom more firmly against the pressure of her hands.

I then sensed that once she had satisfied her immediate curiosity about my intimate appearance, she was at a loss and was unsure as to how to proceed. Shaking my head to clear it of the mists which had enveloped it from the moment she had appeared, I clambered up onto my knees, put my hands on her shoulders to draw her lovely moist mouth to mine and slowly began to help her on the road to sensual knowledge. The bare skin under my hands was like warm, velvety silk; her lips set mine afire with her sweet spittle adding to the flames. I breathed my desires into her breath.

'It's my turn now, my darling. I am going to spank you. On *your* bare bottom. Then I am going to kiss your burning cheeks better; hold them open so that I can see your bottom-hole. Then I shall kiss that. You cannot imagine how delectable a caress that is — especially when all the surrounding flesh is glowing after a loving spanking. Come, my sweet, put yourself across my lap.'

Her acquiescence was unspoken. The rise in the warmth and frequency of her breathings into my open mouth said all that had to be said. I sat on the edge of the bed; she knelt down on my right, kissed me once more and with infinite grace, settled her middle on my naked thighs. I slipped her chemise up to her waist, smoothed my hand over the thrusting mounds of her buttocks and gently laid them bare.

I did not, for some reason which is still inexplicable, cast a lingering gaze over their nakedness, but began straightaway to set them into quivering motion with sharp little spanks. Immediately she began that lascivious weaving and bobbing movement, which delighted me not least due to the feel of her bare thighs, belly and cunny shifting on my lap. My spanks grew harder; I wanted to drive my palm right into the yielding firmness of her intimate flesh and touch the inner core of her sensuality. I revelled in the silken sting as my palm struck her naked buttocks. I knew that the red stain was pleasing her no less than it was delighting me.

As she had done with me, I stopped before she really wished, because I needed above all else, to see, touch and taste her. Every nook and cranny. I tore off her drawers, whisked her stockings off her legs and wrestled the chemise off her shoulders until we were as one in Eve's unparalleled costume and we could use each little inch of my bed to writhe passionately around, clinging as tightly as we could to absorb every sensation the other emitted.

We climaxed at the same time and, wondrously, it was simply our emotions that led us on, for at the time, neither was touching the other's cunny. We did later. I showed her the delicious things I had learnt: I licked her anus; I placed her on her back with her legs so far back that her knees were resting on her bosoms and ran my tongue from bottom-hole to clitty in one sweeping movement; I slipped one finger into her rectum and tingled her love button with another. I had her shrieking her ecstasy to the heavens, as her eyes rolled back in her head and her whole body stiffened quiveringly. She followed my actions on my parts and my reactions copied hers.

Satisfied, but not sated, we clung to each other as our perspiration jointly flowed. We did not speak: there was nothing to be said — even 'I love you' would have sounded trite and inadequate. After an indefinable time of the deepest possible contentment, Arabella stirred and lazily announced that it was time for her to go. The void in my heart almost swallowed me up and I could not bear the thought of being without her, so I decided that I had to take some sort of action to prevent her departure.

Giving her a long kiss, I told her to stay still and bounded out of the room to search for Aunt Grace and ask if Arabella could stay the night as my guest. It was an indication of my euphoric state of mind that I did not even pause to put on my peignoir, but ran straight to her quarters completely naked. It was not until I saw her and Uncle George blink in surprise at my appearance that I realised! And even more telling was the fact that I felt not the slightest trace of remorse or embarrassment at my condition.

I was smilingly told that Lady Arabella was welcome to stay — any time I wished — and that I could ask Cook to organise a supper for us. 'With a bottle of the best champagne' added Uncle George. Squealing with glee, I kissed them both and skipped down to the kitchen. There, my reception was a great deal less restrained!

'Annie, what on earth are you up to?'

'Look at her bottom. It's bright red.'

'Who spanked you, Annie?'

'Turn round, dearest. I want to see.'

I posed with happy abandon. Hands moved around my throbbing parts, stroking, patting, tweaking, probing, separating, prodding. I was pushed across the end of the big table and my fervent naked bottom slapped by all present until the sparks flew through me. Eventually, breathless with the smart and laughter, I wriggled free of the clutching hands and reasserted what little authority I could muster, ordering a platter of cold poached salmon, with potatoes and peas, strawberries and, of course, the champagne, suitably chilled.

Pointing my nose in the air, I walked out, exaggerating the natural sway of my freshly reddened bottom as I went, and I was followed by a chorus of happily sympathetic laughter.

Arabella was curled up on the bed with her back to me and my heart missed at least a beat as I gazed at her, from her tousled curls falling over her lower shoulder, down the gentle curve of her spine with the little bony knobs breaking the smoothness of the surface, to the tight straits of her waist, the flat plane of her loins and thence to my favourite part of her — or any woman's — body. It was still a delicious bright pink, plumped up by the pressure of her weight, the cleft elongated and even tighter. It looked both firm and soft. I moved silently towards the bed, sat gently on the edge and ran my hand over the swelling curve of her hip and over both buttocks. She stirred and her soft sigh was an invitation to continue. So I did, renewing my acquaintance with all of her.

Then a shyly smiling Agatha brought in our supper and, still naked and with no sense of shame, we moved to the table and ate with hearty appetites until the bottle was empty and our plates clean. We talked and talked. She told me that she had not been happy in their family house after her mother had died and had found relative freedom when she moved in with an aged great aunt, who lived in one of their houses in nearby Richmond-on-Thames. The old lady was apparently delightful company, had lived a full life and it had been none other than she who had guided Arabella to our household.

I was bold enough to ask how she had first become excited by corporal punishment and she had me breathless with her tale of the Governess who had had charge of her when she was 14 years old (she was just 21 at this time) and who had been an unashamed lover of spanking and the rod. She had been intelligent enough to lead her young pupil gently down this road and Arabella had soon found herself actively anticipating their frequent reviews of her academic prowess. The desires had not risen again until she had witnessed one of our entertainments, which she had found exceedingly stimulating. She was flattering enough to tell me that watching my bottom being dealt with had caused her to long to meet me. And to spank me if at all possible.

It was at this juncture that Agatha returned to collect the tray and, on her way out, was clumsy enough to spill one of the plates and most of the silver. As she bent down to pick them up, both Arabella and I stared at the breadth of her tightly stretched skirt, looked at each other, smiled with impish delight as we simultaneously recognised the opportunity and moved smoothly into action.

'Heavens above that startled me!' said Arabella, looking surprised.

'And me,' I interjected, trying to look angry as we both stared at Agatha's big bottom. 'That was exceedingly careless of you, Agatha. Lady Arabella has a particularly nervous disposition and does not care to be frightened in such a way.' My new-found friend glared at me for my impudence in making such a slur on her stalwart character and then hastily looked away again as the laughter threatened to erupt.

'I think she should be spanked!' she proclaimed after a brief pause.

'An excellent idea, my dear Arabella. And as my guest, I would be honoured if you would take the first turn. Prepare and position her in whichever way you wish.'

Agatha had stayed in her deeply stooping position while

this conversation was taking place and at my last sentence she peered back past her legs to see what was happening, giving me a glimpse of her slightly apprehensive face. She clearly assumed that this was not going to be one of our usual playful smackings and that we were in the mood properly to redden her bottom for her.

My glance flicked immediately to the even more arresting sight of the naked Arabella marching purposefully across the room, her plump but beautifully firm buttocks swaying most seductively as she went. I sat back and prepared to enjoy the ensuing spectacle to the full. The naughty girl was told to stand up, whereupon Arabella squatted down behind her and groped and prodded the very generously fleshed area under the seat of the tight skirt. This was then folded upwards and tucked securely into her belt, as were her petticoats, until she was standing with only her drawers covering her rump. Not that they provided much in the way of cover, because they were of the split variety and Agatha's bottom was far too big to be contained by them, so almost the full length of her cleft was displayed.

Much though I loved the ample curves of Agatha's bottom, it was Arabella who held my attention almost exclusively. Even if she had not been all bare, I would have watched her and I know that I would have found her natural gracefulness and the happily earnest expression on her truly lovely face as she went about her task nearly as captivating if she had been fully clothed. As it was, I could enjoy the extra elements provided by her bobbing bosoms and the rapidly changing perspectives of her bottom. The combination of a beautiful and entirely naked spanker, a compliant and full-bottomed spankee, plus the frisson supplied by the fact that there was a real intention to punish, added up to a most memorable spanking.

Agatha was made to bend forward and hold onto her

ankles, and given the impressive fleshiness of the naked buttocks so posed, Arabella had a stupendous target to attack and I had an equally splendid sight to behold — especially as there was only the merest hint of darkly haired cunny peeping out between her thighs to distract the eye from the soft whiteness of the bared bottom above.

Meanwhile Arabella had tucked her victim under her left arm and was stooping down so that her intent face was but an inch or two above the proffered bottom, which she was assessing with gleeful concentration, running her right hand over the exposed flesh, poking it with her forefinger and then patting both cheeks gently, smiling at the ensuing quiverings. I moved closer so that I could get a more satisfying view of Arabella's bottom, and as I did so, I noticed that Agatha had cocked her head up and was staring goggle-eyed at the very unusual low view of her punisher's nether portions. After but a moment's thought, I resolved to treat myself to a similar view at the first possible opportunity! Then Arabella opened fire.

It was a brisk and sound spanking. From the outset. Each impact resounded crisply and made the whole area quiver. Each spank left its red mark. Each one caused a quivering bobble in the administrator's own breasts and buttocks. And as the passion rose, they got harder and harder, until I began to worry that poor, gentle Agatha would be seriously bruised. However, I think Arabella's inexperienced hand wearied before Agatha's experienced bottom and she stood back, panting, and then moved towards me to indicate that it was now my turn.

After pausing for a brief kiss, I took her place beside the scarlet bottom awaiting me. Poor Agatha was sighing with the smart and I was certain that she was not looking forward to the resumption of hostilities and, luckily for her, I was so absorbed with the prospect of a whole night with Arabella that I had no desire to punish her further.

182

I adopted the same position that my predecessor had done and immediately realised that it made a charming alternative to the traditional across the knee pose which was all that I had experienced until then. Her buttocks appeared far more widely separated when viewed from above and I only had to lean forward a little to treat myself to a 'full-face' aspect. I noted that while her cheeks were very red, albeit rather blotchy, the open cleft was almost entirely white, so that she did not present a well-smacked bottom to me so much as two reddened buttocks. Much more gently than Arabella's rampant enthusiasm had encouraged, I concentrated my spanks down the gaping division, confident that it was deep enough to offer protection to the delicate little anus. Had this part been on display, I would of course have adjusted her position accordingly. I basically used the ends of my fingers to flick against this especially soft skin which very soon began to blush a delicious bright pink.

I must confess, however that before I finished I found the charms of her buttocks irresistible and jolted her with six good solid spanks on each, before helping her up and kissing her, rubbing her glowing bottom as I did so. I tasted the saltiness of the fat tears which were rolling down her face and soothed her back to her usual soft smile in moments.

Arabella followed suit and when she finally left us, she was blushing with pleasure — at both ends!

We retired to the bed and lay silently, reliving the recent past and gently stroking each other as if frightened of losing contact even for a second.

'I did enjoy spanking her bare bottom.' Her soft low voice broke the intimate silence. 'She really was delightfully plump and soft.'

'Was it better than spanking me?' I teased her.

She smiled. 'Of course not, you silly goose. It was a

different form of pleasure. Becuase I am not in love with her, I seemed able to concentrate much more on her bottom. I did not really care how much I was paining her.' She suddenly propped herself up on one elbow and looked down on me. 'Am I dreadfully callous to think that?'

I smiled tenderly up at her, and it was a little time before I dared to speak, for her casual declaration of love for me had pierced my heart to the core. 'No. She, like all the maids, is well used to having her bottom warmed up, and so it was not as though you were cruelly torturing some little innocent. And I have found the same as you — that there are great differences in spanking a loved one out of sensual pleasure and administering a fair punishment as a means of correcting wayward behaviour . . . and both, in their varied ways, provide a great deal of satisfaction . . . although they do not usually end in the same manner! Now, to prove my point, place me in the same position that you did Agatha and spank me!'

Thus not only did I lead my beloved a little further down that joyous path, but I also chanced on a way of treating myself to a worm's eye view of her naked bottom as she relit the flames in my intimate flesh. Naturally I repaid her in kind and by the time we had regained the haven of my bed we were both flushed and giggling.

'You were right, dearest. It *is* different. Now kiss me . . . and my poor wounded bottom, please.'

'Certainly, my darling.'

I explored her body in all its wondrous detail, having first lit all the gas lamps and every candle, the better to view it. I marvelled at her smooth, firm softness; I inhaled all her variety of scents; I tasted her saliva and the jewel-like little spends from her adorable cunny; I licked her bottom-hole and eased my finger into its hot, clinging depths; I drew her love button right into my mouth and sucked on it until she called out my name in ecstasy.

We dozed in each other's arms, breast to breast, then awoke and she covered my hungry body with caresses. Less used to loving another girl than I, she was sometimes tentative: for example, she knelt over me, holding the cheeks of my bottom open for quite a while before lowering her mouth onto the yearning orifice.

Lying back, spent after our climaxes, we talked as though we had known each other for years, not hours. We dozed again. Awake, we flattered each other with fulsome praise of our respective bodies. This led to a desire for direct comparisons, so we leapt up, arranged all the available glasses and stood, knelt, bent and lay side by side gazing at our images. My bosoms and bottom were bigger than hers, although not by a great deal, and my waist narrower. Her hair was more golden than mine and that on her belly more profuse. Her bottom-hole lacked the hint of brown which characterised mine, and was even neater, as well as pinker. I solemnly judged it to be just the prettiest of all her parts, as we crouched on the floor, our rear ends thrust high into the air, hip to hip with the pier glass just wide enough to encompass the image of our four spread buttocks. She then watched in the glass resting on the floor before us as I reached back and tickled the part under discussion with my forefinger. And her face screwed up with the pleasure. As did mine with the pleasing.

Dawn came on the swiftest of wings and I awoke to find that we were in that nicest of sleeping postures — curled up like two spoons, with her bottom tucked into my middle. My hand was resting on the curls of her love-nest and, as consciousness came, I had the the strangest of passing thoughts — *if only she had a cock, she would be perfect.*

Shaking my head at such a silly notion, I shook her and led her off to share a bath, overcoming her modest objections to walking naked down the empty corridor.

As I watched her gracefully climb into her carriage, I experienced a similar bleak emptiness to that I had known when I was told about my parents' death. For the first time in six months, I did not look forward to the day ahead of me.

CHAPTER 10

My gloomy period did not last long. A day or so later,
the first breach was made by Cook. She, all the maids
and I were in the kitchen after luncheon and I was sitting
quietly in a corner, ignoring the happy chatter around me.
Gradually I became aware that eyes were turning in my
direction and there was an air of suppressed glee pervading
the atmosphere. Before I could really grasp what was happening they had all risen and moved until they were in
a semi-circle around me. Adopting a gravely solemn expression, Cook opened the proceedings:

'Friends and colleagues. We see before us a miserable
specimen of humanity. Whereas she once lit our humble
halls with her merry laughter — and an often naked, glowing bottom — her down-turned mouth and sad eyes are
now casting a gloom upon us. How can we make her smile
again?

'Tickle her.' That was Elspeth. I was just making up
my mind as to the exact penalty she would have to pay
for such an outrageous recommendation when I realised
that they were advancing on me with grim intent. The
thought of being publicly tickled appalled me and I turned to flee. Too late. I was seized and dragged over to the
large table in the centre of the kitchen, flung down upon
it, face up and full length, securely pinned by my wrists,
ankles, shoulders, waist, thighs and arms, and had to lie
helpless while Cook thrust her way through the giggling

mob to begin my torture.

And torture it was. Of the most lascivious nature. I was gradually stripped to the waist and my hands held above my head so that my delicate bosoms and sensitive underarms were exposed. Any fingertips that were not actively occupied in holding me firm were then used on those areas, plus my ribs and belly until I was squawking and wriggling.

Then my lower garments were taken from me, leaving me stark-naked — until my drawers were returned to me, but not in their right and proper position but as a blindfold, cutting me off from the sight of their avid faces, their eyes gleaming as they surveyed my naked body and with ample expanse of white skin and ticklish little nooks and crannies. My cunny tingled in anticipation. But they avoided it, concentrating instead on my thighs, hips and feet, until I was squealing and writhing again.

As I was on the verge of complete breathlessness, I heard Cook order them to turn me over and in a trice I was flipped rather painfully onto my belly and my naked bottom began to tingle. This time the anticipation was correct, except that they did not tickle my cheeks but did what I am sure I would have done in their place, and smacked them. Not hard. Enough to render them warmly pink and to make them glow throughout, before they returned to their planned activity on the soles of my feet again, my calves, the backs of my knees, my loins and back, under my arms and on the squashed mounds of my breasts. I was now helplessly sobbing with laughter and too weak even to wriggle.

Thankfully I was given a brief pause while I did my utmost to get my breath back. Then the pressure of the pinioning hands increased and I moaned aloud in expectation. Then they started on my bottom, which had already been rendered especially sensitive by the volley of slaps.

On this part of me, however, the tickling was purely sensual, especially when it was directed to those folds where thighs and buttocks meet. After I had been moaning and sighing for what seemed at least an hour, the caresses stopped and my tingling bottom was left alone. A moment later, it was invaded by a new and even more blissful sensation, which at first completely mystified me. It was sharper and harder than a fingertip, softer than a fingernail and even nicer than either. It was only when Cook ran it lingeringly up and down the length of my cleft that I guessed that it was a feather and, having reached that conclusion, I could devote the whole of my awareness to the pleasures it was bringing me. These were even greater when my buttocks were eased wide apart and that tantalising implement brought to bear on my eager bottom-hole. My darkness was filled with these delectable surges which seemed to flow from the entrance to my passage right into the very centre of my being. It was very nearly as pleasing as a caress on the same place from a loving tongue — preferably Arabella's.

When they turned me back over, I was limp and fluid in their hands, unable to resist as my legs were pulled apart and then bent back until my knees nestled comfortably against my bosom. Both my secret orifices were open to the staring eyes. Soft fingers touched the lips of my cunny and opened the tight little slit to the feather's probing. It slithered around the lusting opening and crept slowly over the moist flesh and flickered against the love button. I could vaguely hear my distant screams as my spasms made me struggle vainly against the restraining hands.

I must have fainted away because I have no memories of being released and my blindfold removed. Just of opening my eyes and looking up at the smiling faces of my dear friends, and noticing that Cook was still clutching the long, white swan's feather which had brought me such raptures.

The merry little romp did much to restore my spirits, although nothing could possibly drive the memories of that special night from my mind. What I had learned was that I could still enjoy the diversions which were so readily available. I also became aware that I was able to abandon myself wholeheartedly to the entertainments as well as the private visits. Aunt Grace seemed to have an instinctive understanding of what was troubling me, for it was she who started the curative processes. During one of our regular conversations, she raised the subject of the Misses C, who apparently jointly owned a nearby academy for young ladies. They were regular guests and Aunt Grace told me that while they were fervent devotees of physical punishment, they were also particularly solicitous about the well-being of the girls placed in their care. They therefore only whipped or spanked them when it was thoroughly deserved and were very careful not to allow their enjoyment of the procedure to be either influential or noticeable.

'As with all our guests, my dear Annie, they have been most taken with you and would like to re-enact one of their punishments on your bottom, but without the restrictions imposed by the proper exercise of their authority.'

'You mean that they want to enjoy themselves to the full, Aunt Grace.'

'Exactly.'

'How can I refuse!'

And so, we furnished one of the little rooms in the cellar as a close approximation to a headmistresses's study and, one afternoon, I was duly waiting outside the door. My hair was tied up with a gay ribbon, I was wearing the appropriate short dress, ankle boots, loose and thick drawers, a chemise and stockings which reached just above my knees. I was exceedingly apprehensive, knowing full well that my bottom would be crimson and bruised by the end of our meeting.

I was also in a state bordering on exultation at the fierceness of the challenge to my courage and perseverance, welcoming the prospect of severe pain and deep humiliation. Taking a deep breath, my heartbeat hammering in my ears, I knocked on the door, waited impatiently until a well-modulated voice summoned me to enter, opened the door and crept nervously in. I did not have to summon up any of my talents for role-playing! Especially when they showed that Aunt Grace could have taught them nothing about the power of the spoken word in such situations.

'So this is the naughty girl we have to punish.' The game was opened by the lady on my left, a strikingly handsome, if rather severe woman in her middle thirties. She was dressed in black, her hair was pulled back in typical fashion and she was staring at me through a pair of lorgnettes. She was smiling happily and the tip of her tongue kept passing slowly over her lips.

'Yes indeed. And I wager that she has an exceptionally naughty and fat bottom, one which will test our skills to the utmost.' Her sister — who was younger and pretty rather than handsome — was not actually smiling but her eyes were glittering with even greater intensity.

'Do you mean that we shall actually be *seeing* her bottom, sister dear?'

'I think so. She has been exceedingly wicked and it is fitting that she should know the humbling effect of being bare-bottomed in our presence. The pain of the punishment will be even sharper.'

They continued in similar vein for several minutes and by the end, I really did feel like a schoolgirl facing a severe chastisement. My bottom felt numb, heavy and twice its usual size and I genuinely dreaded its imminent exposure.

Eventually they ended the verbal torment and began the physical. As I stood meekly before them, staring dismally at the opposite wall, they removed my dress and rolled my chemise up to just below my breasts.

'I am glad that she has decent drawers. Too many of our girls keep wearing theirs when they have far outgrown them and they no longer cover their parts properly. Look, I have to open the slit wide before any of the flesh of her bottom is revealed.'

'I quite agree, Jane. You hold that side and I'll do the same to mine and we shall be able to see her well enough . . . My, she *does* have a nice big bottom . . . So nice and chubby . . . Like a big bumblebee.'

'Lovely soft skin . . .'

'And such firm flesh. I cannot think of another bottom in the whole school which is half as well shaped.'

Their hands roamed freely over my tingling flesh and whereas in other circumstances I had always found such fondling in some way soothing, their gloating over my discomfited body only added to my apprehensions. At last their inspection was over and they were ready to commence the punishment.

'As the senior, you will, of course, start. But as we both love beginning with a white bottom facing us, may I suggest that we take a buttock each? In that case, we shall both be able to start on virgin flesh.'

'What an excellent idea. I shall have the right one, I think. Now, shall we start off with her across the knee? It has a certain charm and will remind her of the childishness of her sins. We shall progress to greater severity later. Place yourself over my lap, my girl.'

With rare clumsiness, I moved around and obeyed. My position was adjusted, then the two halves of my drawers separated to lay my buttocks completely bare. They were intimately poked and prodded, my position altered to allow the best possible access to the right cheek. I braced myself just in time for the first of an unconscionable number of ringing spanks to land. If their usual punishment routine precluded them from gloating in advance, I rapidly realised that it also stopped them spanking with the hot-blooded fervour which their inclinations demanded. Each spank hurt. Even the very first one. And by the time that the elder of the sisters had finished with my right buttock, my fortitude had already been severely tested and I was exceedingly grateful for the pause while they changed places and I was repositioned with my left cheek prominently posed for its turn. There were several amused and admiring comments on how strange my bottom looked with one red buttock and the other still a virgin white, and the part of my mind not fully occupied with the pain and humiliation of my ordeal wondered at its appearance and resolved to conduct a similar experiment at the first possible opportunity.

The interval was not long enough as far as I was concerned, and too soon, the younger of the sisters was battering her side into near submission. Her spanks were delivered with greater rapidity and with no less venom that her sibling's and I was soon wishing that I only had the one burning buttock.

As soon as the redness was evenly distributed, I was told to rise and place myself over the back of a well upholstered chair, my head firmly buried between my arms and my bottom thrust roundly upwards. They then took a buttock each and slapped merrily away until real tears were flowing down my upper cheeks as my nether ones quivered their way to a fair emulation of a blazing furnace.

I was then turned around and made to kneel on the seat of the chair with my bottom pushed out to the extent that my anus was visible, whereupon this very personal little part was tickled, poked, penetrated and generally commented upon. The fact that the comments were almost entirely favourable did little to improve my lot, especially when the spanks rang down onto the open cleft and the central orifice could not escape a share of the impacts.

Finally I was made to strip stark-naked, to stand in the middle of the room with my hands on my head while the happy pair moved round me slapping away at any area of my flesh which took their fancy, my bosoms included, although to be just to them, the smacks there were perfectly gentle and it was my thighs and bottom which attracted most of their attentions.

Never had I had such a demanding spanking. And never had I welcomed the pain and never had it washed through my being with such intensity. I had forgotten my yearnings for my Arabella early on in the proceedings and the simple challenge of keeping my body as still as possible for my pretty tormentors drove them completely from my mind as I moaned my way to that strange form of climax which usually accompanied a really satisfying chastisement. By the end the blood was flowing through my veins like molten lava and I was pleading with the sisters to finish. But it was not until some inspiration made me offer to kiss their bottoms that they pantingly halted, stood before me, lifted my pain-wracked face and accepted my offer. They watched me wriggle around for long minutes, clutching my burning flesh and allowing the tears to dry up, before they made me kneel behind them and watch while they slowly hoisted their skirts, revealing their naked bottoms to me. As I gazed at the four plump white globes with the long tight divisions, my mouth longed for the silken touch of their skin and the softness of their flesh. With a muffled sob of desire I leant forward to please them, smothering their buttocks with tear-wet kisses, running my tongue down the clefts and along the thigh folds, before suggesting that they bend forward to permit access to their back passages.

Even in my very emotional state, I was able to derive my usual pleasure from parting a pair of plump female cheeks, wondering the while what shape and shade of bottom-hole would be revealed to me. Both sisters were well and equally favoured, with neat, pinkish little orifices, and I was very happy to run my stiff tongue around and in both of them. And judging from the intensity of the gasps from the other ends, both were equally happy with the quality and quantity of my caresses.

To my surprise, after I had brought them both to a climax — aided by the judicious use of my hands on their wet cunnies, they made me lie on the table with my legs brought back to my chest and buried their heads between them so that I had one mouth on my anus and the other on my love-nest. The combination, added to the hot flood of sensation from my burning bottom and thighs, had me screeching in a matter of moments.

When we had all recovered, they thanked me most prettily for providing them with such a happily diverting evening and we bade each other the fondest of farewells. I was pleased that Elspeth was able to spend the night with me, for her familiar and loving form was infiniteley nicer to hug than my bolster. And her soft hands applied a soothing balm to my sore bottom with a rare delicacy.

If I was discovering that my yearning for Arabella somehow increased my desire to experience pain as well as pleasure in feeling those fiery waves pound through my vitals, I also found even greater satisfaction in having my bottom-hole plugged by the male guests. My friend Bertie was a regular caller and I recall his visits with nothing but happy memories. Probably my favourite moment was when I had removed all but my stockings and slowly positioned myself on the end of the bed, gradually thrusting my freshly spanked bottom up to him so that the revelation of the crucial spot was as tantalising as possible. The throbbing waves spread through me as I felt the coolness of the air on my cleft and sensed his gleaming eyes on the hole. Then he let me feel the warmth of his breath on me as he leant forward to salute his target with his tongue; his moustache tickled the sensitive skin on the inner surfaces of my spread buttocks before the pleasure boiled up into the passage. At last, I could hold my breath in fervent expectation as I felt the smooth plum of his cock nuzzling against the tight ring of muscle before thrusting through the barrier and filling me with joy. I learned to 'milk' him by squeezing my hole around the more sensitive parts of his cock and by timing the movements of my hips to match his.

I also found pleasure and fascination in playing with his manliness and his bottom. If my feelings for him did not approach the ones I held in my heart for Arabella, I grew very fond of him and, as I did so, found that I began to lose much of my usual shyness when in the company of the masculine sex.

But my beloved Arabella had not forsaken me. She came for the night whenever she could, and on several occasions when I was taking part in one of our entertainments, my heart leapt when I peeped at the guests and saw her lovely face and we could exchange a secret little smile. On such occasions, I always played whichever role had been designed to me with extra fervour. I tried my best to pose my bottom to give her the best possible view of it under punishment and my enjoyment was inevitably much greater for knowing that her loving eyes were following every blow, every quiver and wobble, every addition to the red staining of my skin; that her ears were listening to every ringing spank or swish of the birch, to every mew and moan that escaped my lips.

When she was with me, it became a custom for one of

the maids to serve our supper and to make some silly mistake. In time, I preferred to let Arabella administer the greater part of the inevitable punishment because I found more pleasure in watching her doing so than in my own participation. Especially when she was stark-naked and the maid just had her bottom bared. I loved the grace of her movements as she spanked away merrily, the bobbing of her breasts and, if she were standing with her victim bent over the back of a chair or kneeling on the bed, the little quiverings in her buttocks. Best of all was the expression on her dear face. There was always a little frown of concentration on her brow, in contrast to the happy little smile on her adorable full lips as she savoured the unique pleasures of administering a sharp spanking to a well-turned bare bottom.

Our love for each other grew. We were totally content with each other's company and the caresses we exchanged were all the sweeter for it. It was with her that I discovered some new sensual touches: for example, one night we were crawling around the bed trying to restore some sort of order to the blankets and coverlet before snuggling down for the night. She was at the head and I at the tail, both on all fours, when we moved backwards at the same time and our naked bottoms bumped into each other Simultaneously we exclaimed at the unexpected pleasure of the contact and, far from moving away with some form of politely muttered apology, we pressed more tightly against the other. Her buttocks felt especially soft and satiny against mine and I unconsciously moved my hips from side to side. At first this just emphasised the yielding nature of the fleshy cushions, but after a moment they were pushed together in an even more intimate and delightful embrace — her left buttock was pressed into my open division and mine into hers. So sensitive is the skin there that I could easily feel the different warmth and texture of her little anus as she thrust it against me. And the feel of her buttock against my little hole was equally pleasing. We knelt for minutes, simply enjoying the sensations.

And it was with her that I took yet another step on the voyage of discovery. On one of her visits, she arrived longing to give me a sound spanking and I had, of course, proffered my bottom to her most willingly. She had smacked it with a degree of enthusiasm which had brought me to the point of tears. Afterwards, as we lay on the bed, me face down and Arabella resting her head on my buttocks so that she could kiss them better at regular intervals, she told me about the dilemma currently exercising her. Apparently, a 19-year-old second cousin of hers had been the cause of many a furrowed brow within the family. She was proving to be lazy, a liar, was suspected of stealing, was so rude to her inferiors that her parents were finding it impossible to keep the good servants and all their efforts to make a good match for her were dismissed with contempt.

'They found a very eligible young man for her, Annie. Lord Darchester's second son. He is in the Grenadier Guards and has a peerless reputation for courage, yet when he pressed his suit with her he was fleeing from her presence — white and shaken — after no more than three minutes. What she said to him I cannot imagine but he would not approach the house again until he had been completely reassured that she had left home. We really are at a loss.'

I thought for a moment. Not particularly hard because it was obviously not a problem which affected me. 'Perhaps her mother should give her a good whipping,' I suggested idly.

'Oh they are both too weak. Perhaps if they had dealt with her properly ten years ago . . . but it is a little late now. She is after all, a grown-up woman.'

I cannot explain why, but suddenly the same thought occurred to both of us. I rolled over, Arabella sat up and we stared at each other with grins spreading over our faces. It may well have been too late for her parents to take action. They may have been weak — but we could try and correct her behaviour and even if we did not succeed, nothing would have been lost. And we were not weak.

And so a week or so later, we were both in a Hansom cab, on our way to Arabella's home. The errant Victoria had been invited there on the pretext that it would be a good idea for her to escape from her family home for a week or so.

I was too excited to take much note of my beloved's home and only noted the elegance of the spacious hall while the footman passed our hats and gloves to an elderly maid, before we went up to Victoria's room to confront her. We paused at the door, looking at each other. We shared the same sense of keen anticipation at the prospect of correcting this wayward girl; of changing her from the hoyden she had become to someone with whom one could be happy to claim kinship. We had also dressed ourselves carefully for the occasion, in plain dresses of obvious quality, the minimum of rouge, hair swept back with a hint of severity. We were ready.

The first stage of our plan was simplicity itself, requiring no more than to get her to Aunt Grace's house, and Arabella had already informed her that she was to accompany us and had told her to ensure that her luggage was ready. Apart from anything else, the initial meeting and the short journey back home allowed me firstly to arrive at some sort of judgement of her character and secondly to establish myself in her eyes as somebody with whom it would be unwise to trifle, so I had resolved to say little but to regard her steadily and appraisingly.

I was not expecting her to be of such striking beauty.

Her hair was as black as a raven's wing and flowed in loose waves over her shoulders. Her eyes were a startling green in shade and her mouth showed great promise of full richness. Her neck was long enough to be only partly hidden by the high collar of her white blouse and there was sufficient evidence of roundness in bosom and hip to hold promise of a splendid chubbiness. My breathing quickened and the hollow feeling of sensual excitement spread slowly through my middle.

'Are you ready, Victoria?' asked Arabella.

The girl simply stared sullenly at her cousin, nodded, stood up and then turned towards me.

'Who is this?' Her arrogant air made my right palm itch but I made no angry riposte, simply raised an eyebrow and smiled sweetly at her.

'This is my friend Annie. She will be taking charge of the arrangements. Now come along.'

Victoria looked at me again. The word 'arangements' had obviously puzzled her a little but she was too proud to question us any further.

The journey passed in silence. I was amused at Victoria's composure — she showed no signs of nervousness, presumably because her innate arrogance did not allow her to feel that she could not control any situation she might be faced with. We arrived and bustled down to one of the small rooms in the cellar, where the first signs of discomfiture showed themselves. She looked round the bare room — the only item of furniture was a tall-backed, armless chair and she opened her mouth to ask the obvious question.

But I was first. 'There is no need for me to go into detail of your many failings, Victoria. You are clearly fully aware that your behaviour has become intolerable. I am going to sit on this chair and you will place yourself across my knees to have your bottom soundly spanked —

something which your parents should have done years ago. Fortunately it is not too late for you to redeem yourself. Nothing further needs to be said, so prepare yourself.'

I had been raised among farm workers, so was not unfamiliar with coarseness of speech. But in the ensuing few moments I learned several words and expressions which were entirely new to me! With her fists on her hips, quivering with outrage, she did her very best to assasinate my antecedents, character and motives. I sighed with theatrical weariness and nodded to Arabella. With smooth efficiency, we extracted two scarves from hidden pockets in our skirts and fastened them round her wrists before she could react to the sudden assault. These were then fastened to two hooks which we had arranged to be fixed to the main beam in the ceiling. She could not escape and it was quite simple to push a rolled-up cloth into her mouth as a gag, to blindfold her with another scarf and then to stand back and watch her fruitlessly struggle against her bonds until she tired. I then added the final touch by uncoiling two more lengths of cloth which had been nailed to the walls at floor level and tying them to her ankles. Again she struggled, and again it proved useless. At last, she hung by her fettered wrists, limp and panting.

'Victoria. I told you that I was going to spank you and I have no intention of changing my mind. If you had obeyed me, you would have saved yourself the pain and degradation of being tied up like a common criminal. You also would have received a far more moderate chastisement than the one I am about to give you. I shall beat you with all the severity I can muster. And I shall beat you on your naked buttocks.'

As I had hoped, the prospect of being stripped had much more immediate effect than the threat of pain. Her muffled wails of protest echoed round the room. It would, of course, have been a simple matter to have pinned up her skirts and underclothing, whisked down her drawers and laid her suitably bare, but we had devised a far more effective approach. Silently we went to a small box which we had hidden in one of the corners, extracted a pair of sharp scissors each, and slowly, one each side of her, knelt down and began to cut off her skirt, starting at the hem and working steadily upwards. It took a little time for her to guess what we were doing but, when she did, her wails and struggles intensified. By the time we had dealt similarly with her three petticoats and had moved to her blouse, she was sobbing and writhing. When we started on her stays, however, the steely touch of the inner blades against her skin proved an immediate reminder of the perils of unconsidered movement and she froze into absolute immobility. After her chemise and stockings lay in tatters at her feet, we stood back and left her in suspense for a while longer while we admired the tautly fleshed naked back and the modestly baggy drawers which gave just the merest hint of the curves beneath.

We then moved back and knelt on each side of her, snapping our scissors noisily to give her the clearest indication of our immediate intent. Once again she writhed against her restraining bonds until the touch of cold steel on her naked thighs stilled her. Slowly we moved up towards her waist, the 'snips' as the sharp blades cut through the material echoing in the silence. We paued at the waistband. The ruined drawers flapped loosely and exposed part of the side curves of her buttocks and we waited until she expelled her pent-up breath in a gusty sigh before making the final cut, and the last piece of protection fluttered limply down to her ankles. Still kneeling, we both moved round so that we could look directly − very closely − at her bare bottom, which proved to fully live up to my expectations. Her skin was flawlessly white, her cheeks firmly chubby, the folds clean-cut and the cleft long, deep and tight.

I reached out and stroked it and her skin was as silken as it looked; Arabella patted it and the flesh quivered firmly. We nodded at each other in approval and stood up to take up our positions, with myself as the spanker to the left and Arabella right behind.

'Now, Victoria. I told you that you were going to be spanked and I should imagine that you now realise that this is precisely what is about to happen to you. Your stupidity is matched only by your wickedness. If you had submitted in the first place, we would not have had to ruin your clothes. You would have been far more comfortable across my knees than you are now — and it would all have been over by now. You would be nursing a sore bottom rather than facing the unfamiliar prospect of an even more painful one. I hope that the next half an hour or so will be a salutory lesson to you.'

I had kept my voice low and warm, in the belief that it would sound more menacing than a show of anger and from the way her full cheeks clenched so tightly that dimples flared over the whole surface, I had not been mistaken. Although it took several moments for the import of my closing statement to penetrate her confusion, when it did, the muffled howl was indeed gratifying. As soon as the strain of clamping her globes together began to tell and they settled back into their usual and most charming form, I let fly with the hardest spank I could muster. It landed with perfect precision in the very centre of her bottom, spanning the divide so that there was an immediate imprint of my palm on the left side and my fingers on the right, reddening with pleasing rapidity and indicating that her skin was as delicate as it seemed. I quietly rubbed my stinging hand and watched the stain grow in colour and fade in definition, while she did all she could to make her feelings known. The gag had been one of Arabella's better ideas!

I struck her in the same way five more times, two above the first and three below and each one made her whole bottom quake and shudder dramatically and left a broad swathe of red on each side of her cleft. Judging from the heat in my hand, her soft and inexperienced flesh was already exceedingly sore and the sounds and movements from her did nothing to make me question my judgement. The opening shots in my campaign had certainly taken effect! It was now time to give her something slightly different to think about. I moved closer to her, placed my left forearm across her lower belly to hold her in place, gripping her hip firmly, then spanked every inch of her bottom, concentrating solely on her left buttock to start with and continuing until the entire mound was a vivid red. As I spanked away the mewlings and wailings from somewhere above me intensified in time with the increasingly desperate jerkings of her naked body. I held her yet more firmly and despite all her efforts, she could do nothing to disturb my aim. I paused to study the effect, which was indeed spectacular, with a brilliantly discoloured left cheek and cleft, then a band of mottled red on the inner curve of the right buttock and after that, an area of the purest white.

I caught Arabella's eye, smiled happily into her flushed face, leaned further forward for better access to the virgin area, and re-commenced the assault, my sharply stinging but not severe smacks landing in such rapid succession that her flesh stayed in a constant state of wild agitation.

Having now reddened the entire surface to my satisfaction, I resumed my first position and aimed another full-strength blow to the plumpest part of her left cheek, waited until the echoes of her screech had faded and her body had settled to a squirming quiver and repeated the delivery to the same part of her other buttock, once more taking great pains to ensure that the whole surface was treated. By the time I had done so, she was sobbing brokenly and was quite clearly washed through with the pain. Certainly the deep crimson colour to which I had reduced her once-white skin was plain evidence of a high degree of burning smart.

In silent concert, Arabella and I studied our victim. Her sobs were causing her taut body to shake and her bottom was jerking spasmodically and trembling visibly. But I had promised her that her punishment would last for half an hour and I have always been taught that a lady should keep her word at all costs. The pause was clearly helping her to recover a little of her composure and because we had still to reach the halfway point, I was quite happy to prolong it for a while. She had certainly behaved badly enough to justify her punishment but I did not wish to move into the displeasing realms of cruel torture. I felt that I had already administered enough severe pain to jolt her out of her arrogant complacency and that a more subtle approach would more effectively break her spirit. I moved round in front of her and contemplated those naked parts which had hitherto remained hidden from me — and was swiftly joined by my beloved partner.

Her front was a beautiful as her rear, with delightfully round and full bosoms, tipped by nipples that were delicately pink in shade and perfectly round in form; a fashionably slender waist supported by a nicely curved belly; a neat but thick triangle of black hair at its base. sturdy, round thighs and shapely legs. She was still sobbing and shaking but far less violently.

'Victoria. You have now — obviously for the first time — experienced the type of chastisement which every young girl should be acquainted with at least once, although in your case, once a week would have been more appropriate!

I do not think that you enjoyed it.' At this, she shook her head violently and I imagine that the garbled sounds which emerged from her gag were meant as fervent affirmation. 'I am sure that you are intelligent enough to understand why your behaviour has been unnacceptable, so I have no intention of wasting my precious time in listing your many faults. Suffice it to say that I will tolerate nothing less than an immediate and marked improvement. To ensure this, I have asked Lady Arabella to keep me informed of your progress. I have also asked her to bring you back here in one week, when I have every intention of putting you across my lap, laying your delightfully fat bottom bare and spanking it soundly. Do *not* make those unladylike noises at me! I shall continue the regime of regular and pertinent chastisement until I am convinced that you have permanently mended your ways. You have beauty. Your form is, I am sure, the sort that men dream of. But, until you have learned that a warm smile is the most important aspect of any beautiful face; until you appreciate that a happy and open heart has more effect on others than the most perfect figure, you will attract nothing but unpleasantness. Now, your bottom will have cooled down considerably now. I am going to warm it up again.'

The walls and sobs were louder than ever and she struggled with desperate violence. However, it was to no avail because my short, sharp smacks had no trouble in landing on the generous, if excessively mobile target before me and I carried on for a good 15 minutes until my arm was aching, my hand burning and her bottom almost purple in hue.

We then unfastened her but with the gag and blindfold still in place, and half carried her upstairs to one of the small spare bedrooms, where we could lay her down and gently apply a soothing balm to her buttocks. When at last she slipped into a sort of sleep, I fixed a strong leather belt around her waist and attached a chain to the buckle in the small of her back and then padlocked the other end of the chain to a bolt in the wall. It was a hot evening and the room was almost too warm, so we left her to sleep stark-naked, helpless and alone with her thoughts.

We had our usual supper in my room but did not spank Connie when she made the accustomed mistake in serving us. As soon as we were alone, I lay Arabella face down on the bed, tucked up her skirts, lowered her drawers and without any preamble, gently parted her big cheeks, gazed lovingly at her beautiful little bottom-hole for a moment and then bent down and thanked her for bringing Victoria into my life.

I soon wormed my hand between her thighs and found her little spot, knowing that she loved the combined 'assault' on both orifices as much as I, and it took less than a minute to bring her to her climax. The feel of her spendings on my fingers added to my joy. The evening's events had exhausted us both and we slept in each other's arms till daybreak.

CHAPTER 11

Beating Victoria had been intensely satisfying and when Arabella escorted her back the following morning I felt very much at a loss. As the day wore on, my thoughts returned to the vision of her wobbling, crimson bottom with increasing frequency and I found it hard to devote myself properly to my various duties. So much so that when I aggravated Aunt Grace to the limit of her tolerance, I accompanied her to the drawing room for the well-merited spanking I was about to receive with feelings akin to relief. It was as though I needed to pay for the pleasures of dominating by being dominated myself. By this time I had lost count of the spankings I had had, and it would perhaps have been natural for me to have found the preliminaries merely routine. I cannot deny that I had lost all sense of modesty about revealing my body, especially to the other members of the household, but on this occasion, I felt all the many sensations involved with most of the keenness of a complete novice.

She bared my bottom with brisk efficiency and I felt myself blush at the exposure. She began the punishment at once and the burning made itself felt in my flesh from the very first blow. And yet my moans were not in protest, for I welcomed the shame and the pain and thrust my buttocks up at her in open invitation.

When eventually she finished with me, I flew to my room and stripped down to just my stockings, moved the looking glasses and gazed fervently at the vivid redness of my bottom and the dramatic contrast with the whiteness of the skin both above and below, watching my hands rub away the smarting. Then the tendrils of desire awoke and I lay back on my bed, my thighs spread languidly apart and slowly stroked my way up the silken skin on their insides until I had found my way into the tight moist slit of my cunny and onto the gently weeping little button.

I had needed both releases and was then able to return to my usual cheerful self. For a time. I still missed my Arabella. I began to long for another opportunity to punish Victoria again, or if not her, another girl whose behaviour was such that I could ignore my instinct for kindness and shared pleasures and spank to punish. It became harder and harder to suppress the gloomy certainty that Arabella meant more to me than I to her and I found that I was often lying awake in the early hours, my feverish imagination planning ever more involved entertainments, anticipating the spicy joys of having my bottom bared and lewdly proffered to the discerning eyes of our guests. I longed for the biting sting of one of Aunt Grace's elegant birch rods and the increasing absorption in the waves of pain which seemed to be the only cure for my aching heart.

The entertainments became even more important to me. Happily my ideas always found favour with Aunt Grace and the maids and, judging from the steady stream of guineas which had already filled my money box three times, with the guests as well.

For example, we enacted a 'play' inspired by the children's rhyme about the old woman who lived in a shoe and had so many children that she did not know what to do and 'whipped them all soundly and sent them to bed'. It was fun both to plan – decorating the stage to suggest a giant shoe proved a worthy challenge to our varied talents – and to act out. Aunt Grace played the harassed Old Lady while we all romped around her in noisy mischief until the obvious finale. To vary the performance a little, Elspeth and Bridget as the slenderest among us dressed up as boys, so when we all had to stand in a line and bare our bottoms for the whipping, there were two pairs of lowered trousers to set off the more usual array of raised skirts. I gathered later that the sight of their small but very feminine bottoms peeking out from rumpled masculine apparel found great favour among those guests present. I played the oldest of the children and so was given the hardest whipping with a fair-sized rod and I could not prevent myself bucking and howling across her ample lap as my buttocks were made to feel as though they had been attacked by a swarm of bees.

My spirits were restored for at least a week after that and were then lifted to new heights soon afterwards when I received a simple note from Arabella:

> My Darling Annie,
> I hope that you will be pleased to lear that Victoria's behaviour has improved beyond recognition since you dealt with her so beautifully. She is, however, showing signs of regression and I feel that she should be punished again. Would tomorrow evening be convenient, at six o'clock? I do hope so.
> With my love,
> Yours,

It was, of course, very convenient! I found that waiting for the appointed hour was not in the least difficult. I did not even ponder overmuch on how I should administer the punishment. I was confident that the close accord between Arabella and myself would help me and I knew that Victoria's demeanour would be of prime influence in my approach and the subsequent severity of the spanking. In the meantime, I busied myself cheerfully with several nondescript duties and, as an hors-d'oeuvre to the for-thcoming main event, found good excuses to give both Maria and Elspeth a brisk spanking. This proved to be especially enjoyable, in that I made them bend side by side right over the back of a convenient settee, with their heads on the seat and their naked bottoms thrust high in the air, while I spanked them in turn. I found the viewpoint charming and was fascinated by the contrast in the feel of their very different bottoms, my hand bouncing off Elspeth's firm flesh and sinking into Maria's. I also derived considerable pleasure from an inspired finale. I made them move round to the other side of the sofa, kneel on the seat with their knees well apart and their backs arched downwards so that their clefts were yawning widely and I could easily see their bottom-holes, Maria's big and dark, Elspeth's small and pink. A few careful smacks to each made them both squeak in delight and felt exceedingly pleasant to my fingertips inspiring some rather delightful thoughts for future treats for Arabella!

They arrived punctually at six o'clock and Connie escorted them to my room. Arabella and I kissed each other as friends not lovers and then we stood alongside each other and surveyed the wayward Victoria. I was told, in calm and unemotional tones, that after a period of almost exemplary behaviour, she had lost her temper with the maid Arabella had placed at her disposal, had smacked her face and pulled her hair viciously. It had required all Arabella's diplomatic skills to prevent the excellent girl from giving her notice.

I listened to my love's low, soft voice and watched the miscreant. To her credit, she made no attempt to deny or justify her actions. Her face reddened with either shame or anger and she stared fixedly at the floor until Arabella had finished, when she raised her head and stared challengingly at me.

'I imagine that you plan to strip me for another beating.'

I returned her stare implacably, while my mind rapidly considered the import of her reaction. She had laid particular emphasis on the word 'strip' and I surmised that it was her nakedness as much as the pain which had affected her.

'No,' I replied eventually. She looked at me with hope softening her expression and giving me a brief glimpse of her natural beauty. 'I shall not strip you. Nor will I beat you. Wait here.'

I sensed that Arabella was both puzzled and disappointed and so took her quietly aside and whispered my thoughts to her, to which she responded with no more than a gleam in her eyes, thus prolonging Victoria's suspense. I swept out of the room and down to the kitchen, where I announced my plans to Cook and the maids who were conveniently gathered there. Leaving a row of happy grins behind me, I returned to my room.

'Follow me, Victoria,' I ordered. The three of us moved steadily downstairs and when we reached our destination. I took the precaution of taking our victim's elbow to guide her firmly over the threshold. It proved a sensible thing to do, for as she saw the row of eagerly shining faces and the armless chair carefully placed sideways-on before them, it did not take long for the significance to strike her. She swayed, stiffened and a wail of dismay burst from her pale lips. I tightened my grip and led her forcefully towards the waiting chair, sat down and transferred my grip from her elbow to her hand, which I grasped with almost cruel tightness. I looked silently up at her to give Arabella time to find a good vantage point, noting the moistening eyes, the quivering lips and the pallor of trepidation. Then I smiled at her. Warmly.

'No, Victoria, as I said, I am neither going to strip you nor beat you. What I am going to do is to put you across my knees and give you a sound spanking on your bare bottom. Lift up your skirts and petticoats, drop your drawers and put yourself in position. *Now*!'

I said no more but simply stared grimly at her, while she fought back the tears of shame and humiliation. I did not even move when she flung a glance back over her shoulder as though to assess her chances of making a successful escape. She evidently remembered the penalty she had paid for resisting the first time and, with a sob of despair, she lowered her trembling hands and began the onerous task of pulling up her clothing. She sobbed again when I made her hold them well above her waist before lowering her drawers, sickened by the knowledge that Aunt Grace, Uncle George, Cook and all the maids would be receiving a perfect view of her bottom as she exposed it.

I was quite happy to wait before seeing it. I held her anguished gaze as she fumbled at the drawstrings then blatantly lowered my eyes so that she would see me looking at her cunny and thighs as she bared herself. And then, to add to her torment, I made her stand there for several moments while she was carefully studied. Even that did not satisfy me. I wanted to see her bare bottom while she was standing upright as I had always found that it is thus that the female posterior is at its most appealing — perhaps because my statue was posed standing. She burst into tears and hung her head. But obeyed and shuffled round, her movements making her fat bottom wobble most delightfully.

I had no regrets over my action. I could see the audience's eyes absorbing the sight of her dramatically dark little triangle and, allowing myself a smile of contentment, I sat back and reacquainted myself with my target. Strangely, when seen looming nakedly from under the folds of skirt and petticoat, it looked even chubbier than it had when she had been completely bare. Her fear was making her tremble like a leaf in a storm and muscular spasms shook her opulent globes. With the lovely, pure whiteness of her skin, the fleshiness of the buttocks themselves, supporting sturdy shapeliness of her thighs and with the tightness of the dividing cleft, Victoria's bottom was a sight for sore eyes and the prospect of spanking it as soundly as she richly merited grew ever more enticing. Eventually I broke the tense silence and bade her to lay herself across my lap. Red-faced, silent tears rolling down her cheeks, she stumbled the short distance to me and plumped herself clumsily down. I was obliged to waste more time adjusting her position so that her body was gently curved, supported evenly between hands and feet and with her bare bottom centrally placed on my thighs. I patted her cheeks thoughtfully.

'Your behaviour has shown a marked improvement, my dear. In recognition of this, I shall treat your lovely fat bottom much more leniently than I did before. It *will* sting. But I want you to show my friends that you can be brave. Try and keep still so that I can direct my spanks accurately. Do not attempt to evade your due punishment. And let this be a warning to you — I shall not be as merciful if you slide back into your old ways again.'

On that last word, I administered the first spank onto the base of her nearer buttock and thrilled anew at the unique sensation as a slight sting warmed my hand when it sank into the yielding softness of her naked flesh. I watched the pink mark flare up and repeated the dose on her other cheek. My spanks were reasonably punishing, although nowhere near as hard as the ones I had given her before, when I had had the advantage of being able to deliver them with a full sweep of my arm but, even so, they rang out loudly. They made her bottom quiver quite violently and her fine skin reddened more quickly than any other I had known.

214

Within two minutes or so, she was bobbing about on my lap and her flesh was the colour of a summer sunset. She had taken the first dozen or so silently but by now was wailing and moaning incessantly, begging for an ending to her pain. Needless to say, I took no notice of her pleas. Instead, I began to cover the entire length and breadth of her big bottom with lighter smacks but delivered in very rapid succession, knowing that the pain from this manner of spanking has a maddening quality because there is no respite at all. It is, however, extremely tiring, so when even the firm pressure of my left arm across the small of her back was no longer sufficient to hold her down, I was glad of the opportunity to rest awhile. I stood her upright, parted my legs, hitched up my skirts a little, brought her round so that she was standing between my thighs and bent her firmly over the left one, with the right one over her legs, clamping them firmly down. I then pushed the upper part of her body until her face was resting on the stone floor. She was now bent at a far more acute angle. Apart from being more restricted in her movements her bottom was spread out noticeably further, to the extent that the cleft opened out and exposed a delectable strip of white flesh between the twin red cheeks.

I immediately aimed a series of deliberate blows from top to bottom of the whiteness and her wails testified to the effectiveness of my onslaught, encouraging me to move directly back up from the bottom to the top. It was time for a more contemplative study, so I paused, easing the burn in my right hand with my left, and gazed down on the crimson area of intimate flesh jutting so provocatively up at me. It was still red rather than violet and certainly looked extremely sore. But she still struggled against my grip until her weariness overcame her and she slumped dejectedly. I then noticed a strange movement of her flesh, around her cleft, a few inches up from the junction of her thighs. I realised that, in her pain, she was pumping the muscle of her anus in and out, presumably because her exhaustion, combined with the severely bent position of her bottom, made it impossible for the muscles of her buttocks to move. I was intrigued. I had never been aware of my bottom-hole acting in that way, even under the hardest of whippings. It also made me want to look at the one part of her rear end which I had not yet seen, and it was a simple matter to open her up and peer down at a surprisingly pink and hairless little orifice. She was too broken even to protest at this intrusion. Her sobs intensified slightly during the period of examination but that was all.

I was sated. I had spanked her to my entire satisfaction and seen her bottom-hole. I had no desire to make love to her in any way, probably because, for all her beauty, her character did not appeal to me. Arabella's assuredly did and after we had bathed Victoria and sent her home in a hansom cab, we retired to my bed, where it became Arabella's turn to assume the mantle of authority. She made me undress her with agonising lasciviousness, kissing each area of delectable flesh as it was uncovered. She forced her stiff nipples into my mouth; encouraged me to suck in a mouthful of delicious buttock flesh and nibble it. I was ordered to try and push my tongue as far as I could up her bottom-hole, before slipping my middle finger up to the hilt in its warm, clinging passage, feeling the tight, pulsating grip of the muscle as she had her first spend. Then she made me undress before her. I had to lie on my belly as she squatted over me and caressed my back, thighs and buttocks with her bottom. I groaned happily at the delightful sensation of tight softness on my skin, with the occasional contrast of moist hairiness as her cunny brushed against me. She turned me over and stood proudly astride my head, treating me to a breathtaking view of her round bottom jutting in cloven arrogance from her thighs — and the delicately mossed cleft of her love-nest in front of it — before lowering herself onto my mouth and enveloping my face in silken skin and scented flesh as I thrust my avid tongue into whichever orifice she chose to place on it.

She climaxed three times before sinking exhausted into my loving arms, where she rested awhile and then caressed me in like manner. Perhaps because of the excitement I had found in spanking Victoria, I wearied more quickly than she. And we slept entwined until Elspeth brought in our supper, after which we revived to the extent that we were strong enough to give her apple-tight little bottom a vigorous spanking, then stripped her as naked as we were, tossed her onto the bed and leapt on top of her to taste her sweet flesh. The climax for all of us came when we had her on her back, her legs folded onto her bosom so that her cunny and anus were openly displayed and had taken an orifice each with our tongues. Her screams were so piercing, her ecstasy so obvious that we had to take turns to be the 'victim'. I was last and so by the time my turn was due, my love juices were in full flow. Thus my climax was again upon me more rapidly than I would have wished, because the sensation of having both bottom-hole and love button simultaneously and expertly stimulated was more than a little pleasing!

At last we slept — the sleep of the 'just after', to borrow Elspeth's somewhat indelicate phrase.

Saying good-bye to Arabella the following morning was as painful as ever and I was fortunate that my melancholy was soon dissipated by an unexpected development. I had asked Aunt Grace to buy me some lace when she next visited London and on her return, she summoned me and confessed that she had completely forgotten my request.

'It really is unforgivable of me, Annie my dearest. I

217

am truly sorry.'

The forgiving words died before they had passed my lips as I looked at her. There was an appeal in her eyes. One that took me moments to comprehend. And when I guessed for what she seemed to be pleading, my heart stopped. I felt sure that she wanted me to punish her. I drew a deep breath, looked across at Uncle George and saw a secret little smile flitter across his face. I knew that I was right and, facing her with a stern expression, told her that I felt that she had been grossly negligent of my needs and that she would now have to pay the traditional penalty. With my head spinning, my heart pounding, I tried to take charge in this totally unexpected turn of events. Aunt Grace had always seemed out of reach; apart from that early fitting session with Mrs Savage when I had slightly rued the fact that I had not even attempted to catch a glimpse of her rear in those surprisingly audacious drawers, I had not even dreamed of any form of carnal contract with this remotely beautiful woman. And now I was suddenly in the position where she wanted me to spank her.

I did, to my discredit, stutter and stumble to begin with, and it was not until she was settled across my lap and I had raised her skirts that I began to regain some composure. When I looked down on the unslitted drawers, with the central section drawn into the cleft so that the shape of her handsome buttocks was clearly visible, I at last started to feel a surge of excitement, which proceeded to increase apace as I eased the fine silk down to her knees, ran my eyes over the swelling mounds and tight cleft then ran my hands over the soft skin and paddled the yielding flesh. When I plucked up courage to pull her cheeks apart and look at her neat and discreet bottom-hole and felt the increased pressure against my fingers as she raised her bottom to me, my heart sang with pleasure and I set about her delicious flesh with a will.

It was by no means the most expert spanking that I had administered and I did not seem to be able to detach myself from my emotions sufficiently to really enjoy it. For the first part, anyway. I was simply aware of nothing but her big bare bottom as it wobbled its way to a splendid red before my eyes. After a while, however, I was able to gather my senses somewhat and to appreciate that the breadth of her rear was preventing me from doing full justice to it, in that her left flank was tucked so tightly against my belly that I could only reach the central area. I made her rise, strip down to just her stays and stockings and bend over the back of the chair, giving me room to deal with her properly. I finished with her kneeling up, sticking her bottom right out with her anus exposed.

Uncle George had been an enthusiastic spectator throughout, making several pertinent comments, for example that her right buttock was redder than her left, and so forth. I found that his presence began to add immeasurably to my enjoyment of the occasion and, towards the end, my own bottom started to tingle. And when I was bending over her fully spread cheeks, directing those special little smacks to the pink-brown centre, my own anus seemed to recall its first penetration by a cock. Suddenly I wanted to be buggered again and, after a final flurry of smacks on that lovely little fold between bottom-hole and cunny, I knelt down behind Aunt Grace and covered her taut buttocks with wet kisses before pleading with her to let Uncle George plug me.

'Be delighted to, my dear,' said Uncle George.

'Only if you give me many more kisses,' said Aunt Grace . . .

So after my lips and tongue had made her wriggle and sigh with pleasure, I stood up and began tearing my clothes off with feverish impatience, only stopping when Aunt Grace walked over to the far side of the room and bent down to open the lowest drawer of the bureau against the wall. The sight of her red bottom as she walked briskly about her business, its swaying and wobbling between the narrowed waist above and sturdy white thighs below, was a magnificent sight. Then she returned with her little box of dildoes, I knelt on the end of the chaise longue and presented my bottom to be oiled and warmed up with the largest implement in her collection. Then I buried my face in my hands and moaned aloud as I felt the warmth of his soft-skinned manhood nuzzling against me before sliding all the way to its hilt in one breath-taking thrust.

To make the occasion even more memorable, Aunt Grace lay down in front of me, with her bare bottom right before my face, so that I had the double pleasure of him working expertly away in my bottom while my hands, eyes, nose and tongue were fully occupied with hers.

After we had all climaxed, I felt exceedingly privileged when they invited me to join them in a bath — which turned into a very merry and rather messy romp, during which I actually dared to smack Uncle George's nice little bottom, and had mine spanked by him in return — and then to go to bed with them, where I was suitably instructed in some new ways to please a man, culminating in an initially startling moment when he spent his passion in my mouth. I was not sure whether the sensation of hot spurts of his come striking the back of my mouth was a pleasant one, nor whether the salty taste was to my liking. But I was slightly disappointed when he proved incapable of rising to the occasion again to give me a second helping!

So when some week or so later, Aunt Grace asked me if I could entertain a male visitor, I was more confident than ever that I would be able to please and satisfy him. I bathed and dressed with especial care and was waiting quite eagerly for him. But even so, I was unprepared for the impact he made upon me. He was tall, well-built, with hair the colour of ripe corn. His clothes were of obvious quality and most elegantly tailored. All this I took in with the first sweep of my eyes. Then they were held by the most captivating smile I had ever come across. I am positive that my heart stopped.

'Hello, Annie.'

My heart melted. I tried desperately to recover some equilibrium. I managed to return his smile. To say hello. I could not ask his name and was hugely relieved when he told me. Philip. It immediately became my favourite. He sat next to me on my bed, took my hand and we sat gazing silently into each other's eyes for an age. My mind was in complete confusion, because apart from my over-whelmingly strong feelings for him, there was a strange familiarity about him. Yet I knew that we had never met. Then my puzzlement ceased to matter. Nothing mattered. For he leaned forward and kissed me and from that moment, there was only him. I was no longer the sophsticated young woman of the world but a shy young girl who has managed to snatch a few brief moments alone with a lover during a Ball.

My memories of the ensuing hours are confused. I know that he helped me undress. And was smilingly gentle. And he did not mock me when I tried to help with his clothes and my trembling fingers made me clumsy. His kisses set me on fire like no other's had done. And I revelled in his firm muscularity and breathed in his scent in gusty inhala-tions. His manhood was hot, long, smooth and rigid and I thrilled to its feel. I suddenly wanted him in me proper-ly and when I felt him nudge it against the aching slit which was its proper destination I was not able to resist him. But he spared me the dilemma by hooking the backs of my knees with his arms and pushing my splayed legs onto my breast, elevating and spreading my bottom. He then moved his cock downwards and thrust it into my bottom-hole.

I had never been buggered in this position and in some ways it was less comfortable than the usual manner. Except that when he thrust himself in to the hilt, his belly rubbed against my cunny and that was delicious. And we could kiss. He moved his bottom up and down and kept his mouth glued to mine until the pressure of my tight and well-oiled passage proved too much and he spasmed and I felt the spattering of his spending deep within me.

Too soon he had to leave. We had not exchanged a single word since he had told me his name and all he said afterwards was, 'I shall see you again, my beauty.' And my heart was at peace.

Understandably, I could not wait to tell Arabella all about my feelings and waited on her reappearance with growing impatience. To my relief, it was only a few days later that I received another note from her, asking me to call round as soon as it was convenient. Guessing that Victoria had erred again, I asked Cook to summon a cab and dressed suitably with indecent haste.

My guess was correct as the errant girl's sulky, woebegone expression confirmed as I entered the drawing room. She had, apparently, been caught red-handed stealing from the great aunt's purse and the old lady had said that unless we finally cured her of her evil ways, she would invoke the full weight of the law. We sent the criminal to her room, ordered tea and discussed the matter at some length. Eventually I suggested that she should be brought back to Aunt Grace's house, kept chained naked to a bed until we were ready to punish her. Apart from the salutory effect on Victoria, I needed time to think of a suitably novel, yet effective punishment.

In total silence, we drove the ashen-faced Victoria back, stripped her stark-naked and chained her securely but loosely to the bed. We then asked if we could see Aunt Grace and, on being warmly welcomed, the three of us

222

settled down to a light supper and an earnest discussion.

'It seems to me,' Aunt Grace said eventually, 'that exhibiting her nakedness touched her almost as much as the pain. When you spanked her before us all and, having bared her bottom, turned her round so that she was facing us, she saw us all looking at her front and her embarrassment was most evident. At the same time, of course, this time the pain must be considerably greater than before. She must suffer enough to remember it whenever she is tempted to stray. And yet it is no less important that she is comforted afterwards. Arabella, you must praise her qualities; show her the benefits of affection; guide her towards sharing your outlook. Be her friend and confidante . . . Annie, perhaps the cane might provide the answer.'

I considered her suggestion carefully. Aunt Grace had obtained a few choice malacca canes from the schoolmistress sisters who had spanked me so soundly some months back, and we had employed them in one of our entertainments. Elspeth, Bridget and I had been schoolgirls summoned to the Headmistress and soundly spanked for some misdemeanour, after which further and more serious crimes were brought to light. We were each made to bend over the table for twelve strokes of the cane on our naked bottoms. It had stung like the very devil and so proved to be a most satisfactory and exciting challenge but we had decided not to use them again. The main reason being that for all the dramatic effect of the instantaneous appearance of the red stripes, the overall redness of a spanked or birched bottom was more appealing. It was also a factor that the pain of each stroke made a dozen about the maximum we could tolerate. And the consequent bruises took far longer to fade than the tracery of marks left by a light birch rod.

'If you make the strokes reasonably light,' she continued,

'you can draw the punishment out for a fair length of time and cause her sufficient pain without damage — and if the bruises last for days, it does not matter for she does not have to present a snow-white bottom for an entertainment soon after her beating.'

It was a sound suggestion and I agreed that a caning would be ideal. I then recalled the maid's birthday and the 'ordeal' of being fastened to the bench for all to play with. A memory of the plump and comely Maria on her back with her legs drawn up and Connie slapping her broad buttocks flashed through my mind and I described it to Arabella and Aunt Grace.

'Yes,' enthused Arabella, 'her cunny would be on display. She would hate that.'

'And her bottom-hole,' added Aunt Grace. 'You will have to be careful not to land the cane on either, Annie.'

'I think we should practise,' I said. All three of us bustled about with enthusiasm, first stripping down to just boots and stockings (and admiring Aunt Grace's fetching garters), then moving a long footstool which would serve as a whipping bench into the centre of the room, finding a cane and some lengths of ribbon. To add to the air of excitement, there was the happy sight of my two favourite women in Eve's costume, with their bobbing bosoms, gleaming white skin and bouncing, wobbling, bending bottoms.

It proved to be a most enjoyable exercise. (Aunt Grace's bottom was of such splendidly ample proportions that her legs had to be tied far further back to expose her fully than either Arabella's or mine.) We were also able to arrive at the right degree of force with which to apply the cane. Sufficient to leave a distinct weal on the tautened skin and to make the recipient gasp at the sting, but without running the risk of severely bruising, or even cutting, the sensitive flesh.

Certainly when I was stretched out to receive, I was fully aware of my nakedness. It was one thing to be in a similar position for a loving friend to run his or her tongue between one's cheeks but quite another to be whipped that way. The feeling of utter vulnerability was overwhelming.

The preparations did not take long. Chairs were laid out so that everybody could sit and get a fine view of the bench positioned before them, while Arabella and I unchained Victoria and led her off for a bath. She protested volubly about her treatment, tried to demand that she should be able to bathe in privacy, objected when we took turns to wash her, cursed when we bent her over to soap her bottom and generally made a nuisance of herself, to the extent that when we were brushing her hair, I was moved to smack the palm of each hand with the brush, which gave me an idea for another suitable implement for an errant bottom!

But as we led her down the corridor towards the staircase, she realised that her punishment was imminent and immediately began to plead for clemency: I stopped, held her naked, trembling body against the wall and spoke with a cold fury.

'You have had two warnings, Victoria. Neither has resulted in more than a temporary cessation in your wicked ways. This is your last chance. Now come along.'

We took an arm each and hustled the wailing girl into the kitchen, where the sight of the eager audience added greatly to the volume of the lamentations. We placed her on the bench with her feet to the chairs, heaved her legs back, fastened a ribbon to each knee and tied them firmly to the end of the bench. Her wrists were bound above her head and a strap fixed round her waist. She was trussed up like a chicken, incapable of any but the slightest movement. We then moved back behind the onlookers to ensure that her position was right. It was perfect. She looked

225

dreadfully vulnerable, with her broad white buttocks providing an excellent target and the very visible cunny and anus in between cruelly emphasising the shame of her total exposure. There could be no doubt that Aunt Grace had been correct in her assumption that she felt the humiliation keenly, for amidst her broken sobs, she was pleading with me to position her more decently and offering to accept a really severe flogging on her back rather than her bottom.

I naturally ignored her, picked up the springy length of cane, took up my position and started. I employed wristy flicks rather than full-blooded sweeps of my arm, but even so, the red lines sprang up eagerly on her snow-white flesh. And it obviously hurt her. The impact of the first few made her gasp aloud with the shock but as I gradually increased the strength of the blows she was soon screeching like a barn owl and writhing in her bonds.

I covered every available inch of both naked buttocks, from measured strokes across the gaping cleft, to sharp little flicks of the tip of the innermost curves near her anus. I shut my ears to her shrieks and howls and concentrated wholly on the spreading redness as the weals joined up and then overlapped. Painful ridge upon painful ridge, each one purveying its own bite and adding to the waves of agony left by its predecessors. I saw where the folds at the tops of her thighs had opened out but had left discernible wrinkles. With infinite care, I left red weals along the whole length of both, just missing the hairy lips of her pouting cunny. I changed sides to even up the effects of the cane's tip. Eventually I grew tired and noticed that her exposed anus was pushing itself in and out at me in a mute expression of her desperation. I placed the implement on the floor and perched on the edge of the bench, looking down on her tear-ravaged and scarlet face.

'Are you truly sorry now, Victoria?' I asked softly. She

could not speak, but her forlorn expression was eloquent enough. I gently stroked her cheek and she pressed it against my palm and her tears flowed faster but they were no longer from pain and anger. Her remorse was, I felt sure, genuine. I moved my hand onto her bottom, smoothing it over the hot and deeply ridged flesh.

'Is this not nicer than being beaten? Would you not prefer to be caressed than thrashed?' She nodded, trying to blink away the tears. I let my fingertips brush against her bottom-hole. 'You can look beautiful, you know. Strange to relate, you do so at this moment. There is an appealing softness about you, unlike the hatred that mars your features normally. Love and you will be loved in return. What I trust will be your final punishment is nearly over. You have been soundly whipped but as a reminder of my power, I intend turning you over and giving you a spanking to finish you off properly. And to prove to you that your bottom can take more punishment that you thought possible. I shall untie you and then I want you to turn over to your belly and offer me your bare bottom. Keep it as still as you can. Do not tighten it. We want to see it wobble when it is spanked. Understand?'

She nodded again. I patted her anus and her eyes opened at the unexpected sensation. Then I unfastened her wrists, waist and finally her legs, gently laying them flat so as not to thump her sore buttocks onto the bench. Groaning as the movements sent hot barbs through her flesh, she obeyed me and made a delightful sight, with her closed thighs leading one's eyes up to the crimson swellings of her bottom, which jerked and quivered involuntarily before she managed to bring it under some form of control.

My spanking was no more than a token one. I had wanted to test her obedience and, as she had not uttered one word, or made a single gesture of protest, there was no need to drive the lesson any further home. Her bottom felt strange under my hand. The ridges left by my firmer strokes added a very different quality to the flesh. But I did enough to make it wobble very prettily for a minute or so and it was certainly redder when I finally told her to rise.

Arabella and I escorted her to my room and immediately applied healthy quantities of Cook's special lotion. As it took effect, her groans changed to sighs and, when we had done, she turned her head and thanked us. We stared happily at each other, certain that we had succeeded in bringing her back onto the straight and narrow path. We both kissed her, told how happy we were to have a nicer Victoria to get to know and love and then returned to the kitchen, where everybody was still in a state of some excitement.

The maids, all of whom had come to adore my Arabella, sensed her pent-up emotions and after we had been plied with wine, guilelessly 'confessed' to all manner of terrible sins of omission and commission. With the broadest, happiest grin I had yet seen on her, she settled down to spank them all. I thoroughly enjoyed watching her ecstatic face and the array of varied bottoms on which it gazed and was bold enough to suggest when the last pair of healthily reddened buttocks straightened up, that they should show their true repentance by each kissing the hand which had chastised them so effectively . . . then the thighs which had supported their wanton bodies so comfortably . . . then the bottom which had suffered so much under their weight. With a squeal of delight, my beloved flung her skirts up, tore her drawers down and bent over the edge of the huge table. With matching squeals, the maids stripped off their disordered clothing and lined up to bury their faces in her bounteous flesh.

When at last we returned to my room, Victoria was fast asleep. Silently we made our toileltte, stripped and joined her, spending the rest of the night cuddling her and starting the process of making her feel loved and wanted.

CHAPTER 12

Punishing Victoria had been an interesting diversion, although it no longer made me wish for further experiences of the same nature. I did not feel any desire to become a governess or schoolmistress and thus have the opportunity to punish girls regularly. Spanking was more than ever a sensual experience and ideally one shared equally by the participants. I found increasing pleasures in the entertainments. My longing for Arabella had been transferred in part to Phillip and having my bottom publicly bared and beaten helped me to forget my yearnings more effectively than anything else. Every time my drawers slipped down my thighs and my plump white buttocks were exposed to the guests, I imagined that Phillip was watching. When Aunt Grace's hand or birch smacked into my hungry flesh, I wished the hand was his. Only when the pain became so strong that my whole attention was devoted to absorbing and conquering it, could I come near to forgetting him. Or when later I was curled up in my bed, with the softness of a maid's naked bottom nestling against my thighs and belly and with my own, equally naked bottom throbbing warmly behind me, then I slept with heart and mind less troubled.

Arabella came to see me whenever possible and, although we romped and caressed with all our old fervour, the main blessing to me was that I could talk to her with a freedom and openness I had never experienced before.

But it was our caresses and our loving which made for the best memories. She was at that time equal to Phillip in my affections and as her love of my bottom matched mine for hers, there was a rare unity of body and soul. Even after a considerable passage of time, when she looked smilingly into my eyes and quietly asked me to take my drawers down, my stomach hollowed and my throat constricted as noticeably as they had done the first time. When I lay face down and felt her soft hands grip my buttocks before prising them apart, before first blowing on my exposed bottom-hole and then greeting it joyfully with her hot tongue, the sensual waves coursed through me like the sea in a storm. And when I did the same to her and felt my fingers sink into her cheeks and that delicious, pinky-brown little opening pop into my view, my heart melted.

We learned to kiss and suck each other's cunnies at the same time and the combination of thrills was almost too much to bear. At one end, there was the silkiness of her inner thigh under my cheek, the glistening pink slit peeping through the damp tendrils of private hair and the tight and cloven curves of the lower part of her bottom right before my eyes. There was the heady scent of her excitement in my flaring nostrils. At the other end, I could feel her cheek on my thigh, and her hair tickling my skin, and the warmth of her breath on my throbbing cunny. Her hands held my buttocks and mine gripped hers. Then there was the smooth, hot, slippery wetness on my lips and tongue and, at the same time, her mouth on me made me gasp in ecstasy.

Sometimes we asked one or two of the maids to join us. But this became less frequent as our pleasures involved more and more around us alone. She spanked me more often than I spanked her, which suited me well. I had far greater opportunity to indulge myself in this particular

231

pleasure than she did and besides that, I found more joy in receiving from her than giving to her! Although, when I did turn her bottom up, the swelling curves of smooth white flesh pleased me to distraction. We were exceedingly happy together.

I did not, however, enjoy the company of male visitors in the way I had done before Phillip entered my life. Once his member had known my bottom-hole, I felt less need for other cocks inside it. My money box felt the deprivation far more than my bottom!

It was the times when I was neither recovering from an entertainment, nor anticipating one, that my life lacked sparkle. My favourite solace was my statue. In the hot days, it was my secret pleasure to remove my clothes, to stand with her on her plinth, to caress her cold, hard curves and to press my warm soft ones against her, sharing the refreshing spray from her fountain and whispering my secret hopes and desires into her sympathetic marble ear.

Then, one evening when I was in my room, having had my evening bath and in only my peignoir before dressing for dinner, there was a knock on the door. My listless, 'Come in' was hardly the most effusive of welcomes and when I looked up and saw the smiling faces of both Arabella and Phillip, my jaw dropped open, my heart leapt and I gaped stupidly at them as they entered. Phillip was carrying a tray laden with filled plates and Arabella two bottles of champagne and three glasses. As if the shock of seeing them together was not sufficient, I was suddenly struck by the resemblance between them. The similarity between the quality of their smiles was amazing. My brain whirled in confusion. They burst out laughing, placed their trays down on the table and stood in the middle of the room, still grinning broadly. With a squeal of delight, I threw myself into their open arms.

After a flurry of kisses and a babble of questions, we

sat down on the bed. In the confusion, my peignoir had slipped open and my front was fully exposed. They both looked, Arabella amused, Phillip with a distinct gleam in his eyes! Suddenly, and for the first time in an age, I felt discomfited with my nudity and scolded them both for staring at me. Even more amused, they solemnly turned their backs and let me dress.

With everything on a proper footing, we could seat ourselves comfortably and settle down to an evening which proved to be one of the happiest of my life. My first aim was to discover why they were visiting me together and, with her smile at its most mischievous, Arabella explained:

'We are first cousins, Annie my dear,' That explained why I had felt that Phillip was somehow familiar when I had met him. 'We have been the best and dearest of friends ever since we were tiny children. I knew that you and he were right for each other and I have been trying to engineer a meeting between the two of you for some months. Fortunately, Aunt Grace proved to be a staunch ally and helped to arrange everything. I gather from Cousin Phillip that it was a most agreeable evening.'

I was dumbstruck. That two of the dearest people in my life had connived together to plot against me behind my back appalled me. I raised my brimming glass and drank a silent toast to both! At the same time, I resolved that, having acquired a taste for the feel of my hand sinking into the ample flesh of Aunt Grace's bare bottom, I would use her complicity in the affair to reacquaint myself with that particular pleasure − and to do the same to Arabella at the first possible opportunity.

'Don't you think that it was uncommonly wicked of me, Annie?' continued Arabella. I stared at her, puzzled. Even if I had decided that she should be soundly spanked, I had dismissed the thought of doing it there and then instantly from my mind. However long and close their friendship,

I could not envisage that she would thank me for turning her up and baring her bottom in front of a man. There was a short silence and I could feel the gentle prickle of a blush on my face.

'I am in complete agreement with her,' said Phillip unexpectedly. 'Annie, your kind and generous nature has obviously blinded you to the depths to which my revered cousin can — and often does — sink. She *has* been uncommonly wicked. And not for the first time. My careworn and haggard features are the direct result of her fecklessness and I am weary with punishing her. I would be most grateful if you could deal with her, Annie. Perhaps chastisement from you will be more effective than it seems to have been at my hand.'

I gaped at them. Again. Arabella was grinning impishly and Phillip had affected the world-weary air of a man who had been overwhelmed by life's vicissitudes. My heart leapt with unholy glee at the realisation that my great enthusiasm appeared to be shared by the man I was increasingly certain that I loved. I also felt that lovely hollow feeling of intense excitement in my belly and my love-nest began to tingle. However, I assumed an expression of resigned disappointment at the revelations of her failings.

'Well, if you insist, Phillip. I shall do my best, although whether my frail woman's hand can succeed where your strength has not is doubtful. Come . . .'

I had been about to lecture her and describe in lurid detail precisely how I was planning to punish her when she skipped across to my chair, hoisted her skirts up to her waist, undid the ties of her drawers and flung herself across my lap as they fluttered down to her ankles. I looked down at her beautiful bottom. The plumpness of the white buttocks, that enticingly tight yet soft-looking cleft, the well-cut folds, all set my senses reverberating with a sensual

234

desire which was all the stronger for Phillip's presence. I looked up and smiled broadly at him and our eyes locked, sending messages to one another, in my case ones of hope that my feelings were not misplaced. All too soon, however, I became aware that Arabella was wriggling on my lap and I could vaguely hear her muttering to herself about the cruelty of keeping a poor girl waiting with her bare bottom sticking up in the air. I returned to the matter in hand and stroked the silken skin for a moment before giving her the most lovingly sensuous spanking I could manage.

I cupped my hand to fit the curves of her buttocks to lessen the smart while making them wobble properly and so agitate the most sensitive parts between and below. I made her spread her legs and so angled my hand that the fingertips landed vertically on the lowest section of her cleft; I used my left hand to hold her right cheek away from its sister and smacked into the open separation. I made her bounce energetically with a volley of proper spanks which pinkened her beautifully. I certainly enjoyed it; Arabella showed every sign of appreciating my attentions and Phillip's enigmatic smile and glittering eyes showed that he was perfectly happy in his role of spectator. As, of course, he should have been, given the outstanding beauty of her bottom.

After the dear girl had clambered to her feet, restored her clothing, kissed me and sat down — she emitted a little squeak as her bottom touched the seat of the chair but then revealed her true feelings by wriggling hard against the reception cushion — there followed one of those awkward silences, when nobody knows exactly which topic of conversation is most appropriate. Then we all started to talk at once, burst out laughing and the evening resumed its friendly and light-hearted course.

I discovered that Phillip's mother was sister to Arabella's

father, that he lived near Petworth in Sussex and had decided that life as an artist was infinitely preferable to helping with the family estates. He modestly admitted that he had already achieved a measure of success and had just completed a major commission for the Earl of T.

'But when I am 25,' he continued, 'I shall come into my inheritance and can then choose only those commissions which amuse me, which excludes painting the awful family of some respectable old codger. Unfortunately, I have two years to wait. On the other hand, this last masterpiece has been rewarding from the financial viewpoint, so that my next picture can be on a theme of my choosing.'

'And what is the theme you have chosen?' asked Arabella.

'The Three Graces,' he replied.

This did not surprise me unduly. Uncle George had shown me several versions in his collection and also had a miniature reproduction of a Greek statue of these three nude ladies in his study.

'Who will act as your models?' There was another little silence while I tore my thoughts away from the lovely statue.

'The two of you. And I will make up the features of the third by combining yours.'

Yet again, I felt a little awkward at the thought of Phillip seeing my unclad person. It did not make sense, for he had not only already seen it but had, of course, buggered me more than once. And in that deliciously revealing position! But, without truly understanding the reason, I wanted his approval for more than just my body.

Uncannily, he must have sensed my thoughts, for having said that he would make the necessary arrangements, the conversation turned to more sociable topics and we ate our supper, finished the champagne and passed the remainder of the evening in a warm glow of simple compa-

236

nionship. I found this a welcome change from the sensuality of the usual atmosphere in Aunt Grace's house. Admittedly, when they made their farewells, I kissed them both with an avidness which contained a large measure of sensuality. Phillip's parting words were that he would contact me with a firm invitation to be his model for one of the Graces. I began to look forward to it.

In the meantime, the only way I could conquer my restlessness was by wholeheartedly embracing the sensual delights so freely available to me. In my next discussion with Aunt Grace (and this time she was across *my* knees as we talked!) I opened up my heart to her and she was, as I would have expected, most sympathetic. While I stroked and patted her soft, white mounds, we discussed an entertainment which would be both challenging for me and rewarding for our guests. She eventually suggested that we could re-enact a judicial whipping, with me as the criminal. It took but a moment's thought for me to agree that this would indeed be a severe test of my fortitude.

During the ensuing silence, I looked down on the bare bottom spread out so enticingly over my lap and felt a wave of warm love for this extraordinary woman who had taken me into her house and led me so gently into a world of undreamt-of pleasures. But it was more than the pleasures themselves which had captured me. There was the pervading atmosphere of real love for all of us, from the shyest maid to her beloved husband. She was the dominant figure in all our lives but could adopt her present position, laid across my knees with her drawers down, without losing a shred of her natural dignity. I was years younger than she and yet did not feel in the least embarrassed. Having discovered the delights of the female bottom and experienced enough to know that hers was of exceptional quality, I could calmly enjoy the sight and feel of her naked flesh. As one who loved attentions to my rear, I could sympathise

237

with her enjoyment, which from her little sighs, the quivering of her ample mounds and the musky scent which stole up into the warm air from between her slightly parted thighs, was growing by the minute.

My burgeoning love for Phillip was starting to move my desires more towards male flesh, perhaps, but as I gazed down at Aunt Grace's bottom, I was again struck at my good fortune, in that providence had allowed me to find such pleasure from both sexes.

We discussed the details of the entertainment as I gently spanked her bare buttocks until they were glowing healthily and, once we had reached agreement, set business matters aside and concentrated on enjoyment. I began the proceedings by separating her hot cheeks until her delightful anus was positively pouting at me and I could tickle it with the tip of my forefinger. Then I remembered having seen a lovely quill pen on her writing table and this reminded me of the joyous ticking that Cook and the maids had administered to me. I bade her rise, we had a race to see which of us could strip naked the fastest and then I told her to kneel on the end of the chaise longue with her thighs well apart and her bottom sticking up and out as far as she could get it. I walked over to collect the pen, its curving white feather beckoning me, and aware that she would be watching me as I crossed the room, added a special sway to my walk, feeling the exaggerated movements of my bottom and shamelessly receiving pleasure from them.

As I returned, she knew at once what I was planning and moaned in keen expectation. I fetched a little footstool and placed it directly behind her, so that my vision was filled with the glorious sight of her out-thrust and very naked posterior. The bright pink cheeks were separated by the strip of whiteness that had been the inner parts while she was being spanked, and that strip was broken by the wrinkled brown orifice. Then a little fold of skin led my eyes downward, to the pouting cunny, its glistening pink slit showing through the dark hair, and thence to the broad white spread of her womanly thighs.

Sighing deeply with pleasure, I leaned forward and applied the stiff tip of the feather to the little knob that showed the end of her backbone and worked in little circles downwards. By the time I had opened up the wet lips of her love-nest to expose the tiny hooded button, she was crying out her ecstasy to the silent room and I watched in fascination as her climax came, her whole bottom jerking spasmodically and her bottom-hole pumping, until she slumped face down and panted her way to recovery.

We changed places and again I found that the pleasures of receiving were no less than those obtained from giving. She spanked me, which was especially enjoyable when laid across her naked lap and even more so when she took my left hand and tucked it under her bottom, where it was deliciously squashed by her soft weight. Then the tip of the feather honoured my stretched division, anus and cunny until I followed her in casting my length along with the knowing upholstery of her chaise longue.

She sat me on her lap afterwards, and I rested my head on her shoulder and felt some of the safeness of a child embraced by a loving mother. Until the feel of her naked skin against mine, especially that of my bottom on her lap, with her cunny hairs tickling the side of my buttock, encouraged me to cup the fullness of her breasts and we moved over to the soft rug by the fireplace and made love.

I was torn between conflicting needs and desires. Part of me longed for her touch on my body and part yearned to caress hers. By the time we had settled down, I wanted most to show my love for her by pleasing her first. I encouraged her onto her front and knelt beside her, moving my gaze downwards from her face, which rested on her folded arms but was turned towards me and smiling soft-ly. Her back was a white plain of smooth flesh, divided by the well-covered ridge of her spine then curving gracefully up to her bottom. The effects of my spanking had all but disappeared and it was merely a charmingly delicate pink in colour. Once again, I was struck by the special beauty of the feminine cleft. I had little knowledge of the male posterior but from those I had seen, the hairiness which characterises the stronger sex, does reduce the attractions of this particularly exciting and aesthetically rewarding part of the human anatomy. Aunt Grace's was lovely and my eyes devoured the soft tightness for several minutes before continuing their downward path to the long folds at the tops of her thighs, then onto those broad and shapely columns, her neat calves and dainty little feet.

I tucked my left hand under her breast and let my right one follow the journey my eyes had taken, marvelling at the variations in the feel of her different parts. Her flanks, for example, were notably cooler than the middle of her bottom and in the recesses of her cleft, the skin was warmer, softer and had a unique moistness. My lips followed my hand and my tongue retraced the same path. We then lay on our sides and kissed with growing pas-sion, while our hands groped, squeezed and stroked bosoms, bellies, thighs and buttocks. I introduced her to the delights of kneeling back to back and rubbing bottoms. We buried our heads between each other's thighs and kiss-ed the glistening love-nests in front of us. We each open-ed the other's bottom and thrust our tongues into the tightness of our bottom-holes. We both had enough climaxes to weary us.

Afterwards I mused on my feelings. If Phillip stirred me in new ways; if Elspeth was my mischievous scamp of a friend, whom I could order to do my will; if Arabella epitomised the all-embracing love that one girl can have for another, then Aunt Grace combined the role of second mother, confidante, mentor and sophisticated lover. If, for example, I opened up Elspeth's bottom to look at the hole, it was because I wanted her to obey me. With the other maids it was as much as anything to satisfy my curiosity as to the form and nature of their bottom-holes. With Arabella it was because she had the most beautiful anus in the world and I wanted her to know that I loved it as well as her. With Aunt Grace it was almost subservient. In each case I found pleasure in slipping my tongue into their bottoms. But it was a different pleasure, appealing to a different aspect of my character.

And so, I prepared myself for the entertainment on the following evening. Aunt Grace and I decided that we would set the 'scene' in Russia, where apparently the birch was still used to punish criminals. We had agreed that we would not be giving our guests full value if my flogging was the only event, so had developed a scenario where she would play the Governess of a penal establishment for younger female criminals and four of the maids would be dealt with before I made my appearance.

Uncle George had some talent as a carpenter — although where a gentleman would learn such skills I dared not ask — and had manufactured a splendid whipping bench for the occasion. It sloped downwards towards the head so that the errant buttocks were even more prominently upraised, and the end facing the audience was well padded and had ample space beneath to fasten the legs in a variety of positions and thus adjust the tightness of the bottom. Unupholstered, it was starkly functional and added considerably to the threatening atmosphere.

Four maids were to provide the hors d'oeuvre to my main course, namely Elspeth and Bridget as representatives of the more slender female shape, Connie as the medium

241

and Agatha as the plumpest and most wobbly. The action opened with the five of us before Aunt Grace while she detailed our various 'crimes' — mine was, of course, by far the most serious, in that I had made several derogatory statements about the Tsar — and then pronounced sentence. The other four were to be whipped, and I was to be flogged until she felt sure that I had fully repented. The curtains closed, the remaining maids changed the furniture and adjusted the lighting so that the stage became a good facsimile of a punishment cell and we reassembled. We were all dressed in coarse, shapeless dresses, thick knee-length stockings and nothing else, so baring our bottoms was a simple matter. One by one, the maids approached the waist-high bench, hoisted their skirts and stood quietly while Aunt Grace selected a rod from the iron bucket placecd under the bench. Each watched nervously, with bare bottom clenching in anticipation as the implement was tested by whistling it through several practice strokes. Then the first maid was signalled to present her buttocks and lay the upper half of her body on the bench, with her legs straight out behind her to present a nicely relaxed target and slightly parted to give the audience a glimpse of the furry lips between her thighs.

She was then birched, slowly and very effectively. It was not the first time I had watched a girl receiving the rod and although my view was restricted to the side of her bottom — we were all lined up well to the side of the bench — I thoroughly enjoyed the quiverings, the jerks and bouncing and the dramatic reddening of the naked flesh. I also noticed, and was fascinated by, the way Aunt Grace's rod and the punished bottom soon began to move in rhythmic concert. After each stroke, the buttocks momentarily clenched, then relaxed and raised themselves slightly as if to greet the next blow.

As each maid was punished, I moved my gaze

periodically from the girls' rumps to their faces and saw that their expressions changed as their whippings progressed. The tautness of their initial apprehensions changed to a softening of the features after the first stroke, which I knew from my own experiences was more pleasing than painful. Then as the biting smart increased, their eyes alternated between screwed up and wide open; their mouths between an 'O' of surprise and a rictus grin of pain.

When each had been dealt with, she had to come to my right and kneel on the floor, with her buttocks still naked, while the next victim was whipped. Agatha was the last and her big soft bottom wobbled noticeably more violently than the others and, judging from the muted sounds of approval behind me, excited the guests more than somewhat. Then it was my turn and all thoughts of other girls' bottoms left me as a white-hot lance of real fear was thrust into my bowels.

I could hardly breathe. My mouth filled with saliva but my throat was so constricted that I could only just swallow; then it dried up completely. My hands trembled as I lifted the skirts of my horrible dress to bare my bottom; my perceptions of my form seemed to change — I felt that I consisted of little more than a softly vulnerable, hugely shapeless and dreadfully naked pair of buttocks. I knew that they were quivering in my terror and, like the others, as I watched Aunt Grace pull one of the longer and thicker rods from the bucket and swish it thoughtfully, I clamped the cheeks together. I was almost glad when I was signalled to lay myself across the bench. The agony of the waiting was appalling. She tested me to the limit as she squeezed my nervous flesh to test its resilience and eased my thighs a little further apart to allow a better view of my cunny. Then her hands left me and I screwed my neck round to watch her as she set about flogging me as I had never been flogged.

She carefully measured the long rod against the centre of my quaking bottom and I shuddered slightly at the cool, damp, prickly touch. She slowly raised it to the level of her shoulder then paused, her eyes fixed glitteringly on the expanse of white flesh proffered so blatantly. She brought it down in a smoothly graceful sweep; it bit into me. It was notably more painful than her usual birch. I gasped aloud. She let her weapon hang down by her leg as she watched the mass of little red weals leap into view; she waited until the smart had faded to a tingling throb; she raised her arm, paused again and then struck the lower portions of my bottom. Then repeated the movements and hit the upper slopes. Three had been enough to cover the whole of my big bottom and now the supple twigs began to land on parts which were already flaming. I looked beyond her and could just make out the shining eager faces of the guests.

My neck began to ache, so I rested my head between my outstretched arms, closed my eyes and concentrated on the sensations invading my naked bottom. It was already burning brightly and I sensed that I was beginning to do the strange, rhythmic dance that I had noticed in the others. Aunt Grace had speeded up the delivery of her strokes and made them lighter so that the level of pain was increasing steadily rather than in spurts. She was making her usual little changes in her stance so that the tips of the twigs were not sinking into the same areas of my flesh. When she moved back and hit the left buttock and the tips landed mainly in the cleft of my bottom, it was especially painful.

The tops of my thighs were sore. Not the same soreness as I felt in my bottom. Not as nice. My bottom was even more swollen. And even more softly vulnerable. I heard moaning and groaning in the far distance. Was it me? I really had to fight the pain. It was overwhelming me and

I had not reached the state of near euphoria. Not yet. Aunt Grace then moved to the other side and was bringing the rod across her body. She was not as accurate. The strokes bit into my flanks; thighs; loins. Mainly my bottom, though. She stopped. I felt a surge of disappointment. I had not yet arrived at the other side of the dividing line between pain and pleasure. I felt her hands on my legs, adjusting my position, bringing them under the bench, tying them at the knees. I was bent nearly double. My poor bottom was much tighter. My cunny must have been in full view. Was my bottom-hole visible? I hoped not. I did not think so.

She resumed. I began to call out at the added venom of the whippy twigs on taut flesh. Then the warm waves started to wash through me. My cries were replaced by moans and my movements became more languid. It was better being tied. The helpnessness helped.

Again I heard that far-off voice: 'Oh my poor bottom . . . It burns . . . I'm sorry . . .'

There was silence. No more 'thwicks'. The agony stayed at the same level. But I did I hear a dry rustle? Had she taken another birch from the emptying pail? Yes. I sensed that she had moved and was standing closer to my side, but did not have the strength to turn my head. I was perspiring. My hands could hardly grip the rail.

My bottom boiled again. And again. And again. Then it was different. All in the centre. In the cleft. My anus throbbed. My cunny burned. The waves crashed and thundered. I swooned.

I first became aware of my breathing sawing hoarsely through my throat. Then I moaned as I felt the fires in my bottom. Then gasped as it was enveloped in a cold dampness. I turned my head and found that I was still tied to the bench, the guests had gone and Cook was bathing my rear end with a wet cloth. It was delicious. When the

245

flames had been reduced to tolerable levels, I was unfastened, helped down and with Elspeth supporting me, hobbl-
ed painfully up to my room. After the first step, my dress
fell down and I cried out at the touch of the coarse cloth
on my tortured buttocks, so it was removed and I completed the journey with nothing but my stockings, stopping at frequent intervals to let the maids inspect the ravages
left by my ordeal.

I collapsed face down on my bed, weary beyond belief
but also at ease. For all the pain, I felt the highest degree
of exhilaration that I had ever known. I asked Elspeth to
light all the gas lamps, every candle, to hold the mirror
for me while I stood before the pier glass so that I could
have a good look at my bottom. I gasped at the first glimpse. The buttocks were purple. There were so many little
weals that they had become as one patch. I could discern
the array of individual marks on my thighs and loins. I
was enthralled at the dramatic discolouration, to the extent that the urgent throbbing faded to the back of my
awareness. I bent forward and saw that even the innermost recesses of my deep cleft were as sorely afflicted
as the main parts of my cheeks. Painfully I knelt down
and thrust my hips into the air, with Elspeth cleverly
following my movements with her mirror so that I only
lost sight of myself for an instant. My anus was red. I
could vaguely see red marks on the lips of my cunny and
exclaimed aloud. She told me that at the end, after my
legs had been brought forward, Aunt Grace had stood
beside me and brought a small, delicate rod vertically onto
my bottom, working from the outside of each buttock in
turn, before giving me six little flicks down the full length
of the division.

I then understood why I had felt the flames on those
two orifices. And why I had swooned. The combination
of pain and pleasure had overcome me. Elspeth was as

solicitous as ever and spent the night watching over me, with cold wet cloths, soothing lotions and distilled witch hazel to ease me back to a semblance of sleep whenever I was awoken by the pain. I could not love her. I was completely spent, physically and emotionally. But her presence and attentions warmed my heart and I knew that she was aware of my deep gratitude.

It was only the next day that the discomfort became nearly unbearable and Cook gave me a sleeping draught. I slept the rest of the day and all the following night and woke at peace with myself.

Some days later, my bottom had healed. And Arabella and Phillip arrived and announced that he was ready to start on what he modestly referred to as his new masterpiece and that my presence was required in Sussex. My feeble protests were overcome and in a flurry of activity I packed my portmanteau, ignoring his forward suggestion that I would only need clothes for the journey, so my smallest case would be perfectly adequate. I said happy farewells to everyone, clambered with scant dignity into the waiting carriage and set off, chattering like magpies throughout the long journey.

Phillip had described his abode as a cottage, which was uncommonly modest of him, for it turned out to be a perfectly charming old house, with a lovely garden, woods behind and fields before and with splendid views of the rolling hills to the south. I was made most welcome by his housekeeper, a very pretty woman of about 30, with warm brown eyes, a lovely smile and a voluptuously plump figure. She had prepared a cold supper for us and so, once she had shown me to my delightful room, she left to return to her home on a nearby farm. Phillip said solemnly that to have her living in the house would not be convenient!

We walked round the garden to ease the numbness that the long journey had left in our limbs, then opened the first bottle of champagne and drank, ate and chattered until the sun went down and we yawned our way upstairs to our rooms. I bathed, put on my nightdress and stood by the open window, looking at the beautiful view bathed in moonlight, breathing in air that had all the pure sparkle of the wine and was overwhelmed with happiness.

The next morning, we were up at dawn, ate a simple breakfast and Phillip led the two of us to his studio, which had been, I believed a summerhouse, so was set in a far corner of the garden, where the light was perfect and privacy assured. As soon as we arrived, Arabella began to remove her clothes, smiling happily at me as she did so. Unaccountably, I was again overtaken by untypical modesty and although I could not bring myself to demur, stripped awkwardly, with fumbling fingers and a face which was flushed with embarrassment. It did not last long. Neither of them saw fit to chide or tease me for my silliness — after all, he had buggered me and seen my bottom-hole at very close quarters, so it was silly to feel ashamed at being all bare when the reasons for it were most honourable. And then Arabella tweaked my nipples, I slapped her naked bottom (but gently), we giggled and suddenly it all seemed perfectly natural.

I could never have imagined how strenuous posing could be. Our poses were not difficult to maintain — we were standing with our backs to him and an arm round the other — but to keep perfectly still proved most tiring. Fortunately Phillip proved to be very considerate and allowed us regular pauses to move and stretch. As the morning wore on, the warmth of the summer air, the glorious peace, the contact with Arabella's nakedness, all brought out the coquette in me and by noon I was feeling mischievously sensual. At the next break, I found myself stroking Arabella's delicious bare bottom, which inspired her to stroke mine and Phillip to stroke both of us. He then said that Mavis had been asked to do no more than tidy up the house and prepare a cold luncheon for us before having the rest of the day to herself, so that there was no need for us to dress again. He fetched a rug, food, and some wine and we had the delightful picnic *au naturel* on the grass near the studio, in the shade of a handsome oak tree,

He worked even harder in the afternoon, but the pauses became gradually more lascivious, and we eventually prevailed on him to join us in a state of nature. I loved seeing him bare. His fine body, rounded and smooth bottom, long limbs, golden skin and splendid cock took my breath away. And yet did not detract one iota from my accustomed enjoyment of his cousin's softer and more rounded charms.

By tea-time he had wearied. Without any hesitation, we left our clothes and walked round the garden. Instinctively I fell behind as they wandered hand in hand. My eyes were glued to their naked bottoms, marvelling at the differences in shape, texture and movements. Loving them both. Then Arabella turned and smiled at me.

'I want to look at your bottoms now,' she said.

I smiled lovingly at her, thrilling at yet more evidence of the closeness of our hearts, minds and desires. Phillip's strong hand closed on mine. My heart was full as I assumed an extra sway and wiggle for her benefit.

The evening grew cool and we went back to the house, with time to bathe and dress before Mavis returned to cook a delicious dinner. We were so completely at ease together and it seemed natural for Mavis to eat with us, contrary to normal custom. Somehow one expected artists to make their own conventions and I found myself in full concorde with Phillip's, although his ease of manner with the lovely housekeeper provoked a little flare of jealousy.

But then, later in the night, he slipped tentatively into my room. My heart raced with joy. I lit a candle to see him better, removed my nightdress, undressed him and we embraced, gently to begin with but with growing passion. Again, I felt the velvet-covered iron of his manhood nuzzle at my love-nest's portico and I stiffened.

'Please, my darling . . . Put it in my bottom . . . I am not ready.'

He kissed me, hooked his arms under my knees, drew them gently up to my bosom, bent down and laved my straining hole with his tongue until it was slippery enough — and I was sobbing with love and lust — and filled me. I did not reach a full climax, even though my bottom-hole and cunny both thrilled to the various pressures his body was applying when I clasped his shuddering body and felt the hot spurts of his pleasings in my clinging passage, I felt a fulfilment that was new to me. And greater than anything I had known.

From that moment, the last traces of inhibition flew away. I had accepted and begun to enjoy our nudity and was only unsure as to the extent Arabella could accept my growing passion for her cousin. As we settled to sleep in the sort of close embrace that was like, but so different to, the ones I had enjoyed with my friends of my own sex, I determined that Phillip's love was even more important to me than Arabella's. Had she sulked, I would have been desperately sad but would have continued to woo him to the best of my ability. It was indeed a blessing that such a choice was never forced upon me.

The next morning Arabella skipped into my room with the happiest of dispositions, clambered into bed with us and immediately requested that one of us enlighten her as to the events of the night.

'And you must not spare me *one* detail,' she concluded. Blushing like a bride, but secretly glowing with delight, I protested that even to think of making such a request was indeed the height of impudence and that I would turn her over my knee if she persisted. She did. So I did, with Phillip gleefully holding her legs while I bared her bottom and spanked it to the rosy hue which became it so well. Her squeals were from happy laughter rather than pain and when I stopped, she demanded that we both kiss her bottom better. Which we did, pausing at frequent intervals to kiss each other, something which was always a joyful act for me and improved more than a little by the feel of her soft, warm buttock under my chin.

When she removed every vestige of clothing, I welcomed it. When she examined Phillip's cock with an air of familiarity, I felt not one pang of jealousy. When she ordered the two of us to lie side by side so that she could compare our bottoms at length and in detail, I complied excitedly and found that kissing my first love while having my naked bottom played with by my second was truly pleasurable. It inspired to make her change places with me so that I could make a similar investigation, after which I once again thanked providence for allowing me to love both male and female forms. Both bottoms charmed me. At last we rose, breakfasted and trotted off to the studio.

The week sped towards its conclusion — my departure. If I had been happy at Aunt Grace's house, I was in seventh heaven with Phillip and Arabella. I could hardly bear the thought of leaving them, with all the uncertainties of never knowing when I could see them again.

In fact, I had no cause for concern. Two nights before it was time for me to leave, Phillip and I were lying peacefully in my bed, my bottom-hole was aching deliciously after his loving attentions and my love nest was pulsing deliciously after a prolonged tongueing. I was rather sadly thinking how lovely it would be to have the privilege of being his housekeeper, when he held me closely.

'Annie, I hope that you have enjoyed your visit.' All I could do was to squeeze him even more tightly.

251

'Good . . . I am delighted with my progress with the painting. I seriously believe that you and Arabella have inspired me. Your skin . . . it has a luminous quality . . . your bottom . . . it is perfect . . . you both are . . . I am sorry, I digress. Annie, I cannot bear the thought of my house without you . . . Will you marry me?'

I was in such a state of shock that I accepted at once! Phillip hugged me so tightly that I thought my ribs would split asunder, then gave a whoop of delight, leaped out of the bed and ran out of the room. At first I assumed that he had taken leave of his senses and it was only when he returned with a sleepy but very happy-looking Arabella that I really understood what she had meant when she had described the two of them as the 'best and dearest of friends'. They clearly shared their joys as well as the few sorrows which came their way and so it seemed utterly natural that she should be as one with Phillip and me in the happiest moment of our lives.

We lay awake for most of the night, making plans, laughing, kissing and stroking each other. My hands roamed freely over the naked flesh of my loves as theirs did over mine. My senses reeled with the feel, sound and scent of them. My heart sang.

Neither of us desired more than a quiet wedding ceremony. I had no known relatives and he disliked most of his. Aunt Grace, Uncle George, Cook and all the maids came, there were some raffish friends of Phillip's and Arabella was my Maid of Honour. After a merry party, at which Aunt Grace and all the others begged me to go back and see them as soon as I possibly could, my husband, Arabella and I took our carriage back home.

We were met by Mavis who had left the reception just before us and had arrived in time to prepare a light supper and to cool a bottle of champagne, before joining us in the drawing room where we cheerfully discussed the day's momentous events. I found myself increasingly attracted to Mavis's soft beauty and was just wondering whether her naked body was as appealing as it was when clad, when I became aware that my beloved husband was addressing me.

'Annie. It is an old custom in these parts for a new bride to receive a sound spanking from her mother on the day of her wedding. In the circumstances, Mavis will do the honours on your bottom.'

He was smiling at me; Arabella was grinning broadly. I grinned back at them as my bottom started tingling in happy expectation. I faced my chastiser and recognised the gleam in her eyes. I kissed her soft lips and stood back to allow her to fetch a suitable chair, place it close to the audience, seat herself and pat the full curve of her right thigh in invitation.

I placed myself in position with all the gracefulness I could muster, lifted my hips to let her ease my gown and petticoats onto the small of my back and as my drawers slithered down my thighs and the receptive flesh of my chubby buttocks felt the freshness of the country air, I remembered my initiation at Cook's hand. I laughed with pure joy as my bare bottom wobbled under Mavis's vigorous palm, sending silent thanks to dear Cook and all my other friends.

My chastiser was clearly unaccustomed to spanking a bottom as experienced as mine, for her spanks were light and there were too few of them for anything approaching satisfaction! Even so, the accumulated joys of the day (including, I admit, a fair quantity of excellent champagne) made the spanking a singularly enjoyable one. She had a most receptive lap and knowing that Phillip and Arabella were watching so avidly added a zest to my reactions to the proceedings. I was not in any pain but the feel of

Mavis's hand and the delicious wobbling it was imparting to my bottom, made me bounce it around with abandon.

Almost too soon she was helping me back to my feet, as my audience applauded us. Then she kissed me most sweetly, wished me a lifetime of happiness, bade the others good-bye and slipped away. Phillip then gathered me up in his arms and, with only an occasional stagger, carried me upstairs to his — no *our* — bedroom. We undressed each other silently; we kissed as our hands roved with practised skill; he kissed and licked my cunny. And then, just as I was about to scream for relief, he raised my quivering legs, probed gently at the welcoming entrance and, in one gently firm thrust, took my maidenhead from me. There was a brief stabbing moment of delicious pain and then we were as one.

At some time in the long night, Phillip slipped out and returned with Arabella. She kissed me in such a way that I knew that we would forever be the closest threesome ever. And we spent the rest of the night with each other.

Together.

NEW BOOKS

Coming up from Nexus and Black Lace

Amazon Slave by Lisette Ashton
June 1998   Price £5.99   ISBN: 0 352 33260 3
Stranded, alone and penniless in the Amazon basin, Emily thinks things can't get any worse. It is only when she boards the *Amazon Maiden*, however, that her dark journey truly begins. The captain expects only one thing from his crew: absolute obedience. Insubordination is not tolerated; punishment is delivered swiftly and mercilessly. Captivated by the beautiful Emily and her arrogant defiance, the captain is determined to enjoy her submission. By the author of *The Black Room*.

A Master of Discipline by Zoe Templeton
June 1998   Price £5.99   ISBN: 0 352 33261 1
When naive young schoolteacher Ruth is sent by her employers to Damocles Priory to learn how to administer punishment, she has no idea that the emphasis will be on practical experience. After her initial reluctance, she allows the masterful clergyman Reverend Mould to help her live out her submissive fantasies and to explore her most perverse desires. Damocles Priory is not all it seems to be, however, and the lewd reverend is taking an unusually personal interest in Ruth's education. Will she learn to take the upper hand before it is too late? By the author of *A Degree of Discipline*.

There are three Nexus titles published in July

Penny in Harness by Penny Birch
July 1998   Price £5.99   ISBN: 0 352 33271 9
When naughty Penny Birch is walking in the woods one day, she is surprised to find a couple pony-carting. Penny is so excited by watching this new form of adult fun that she has to pleasure herself on the spot. Realising how keen she is to discover for herself what it is all about, she begins to investigate this bizarre world of whips and harnesses, of crops and restraints. Firstly punished by the mysterious pony-girl enthusiasts for misbehaving in the woods, she is soon accepted into their fold after demonstrating her enthusiasm for being made to act in a lewd manner.

Chains of Shame by Brigitte Markham
July 1998   Price £5.99   ISBN: 0 352 33270 0

As innocent but cheeky teenagers Laura and Helen enjoy the sun-drenched beaches of Corfu, Helen's aunt, Angela, has a novel agenda for them – she wants to oversee their sexual awakening. She finds them keen to experiment with their new discoveries; eager to be oiled and depilated; to explore their lesbian lusts; and to be introduced into the dark arenas of punishment and bondage.

Eroticon 4 Anon
July 1998   Price £5.99   ISBN: 0 352 32563 1

This remarkable compendium takes the reader on a journey into the sexual imagination, presenting a panorama of exotic scenes drawn from over a century of the world's finest erotic writing. Here are lovers and maids, rakes and whores from texts known only to connoisseurs of the forbidden. Look out for *Eroticon 1, 2* and *3*, also from Nexus.

There are three Black Lace titles published in June

Masque of Passion by Tesni Morgan
June 1998   Price £5.99   ISBN: 0 352 33259 X
Lisa Sherwin is finally having second thoughts about her forthcoming marriage to rugby-playing Paul, especially as he sees her prodigious sexual needs as unimportant. The rural English village in which they live is home to some eccentric characters, one of whom, David Maccabene, introduces her to new and kinky ways of loving. In a bid to escape the stuffy conservatism of Paul's overbearing family, Lisa begins to seek the total satisfaction she has only just realised she can achieve.

Circo Erotica by Mercedes Kelly
June 1998   Price £5.99   ISBN: 0 352 33257 3
Flora is a beautiful lion-tamer in a Mexican circus. When her father is mauled to death by one of the lions, he dies owing a large sum of money to the cruel ringmaster Lorenzo, who takes Flora as compensation to satisfy his unnatural sexual appetite. His accomplice, the perverse Salome, also has designs on the young woman. Will Flora ever be able to come to enjoy their bizarre games?

Cooking up a Storm by Emma Holly
June 1998   Price £7.99   ISBN: 0 352 33258 1
The Coates Inn restaurant in Cape Cod is about to go belly-up when its attractive owner, Abby, jumps at a stranger's offer to help her – both in her kitchen and in her bed. The handsome chef claims to have a secret weapon: an aphrodisiac menu that her patrons won't be able to resist. It certainly works on Abby, who gives vent to passions she has denied for years. But will Abby be able to tear herself away from the object of her lust long enough to understand his true motives?

The Barbarian Geisha by Charlotte Royal
July 1998   Price £5.99   ISBN: 0 352 33267 0
Entranced by the beauty of a naked English girl when he finds her
washed up on a beach following a shipwreck, Lord Nakano takes her
to his fortress home, where the Mamma San is to teach her the art
of giving pleasure. She is an enthusiastic and willing student, but the
world of Shimoyama is one of political intrigue and danger. Will she
ever be accepted as a barbarian geisha? By the author of the bestsell-
ing *Invitation to Sin*.

Drawn Together by Robyn Russell
July 1998   Price £5.99   ISBN: 0 352 33269 7
When Tanya Trevino creates a sexy alter-ego in the form of Katrina
Cortez, private investigator, she begins to wish her own life were
more like that of her comic-strip character's. Kinky Stephen Sinclair,
who works with Tanya, is her kind of man. Trouble is, Tanya's just
moved in with her executive boyfriend, who expects her to fit in to
his corporate routine. But she can't get Stephen out of her increasingly lewd fantasies. Can she learn to obey her desires?

NEXUS BACKLIST

All books are priced £4.99 unless another price is given. If a date is supplied, the book in question will not be available until that month in 1998.

CONTEMPORARY EROTICA

THE ACADEMY	Arabella Knight		
AGONY AUNT	G. C. Scott		
ALLISON'S AWAKENING	Lauren King		
AMAZON SLAVE	Lisette Ashton	£5.99	June
THE BLACK ROOM	Lisette Ashton		Mar
BOUND TO SUBMIT	Amanda Ware		
CANDIDA IN PARIS	Virginia Lasalle		
A CHAMBER OF DELIGHTS	Katrina Young		
THE CHASTE LEGACY	Susanna Hughes		
A DEGREE OF DISCIPLINE	Zoe Templeton		Feb
THE DOMINO TATTOO	Cyrian Amberlake		
THE DOMINO QUEEN	Cyrian Amberlake		
EDUCATING ELLA	Stephen Ferris		
EMMA'S SUBMISSION	Hilary James		
EMMA'S SECRET DOMINATION	Hilary James		Jan
FALLEN ANGELS	Kendal Grahame		
THE TRAINING OF FALLEN ANGELS	Kendal Grahame		
HEART OF DESIRE	Maria del Rey		
HOUSE OF TEMPTATIONS	Yvonne Strickland		
THE ISLAND OF MALDONA	Yolanda Celbridge		
THE CASTLE OF MALDONA	Yolanda Celbridge		
THE ICE QUEEN	Stephen Ferris		
JENNIFER'S INSTRUCTION	Cyrian Amberlake		
JOURNEY FROM INNOCENCE	Jean-Philippe Aubourg		

EDWARDIAN, VICTORIAN & OLDER EROTICA

ANNIE	Evelyn Culber	£5.99	May
ANNIE AND THE COUNTESS	Evelyn Culber		Apr
BEATRICE	Anonymous		
CHOOSING LOVERS FOR JUSTINE	Aran Ashe		
THE CORRECTION OF AN ESSEX MAID	Yolanda Celbridge	£5.99	May
DEAR FANNY	Michelle Clare		
LYDIA IN THE BORDELLO	Philippa Masters		
LYDIA IN THE HAREM	Philippa Masters		
LURE OF THE MANOR	Barbra Baron		
MAN WITH A MAID 3	Anonymous		
MEMOIRS OF A CORNISH GOVERNESS	Yolanda Celbridge		
THE GOVERNESS AT ST AGATHA'S	Yolanda Celbridge		
PRIVATE MEMOIRS OF A³ ✳ KENTISH HEADMISTRESS	Yolanda Celbridge		Feb
SISTERS OF SEVERCY	Jean Aveline		Mar

SAMPLERS & COLLECTIONS

EROTICON 3	Various	
THE FIESTA LETTERS	ed. Chris Lloyd	
NEW EROTICA 2	ed. Esme Ombreux	
NEW EROTICA 3	ed. Esme Ombreux	

NON-FICTION

HOW TO DRIVE YOUR WOMAN WILD IN BED	Graham Masterton	
HOW TO DRIVE YOUR MAN WILD IN BED	Graham Masterton	
LETTERS TO LINZI	Linzi Drew	

Please send me the books I have ticked above.

Name ....

Address ....

....

....

.... Post code ....

Send to: Cash Sales, Nexus Books, 332 Ladbroke Grove, London W10 5AH

Please enclose a cheque or postal order, made payable to **Nexus Books**, to the value of the books you have ordered plus postage and packing costs as follows:

UK and BFPO – £1.00 for the first book, 50p for the second book, and 30p for each subsequent book to a maximum of £3.00;

Overseas (including Republic of Ireland) – £2.00 for the first book, £1.00 for the second book, and 50p for each subsequent book.

If you would prefer to pay by VISA or ACCESS/MASTERCARD, please write your card number and expiry date here:

....

Please allow up to 28 days for delivery.

Signature ....